TO THE BOYS
WHO WEAR PINK

ISBN: 978-1-7770279-0-2 (Paperback)
ISBN: 978-1-7770279-1-9 (Epub)
ISBN: 978-1-7770279-3-3 (Hardcover)
ISBN: 978-1-7770279-2-6 (Mobi)

Edited and Published by Riley Palanca
7834 avenue de l'épée
Montréal QC

TO THE BOYS
WHO WEAR PINK

Revan Badingham III

Track List

01 | Get The Party Started
02 | Just Like A Pill
03 | Stupid Girls
04 | Dear Mr. President
05 | So What
06 | Who Knew
07 | Try
08 | Fuckin' Perfect
09 | Please Don't Leave Me
10 | U + Ur Hand
11 | Trouble
12 | Slut Like You
13 | Glitter In The Air
14 | Lady Marmalade
15 | What About Us
16 | Family Portrait
17 | Funhouse
18 | Just Like Fire
19 | Just Give Me A Reason
20 | Don't Let Me Get Me
21 | Are We All We Are
22 | Revenge
23 | Sober
24 | Beautiful Trauma
25 | Blow Me (One Last Kiss)
26 | Raise Your Glass

To The Outcasts

"So, baby girl. We don't change. We take the gravel and the
shell and we make a pearl."
(P!nk, VMA 2017)

Get The Party Started

"JESUS, LORD, SODOMITES, AND BEDWETTERS!"

With his eyes fixed on the mirror, Ryan plucked a solitary hair that his razor had missed. Though the mirror had never been kind to him, Ryan would still get wounded every time their faces met. Yesterday, his teeth didn't line up. Today, his hollow eyes were flanked by wrinkles. God only help what he'll see tomorrow.

"Lord Jesus, fuck us all." Ryan slumped on the vanity, his hair dripping water down his naked body. Purple paint on his bulging stomach had hardened, and it wouldn't come off no matter how much he scrubbed.

The mirror and Ryan used to be best friends. Six years ago, he'd preen in front of it, shirtless and toned, face unblemished by solitude, and a smile that could've shattered the mirror's face.

Adorned with ornate gold figures, the mirror occupied a queenly post in Ryan's studio. Everything else, from the rotting bed to the mismatched dining chairs, would've blushed. The only item that rivaled it was Ryan's easel. After a long day of cursing and countless splatters that assured his damage deposit wouldn't be returned, the easel slept with Ryan's newest child beside it.

Ryan's misery was interrupted by the buzz of his phone. A text from Percy. "They've arrived. Let's get this party started!" He flung the phone back on the dresser before staring at a soon-to-be pimple on his reflection. *Of course.* Of all the nights, it had to be this one.

Furious at the blemish, Ryan moved his attention to the photos surrounding the mirror. The one to the right was him and his best friend, Eyes, on their bikes back in high school. Below that was another from a Halloween party where he went as a Picasso painting. "Stunner #1 Superstar!" was scrawled on it with lipstick. On the mirror's left was a torn picture of him with another artist with emerald hair peeking from behind. This was taken at a gallery opening—the missing half (an ex he'd rather not think of) was hidden in a drawer.

The blown-up photo at the top drew the most attention. Not long after university, the gang got together for a Madonna concert, with backstage passes thanks to El. Everyone was there: Ryan bear-hugging Eyes and a glammed-out Percy; Sugar and Vyn shrieking as they flanked Madonna; even El and Long, both too drunk yet managing goofy smiles. Ryan creased his brows. *Where was King? Ah.* Someone needed to take the photo. King always got the short straw.

His phone buzzed again. Percy. "Where are you! We're waiting…"

Ryan slammed the phone down, though he managed to get away from the mirror's judging eye. Percy was like that. Always on time. Always a shrill, "Where are you? I'm here. I've been here for hours. Where are you? Why are you late!"

Still. It wasn't often they got to see each other. He walked to the closet where he rummaged through his clothes. He owned no clothes of note; his agent always nagged him about his lazy ensemble. At any other party, jeans and a t-shirt were fine, but he shuddered imagining the look on Percy's face if he were to enter in anything less than the mode.

He took out an old wool sweater. It had a snag on its neckline. Ryan played with the loose threads. El's barbecue. *Fun times*.

◄◄

It had been back in high school when he had last worn that sweater. He had been driving to El's barbecue, Eyes riding shotgun, with Sugar, Vyn, and Long in the back. As usual, he was late, and Percy's texts graduated from mildly annoyed to a demonic rage. "Where the fuck are you? Don't you dare leave me with El! Or King!"

"Percy is so anal." Eyes flicked his cigarette ash out the window. "No wonder he's a bottom."

Right behind him, Long laughed, slapping the headrest in front of him.

"My dear, control yourself." Eyes rubbed the back of his head. Long sometimes didn't know his strength. "You're one fuck away from being a powerbottom."

Ryan's seat shifted forward as Vyn tapped Eyes's shoulders. "Eyes! Eyes, Eyes, Eyes. What do you call a top with no bottom?"

Taking a long drag, Eyes looked at Ryan. He needn't say anything. He was annoyed. "I don't know, my dear, what would you call a top with no bottom?"

"Masturbation!" Vyn, Sugar, and Ryan sang out. Long laughed again.

They passed the old country stop. If Ryan's car had been in better condition, they should've arrived by now, but its rickety engine prevented it from going top speed. Accustomed to Ryan's aging vehicle, his friends filled the times with jokes they'd been telling for years.

Always the lewd one, Vyn was in the middle of a gold mining story when Sugar interrupted him. "Sweetie, Percy's texting."

"What'd he say?" Ryan asked.

Putting on his best Percy impersonation, Sugar read, "Where is that bitch? Is he stopping every five minutes to give each trucker he passes head? Please. He was never good at it."

"Tell him five minutes," Ryan said as Long roared in laughter again. "Five minutes and fuck you."

With Vyn resuming his story, Eyes leaned toward Ryan with a smirk. "I beg to differ."

Ryan blushed. He felt Eyes's fingernails slide on his neckline. His neck grew warm. Getting distracted, Ryan pushed Eyes back. Eyes's nail caught on his sweater, ripping a hole in the neckline. "Jesus, lord, sodomites, and bedwetters!"

With no remorse, Eyes puffed smoke out the window. "Now, my dear, we're even."

▶▶

Ryan tossed the sweater away. *Maybe it needs to be burned.*

Near him was the painting he had finished earlier. It was of that car ride, though liberties were taken. Sugar was plumper, Eyes's cheekbones higher. In contrast, the Ryan in the painting was gaunt, sleep-deprived, and pimply. The easel could be worse than the mirror. Ryan hadn't decided if he was putting this in the exhibit. Though he still needed a centerpiece, that was a decision for tomorrow.

His phone vibrated again. *Bloody Percy*—Ryan raised an eyebrow. It was Sugar. "Sweetie, we're all here. Where are you?"

He dropped his towel and put on an old pair of boxers. No one would see his underwear anyway. At least that was one thing. He unfurled a pair of argyle socks. Two things.

Rifling through his other shirts, he came upon a dusty white hoodie. He didn't bother taking it out. *Nope. Never.*

"Please don't tell me that was Wallace. It was, wasn't it?" Ryan had asked El a few years ago as they sipped coffee on the patio of a local coffee shop. On break from university, they were on the way to El's cabin when Vyn complained about the variety of snacks Long brought.

Small independent coffee shops were the perfect place for a stopover. Eyes sat beside Ryan, sharing a cigarette with Sugar. (They didn't bring enough and had to conserve the smokes for the trip.) El sat in front of them, in between Vyn and an empty chair with Percy's bag.

"Wallace!" Vyn poked El in the ribs. "Rimming Wallace! Sucking Wallace!"

"Another lost cause, my dear?" Eyes asked.

El swatted Vyn's hand. "Wallace is, okay, stop it, Vyn, Vyn! Vyn! He's not a lost cause. Okay, maybe he is, but it wasn't Wallace."

"Lost causes aren't your problem, my dear." Eyes took a deep drag before passing the cigarette to Sugar. "The real problem begins when you find these causes."

El had Vyn's hands pinned down. "And you're smooth as Don Juan. List yours down. Timmy. Joule. Ryan, of course—"

Eyes was fast. "Oh dear. The time! Shall we go, my dear?"

Ryan grunted. What was to be a pit stop for coffee had now been an hour. King and Long had yet to make it back from the sex shop next door. Only Long was brave enough to go with King. If history were to be trusted, the two needed saving after that long. Or a lawyer.

"Oh, and Percy!" Sugar added. "Don't forget him and Si. They're taking so long." Percy was changing in the bathroom assisted by his then-boyfriend, Si.

"Should I knock and ask if they want a threesome?" Vyn asked.

Eyes sighed. "Probably, my dear. But not with you."

As Vyn continued pestering El to admit who he slept with, Ryan kept checking his phone for the time. While he didn't enjoy sleeping in the middle of the woods, the surrounding lake always refreshed them on a hot day. It'd been a while since they went swimming and a dip in the lake was more calming than an hour at the local pool. Ryan could almost feel his feet soaking.

His dreams got jolted by the arrival of the barista, asking if there were anything else they needed. The barista was the reason they came here often. He was tall, bald, really good-looking, and, most importantly, smelled like freshly brewed coffee. They had a bet on what his name was: his nametag just read "CC".

"You can get me something," Vyn said. "Mmm. How about an extra-large extra-long with extra, extra frosting?"

"Ignore him," Eyes swooped in. "We're good. Just waiting on friends."

CC looked toward the restroom. "They've been a while, haven't they? Want me to check—"

A collective "No!" rose from the table, followed by nervous laughter and cover-ups such as "Oh, indigestion.", "He's snorting cocaine—ouch!", and "You don't wanna go in there, my dear. Trust me."

"Well, I guess I'll get these out of the way." CC bent over to pick up the coffee mugs. Instinctively, Ryan checked out his behind. *Not bad. Not bad at all.*

"What does CC stand for?" Vyn asked. "Does it mean cut co—"

Thank god for El, who covered Vyn's mouth before he could embarrass them further. Sugar looked scandalized, Eyes barely amused, but Ryan grinned. Vyn's mouth got them into trouble, yes, but it was a riot the whole way through.

"What's he gonna do, spit in our coffee?" Vyn snarled after El took his hand away.

CC laughed, saying it was a secret. As he picked up Ryan's plate, he smiled. "Nice hoodie. Banana Republic, right? Got one too."

Ryan's hand shook as he put his cup to his mouth. *Drat.* Empty. Eyes raised his brows in encouragement. "Figured, white, summer, fresh, y'know."

"Looks good. Especially on you." CC tugged on one of the hoodie's drawstrings.

Vyn shrieked. "Okay, Mr. Barista, please give our friend your number! Wanna see that hoodie on your bedroom floor—"

"What our tactless friend is saying, my dear," Eyes said, "was perhaps you'd like to meet up with our artist friend here. He can draw while you make coffee, he can even draw you in a cup—"

"Stoooooop." Ryan buried his face in his hands. His back was sweating. He hated being the center of attention. (He once had to do a play for Eyes and was shaking the entire time onstage.) All thoughts of the lake, swimming, and escaping the heat were gone. All he wanted was to sink through the hardwood floors into the jagged rocks.

"Sure," CC said. Having gathered all the dishes, he started heading inside. "Hit me up before you go." With those words, the cute barista disappeared into the kitchen.

"Oh, my god!" Vyn almost overturned the table with his fists. "I cannot take this. I cannot! I cannot!"

"Just espresso yourself," El said. "And you'll have a latte love."

Even Sugar piped in, "Oh, sweetie, do go for it! You've been single for too long."

Ryan was exasperated. He wanted to go. But the guy was cute. Really cute. And the booty didn't hurt. He turned to Eyes. "Well? Anything to add?"

Eyes snuffed out his cigarette. "Personally, he and I would make a better couple. But you two will do."

"Jesus, lord, sodomites, and bedwetters!" Ryan banged his head on the table.

⏵

The mirror welcomed Ryan back. He was wearing a purple shirt he'd been reserving for the upcoming exhibit. It wasn't ironed, but it'd have to do. His tight jeans would hopefully distract from his tummy. And a pair of white trainers because what gay guy didn't wear white trainers?

The phone vibrated. This time King. "You at Percy's? Got the stripper? Let me know if there's problems, got names for backup. Also, sorry but I kinda told the twins about the party. Yeah, they're coming. Tell Percy! Ciao!"

Ryan groaned. *The stripper and now the twins!* He opened his desk bureau hoping for a bottle of aspirin but he had drained the bottle yesterday while painting the lake by El's cabin. Landscapes weren't his forte.

Vibrating phone! El. "Percy's about to throw a fit. He unbuttoned his collar. His COLLAR! Where are you?"

Ryan checked himself out in the mirror. Decent. Presentable. Almost hot. *I'd fuck someone who looks like me.* He swore the mirror almost laughed.

Another text message. *Balls, I'm coming up, I'm coming up.* Long this time. "On your way? Bring tequila. And brandy. And whatever you can! Percy's taste in booze…"

Here we go, here we go, deep breaths. Ryan envisioned the party, meeting the old gang, El and Sugar and Vyn and everyone else he hadn't seen in years. He had a thousand things to do for his exhibit, but he needed this. Even if it meant more 4 a.m. adrenaline-pumped painting sprees.

What happened to us? Our parties were legendary. They'd had the police bang on their door, bartenders chase them out into the streets, and even random strangers join in on the merriment. Everyone came, everyone had a drink at all times, laughing and kissing and gyrating on the dance floor.

Tonight will be the same. And it won't end, as Vyn used to say, until every single cup and cock were dry.

"You can do this," he said to the mirror.

He put his phone in his pocket, checked his wallet, car keys, all good. Something was lacking, though. He still felt like his dick and balls were hanging out for everyone to stare at. Scrambling through a drawer, his fingers hit a gold ring tucked in the back.

Eyes had given it to him a few years ago.

"It's like a friendship bracelet, my dear, except we're grown men and not six-year-old girls," he'd said while kissing him on the cheek. "Love you."

Ryan fondled the ring, debating whether to wear it. *Oh, go on then.* First time in a long time. A really long time. *There we go.* Now he was ready.

His phone rang. A call this time. Percy.

"Hey, Percy, yeah, yeah, I'm sorry I'm late. Yeah, I'm on the way, I'm like—err, I'm driving right now, I'm five minutes from you, okay? Yeah, talk to you later, driving!"

Goddamn Percy.

Just Like A Pill

THERE WERE FEW THINGS in the world Percy desired. Unfortunately, those tended to be the rarer things in life. Throwing money at everything his gut wanted didn't guarantee he could wrap them up in a pretty bag.

Take his attire. Perfect. A crisp white shirt with baby blue polka dots, tailored slacks, and oxford shoes. His light beard was trimmed to millimeter accuracy and his hair was professionally styled. A look meticulously curated after a J. Crew ad. *Stunning.*

At the opposite end, take tonight's pending disaster. He threw a party for his friend and Ryan had the audacity to show up late. Fuming, he checked his phone for any update. Nothing. *Insensitive prick.*

The doorbell rang. Percy strutted over. *Please be Ryan.* That way, he could deal with the guests. Percy shuddered after he had read Ryan's guest list. *Nope, not my problem.*

Instead of Ryan, a mousy-haired guy stood at the door. "Yes?" Percy demanded.

"This is the, uhm, party, right?" the guy asked.

"Yeah, come in." Percy gestured him in. The guy entered and stood at the welcome mat scratching his head. Exasperated, Percy gave a quick tour. "This is the hall. Put your coat there, don't drip on the carpets. Upstairs is off-limits. Obviously. The rooms here are off-limits. Well, you can use the bathroom but no further."

After the coat was hung, Percy led him to the living room. A few guests had arrived but as the guest of honor had yet to make an appearance, Percy deemed it improper to get the festivities underway.

Percy's open concept living room allowed the guests to mingle in clusters. Immediately across the hall was a lush burgundy sofa set, the signature piece of Percy's favorite interior designer. Behind the sofas were patio doors leading to the pool. Dotted around the room were a grand piano, a billiards table (specifically bought for the party), a massive sound system, and a buffet table. Dead center was a fully stocked custom bar, its contents Percy curated earlier.

Percy counted the guests. *Why did I agree to host?* Well, Ryan was his closest (if only) friend. They had coffee every other week and he helped the clueless boy shop for clothes. But no matter what he did, they lacked the closeness Ryan had with Eyes. That one, everyone would say, was for the books.

By the sofas, Long was flipping cards with Vyn as the mousy-haired newcomer approached them. Long hadn't changed. Percy wouldn't say it, but he was envious Long held on to his muscled physique. In contrast, Vyn had lost a ton of weight. His body was so gaunt, his flesh sagged. His loose shirt, a relic of healthier days, only highlighted the change further.

Unlike Long who was immediately chatting up the newcomer, Vyn was staring directly at the wall. Though Percy hadn't spoken to either for years, he was surprised by the blank way Vyn greeted him when they had arrived. Every time he passed by them, only Long's thundering voice could be heard.

Drastic weight loss and an absentminded gaze. These are symptoms of—No. Percy shook himself. He wasn't working tonight.

Across from them, Sugar was playing the piano. Percy liked him, although it was impossible to dislike Sugar. He wasn't like Vyn or Long or (Percy rolled his eyes) King, who preferred loud dive bars to the cocktail lounges Percy frequented. Whenever Sugar played the piano, Percy's headaches would temporarily leave. Sugar was a virtuoso and, if he'd had the opportunity, he'd be playing the national orchestra.

Percy walked past Sugar, the rising melody removing Ryan's lateness from his mind. Sugar waved at him before turning to the guy leaning on the piano. Sugar brought him—*from work? Or did they live together? His name was, oh, Percy, come on, think. What was it? Something silly and pedestrian, was it Drew or Dave or something?* He'll ask Sugar later. Or not. The music stopped. He didn't care anymore.

At the bar, El was talking to Badger. Percy bit his lip. He wasn't sure about El. In their group, he liked Ryan and Sugar, tolerated Eyes, disliked Vyn and Long, absolutely despised King, but El was tougher to pin down. Ironic, given he'd known El the longest. Since they were kids, their families ran in the same social circles: regattas, fundraisers, late-night soirees at each other's mansions. Yet, unlike Percy, El didn't behave in accordance with his status. El's family was richer but El's rugged nature made him more at home in the streets than the boardroom.

Distrust. It was distrust. Percy distrusted El.

On the other hand, Badger was Si's old basketball teammate. Even though Percy's friends lacked certain sophistication, they seemed almost upper class compared to Badger and his fart jokes, greasy hair, and uncut nails. Just about the only good thing about not dating Si anymore was not having to put up with Badger.

"Everything on track?" El asked Percy.

Headache notwithstanding, Percy smiled. "Just peaches."

El unfurled a piece of paper. "By the by, can I get your signature for——"

"Oh, you must tell me absolutely everything later," Percy said, in perfect grace. For one, he had little interest in whatever cause El was championing this time. But more importantly, his phone was vibrating. Ryan. *Finally.* "Almost there. BTW, King's bringing the twins."

Percy's blood pressure rose. He knew the symptoms first-hand. *The twins, the goddamn twins.* Percy bit his lip again. *Do I have time to tell King the party's canceled? No, goddamn it. Long already posted on Instagram.*

He dug into his pocket and popped a Vicodin before pouring a glass of whiskey. The ice cubes jingled in the glass the same way his brain was bouncing around in his head.

"What happened to margaritas?"

For the first time tonight, Percy relaxed his shoulders, his head also calming down. He turned to see Si returning from the bathroom.

"Margaritas are fine." Percy picked up his drink. "But to-night, I'm courting danger."

Percy and Si met in high school when things were easier, and yet, ten times more difficult.

Eyes dragged him and Ryan to a basketball match. Percy despised organized sports. It was unbecoming for a civilized society to declare superiority by regressing to such physical bouts. Yet Eyes told him to stop thinking of it as a game but rather "a performance piece where all the actors are beautiful, beautiful boys."

After the match (a record win for their school), they were heading out for a snack when Percy realized he'd left his bag in the bleachers. He ran back into a deserted gym and scoured the seats. It wasn't there. That bag was an authentic D&G. No one——no one in this school could appreciate it.

"Looking for this?" Across the court stood one of the basketball players, jersey still drenched with sweat, holding his bag. "Thought it was a chick's, but it looks better on you!"

Had it been anyone other than Percy, they would've fainted. This was Si, captain of the basketball team and clear front-runner for prom king. Even Percy had to steady his knees. "You thought something that chic could only belong to me?"

"No!" Si yelled, his voice echoing throughout the gym. "It's the only thing left behind!"

Percy strutted across the court. "Well then," he said, face-to-face with the hunk. "Guess you're every guy's hero."

Si laughed. "I've been called many names. I could add 'hero' to the list."

Percy snatched his bag away from Si's hands. Thankfully still in pristine condition. *No jocks needed to be killed today.* "They call me Percy."

Si flexed his arms. His sweat sparkled in the dim lights. "Maybe I can call you tonight?"

"Si!" A booming shout came from the locker rooms. Percy was grateful. He had no ready retort.

They turned toward the cause of the noise. Badger stood in a towel outside the locker room. "Si, team picture!"

"Yeah, well, you're naked!" Si yelled back.

"Yeah, 'cause they said they wanted the big shots!" Badger grabbed his dick.

Percy rolled his eyes. "Yeah, then why'd they want you?" Between a naked Badger and a fully clothed Si, everyone would choose the latter.

Si doubled over in laughter. Badger grunted, hitting the wall in frustration before heading back. "He's an ass, but I do have to go," Si said. "I'm glad you left your bag."

Holstering it over his shoulder, Percy walked away. "What makes you think I didn't leave it on purpose?"

"Hey!" Si yelled at Percy's back. "Hey! You didn't give me your number!"

Game. Set. Match.

Percy may have won Game 1, but the tournament wouldn't be that easy. Though he couldn't be the queen of their group (not with Eyes holding the throne) for Si, he was royalty. Si was the only person Percy had ever shown true vulnerability.

Percy had needed him the day of his mom's funeral, where he stormed out after delivering a broken eulogy. He'd needed Si when he got mugged while walking home drunk. Though he had shaken off the attackers, Si's arms made his head stop exploding in grief, stress, and fear.

Percy had needed him that night his friends had been in a car accident. He, Si, and Sugar were at the cabin waiting when Ryan called him. With a shaky voice, Ryan told him to hurry to the hospital. Pale and frozen, Percy relied on a sturdy Si to carry him to the car and drive him to the hospital.

The months following that accident, Percy had depended more and more on Si. Si would feed him, bathe him, and cuddle him to sleep. Percy had resented this, his weakness turning into bitterness. *What kind of queen needs their subject to take care of them?*

Percy blamed that dependence as the reason they broke up. Instead of getting better, Percy fell into his own paradox. Si didn't need a queen. He needed a boyfriend. And eventually Si found another one.

Percy understood. *Maybe this time, Si needn't always be the caretaker. Maybe Si didn't need to constantly pick them up to make them better.* Si left, and Percy's head was cracking, his whole body in revolt. That night, Percy ran. Just kept running through the night, with nowhere left to go.

Sitting at the bottom of the hallway stairs, Si drummed his fingers on his thighs while Percy sipped his whiskey.

It'd been ages now since they'd seen each other, but Percy still remembered every detail of Si's body. The flat stomach that once had a six-pack, the lanky limbs, the graphic T-shirt he himself had designed. Every bit of the Si he once said goodbye to was sitting two feet from him.

"Gum?" Si asked.

Percy looked at the Mentos Si was offering. Convenience store drivel. "Why? Are you gonna kiss me?"

"I forgot." Si put the gum away. "You were always—"

"—Minty fresh," they said at the same time.

Percy sat beside Si. There were things he should've asked, maybes and what-ifs that lingered from the past. Si continued drumming, but his feet fidgeted. They'd been together long enough for Percy to know Si's nervous ticks.

At the worst possible time, the doorbell rang.

Si jumped up. "I'll get it!"

"Sit your pretty ass down." Percy stood reluctantly. "I'll get it."

My party, my rules. Percy pushed Si down. Si pretended to fall, clutching his chest. Percy sighed. *These antics. This childish behavior.* He missed it. He walked to the door. *This better be Ryan and this better be good.*

It was not Ryan and it was not good. Percy opened the door to Angelo and Reyes, more guys from their high school who were, frankly put, losers.

"What?" Percy demanded.

"Hey, Percy, can we come in?" Angelo asked. He was a fat guy with thinning hair and rather strong cologne. Beside him, Reyes was in cargo shorts, a t-shirt, and mismatched socks. Unlike Angelo who was tentative but eager, Reyes looked like he'd rather be anywhere else.

"Why?" Percy asked. He hoped his tone would cause both to leave. His head prayed for relief and it wasn't these two.

"We were invited," Angelo said. "Ryan invited us."

Frustrated, Percy gave in. "Very well. Come on in. And don't break anything."

Why on god's green earth would Ryan invite these two? He needed to have a talk with him. Inviting a stripper was bad enough, bringing the goddamn twins was worse, but now having the bottom-feeders at his party? *Enough was goddamn enough.*

And where the hell was Ryan? Percy checked his phone. Nothing. *Goddamn. Goddamn Ryan. Late to your own goddamn party and no courtesy to tell me where you are.* Percy clung on to the doorframe. His head was pounding. It'd been hurting all day but now it was unbearable. He was dizzy and his knees were failing. To top it all, Angelo's cologne made him want to puke.

He dug out his unlabeled bottle of Vicodin. His hands were used to the routine by now. Uncork. Take. Swallow.

◀

There wasn't just one reason he needed pills. Med school, losing Si, the accident. And the goddamn chronic headaches. As a teen, he used to steal some of his dad's Vicodin and it'd helped, if only for a while.

In med school, all he needed was to hand a discreet bill to the local pharmacist. One pill before an exam. One pill before watching surgery. One pill before the Hippocratic Oath.

Now that he was working as a resident at the local hospital, getting hold of them was ironically more difficult. He might've tried to get the pills the legal way when he met Naveen. Naveen was a doctor who'd been at the hospital for five years. Percy had no interest in socializing with his coworkers, yet when you're friendly with a senior, swiping pills is child's play.

What started as a fling in the supply closet became serious. Naveen was of the age where he wanted to be with someone. And Percy was at a time where he needed to be someone.

Through the haze of Vicodin hallucinations and flashes of depression, Percy had tried to find the same serenity he got from Si. Naveen was different; older, surer of himself. Percy desperately wanted to want that.

A week after they became a couple, Percy thought the pain was gone. He threw out his pills—a decision he regretted a couple of hours later when Naveen held his head over the toilet.

"Alright?" Si stood behind him.

Not in the mood for a confrontation, Percy hid his pill bottle. "I'm always alright. Just headaches."

Si pressed his hand against Percy's. Gentle, like the tap of rain on a leaf. "I'm sorry you still have them."

Maybe it was the Vicodin, maybe it was Si, but Percy's head cleared. "You always found a way, Si, to make me feel better."

It was just that morning when Percy collapsed on the bedroom floor, disheveled, snotty, and in pain. The bed was untouched. He couldn't sleep last night, and Naveen was at a conference.

His pills mocked him from the table. He'd already taken three or four, and he'd risk his sanity if he took more.

He breathed deeply, forcing the pain to stop going to different places. One moment, it was his neck, and the next, his legs were in agony. His phone vibrated as Naveen sent him a GIF of a cat holding an "I love you" sign. He threw the phone away. He had no use for fucking memes.

"You have a party to plan," he said to no one in particular, except the chandelier. "Get the fuck up, Percy."

At that moment of helplessness, Si came to mind. Good Si, dependable Si, the Si that worshipped him and made him a queen.

And that was when Percy made the mistake of inviting him.

Percy and Si were holding hands, their fingers woven with each other. The ecstasy of Vicodin was kicking in and he was pulled irresistibly to Si's face. They shared a metaphysical moment, something Percy didn't learn from multiple volumes of human physiology. *Addiction is human. Needing someone is divine.*

Percy refused to think. Clarity was rare and he refused to spend it on silly philosophy. It shouldn't be spent on anything but itself.

Si's face hovered above Percy's. That face. Those lips. Those eyes.

And then the doorbell rang. The moment was over. Percy untangled from Si's hand.

As he walked away, he was surprised about the lack of disappointment. Of the few things Percy wanted, Si ranked highest, but with the ring of the door, Si was plopped out of his consciousness and re-created in the cosmos before being planted back. It was just Si. It was nothing more.

Percy straightened his shirt and opened the door to a very late Ryan.

"Well, thank you for showing up."

Stupid Girls

BADGER WAS TRYING TO ENJOY his conversation with El, who'd been spending a good half hour discussing agrarian reforms. Badger was smiling and nodding, but mentally, he was replaying last week's play-offs and wondering *what the fuck happened to this crowd's parties?*

"So, can we count on your support? Badger?"

El's direct address brought the former jock to reality. No matter how hot El was, the rich boy's speeches dragged on for so long even a boy who spent his weekends memorizing basketball statistics would zone out.

"Mmm? Yeah, I guess, sure." Badger missed the latter half of El's speech, but one never argued with El.

El brandished a sheet of paper. "Perfect. Sign here and we're one person closer toward genuine agrarian reform."

To Badger's relief, Percy announced the arrival of Ryan. El rushed to give Ryan a tight hug, saving Badger from committing to a cause he didn't support.

"Where've you been hiding, you!" El rocked Ryan left and right.

The commotion drew more attention as a hiccuping Long stumbled toward them. *Fuck, was he already drunk?* Sure seemed that way as he jumped around in a circle with Ryan and El while Percy pursed his lips.

From the opposite side of the room, Sugar stopped playing the piano to come greet the new arrival. *Oh, shit.* Sweat dripped from Badger's collarbone. Though he'd been aware that Sugar'd be here, he'd hoped to avoid him. This proved wrong as the blonde boy headed toward them.

Furtively, Badger checked the room for a distraction. Nothing. Everyone was coming their way. *Bathroom!* No one'd look for him there. "Fellas, I gotta—"

"Badger!" Ryan called out. They faced each other in an awkward stand-off, unsure if they were close enough to hug. Ryan settled the matter by tapping him on the shoulder. "How're you, man? Good to see you. Heard you're at the foreign ministry—"

"Hi, Ryan." With Sugar only a few meters away, Badger was stumbling over his thoughts. "Yeah, the minister's. So, uhm, hey, happy birthday. Or congratulations, was it? Fuck, I forgot, sorry, dude."

Ryan laughed. "'Hi, Ryan' would do."

Badger's toes were twitching. He had to tap out and this hippie painter he hardly knew was making it impossible to leave.

"Sorry for cutting, gotta piss!" Badger backed off quickly. And not a moment too soon as Sugar was now giving Ryan a peck on the cheek. Then laughter, followed by the pop of a champagne bottle. *Guess the party's officially starting.*

As he was scurrying out, he noticed a tipsy Long run back to the sofas to grab Vyn. *What happened to Vyn?* Back in high school, he was the worst, the most obnoxious flaming little fairy he'd ever seen. Always cackling or gossiping or twisting everything to a sexual metaphor. Now he looked like he should be committed.

In the hallway, he held the banister to catch his breath. He'd been rushing (hopefully no one noticed) and his lung capacity wasn't on par with when he used to paint the court with his three-pointers. He clutched his belly, making a mental note to hit the gym tomorrow. He was lying. He hadn't been there in years.

"Excuse me."

Badger turned to see a mousy-haired stranger. *Wasn't this a class reunion?* With a beer in one hand, a phone in the other, he looked older than most of the boys here. "This is weird, but are you TigerClaws69? From Grindr? It's me, Zk10inches"

None of those words made sense. "Tiger what?"

"From Grindr?" the guy repeated. After Badger didn't reply, the guy followed with, "The app? Grindr, the dating app?"

Badger clutched his stomach. Laughter pained him. A dating app. *For fuck's sake.* A chuckle escaped him. *Ouch!* "I don't use those."

"Stupid, stupid Zeke!" The guy punched the wall. *Psycho.*

"Got stood up?" Badger asked. Zeke nodded. "Didn't show up, eh? Or maybe he saw you and ran? Maybe he figured he'd have better luck with those porno paparazzi boys."

Zeke clutched his chest and took a few deep breaths. "Know anyone here?" he asked after calming down.

"Try everyone," Badger replied. "Well, except you and the creepy guy by the piano." He was referring to the guy hanging around Sugar. From one look, Badger distrusted him. His messy hair and psychedelic colored shirt raised every flag in Badger's head. Being with Sugar might've also triggered that.

"Why aren't you with them?"

Badger shrugged. "Cause I'm talking to you, you dolt. Gimme a swig of that, wilya?"

Zeke handed Badger his beer. A little over half was left. He took a long swig. From the bar, another round of laughter rang out. "Stupid, stupid, stupid," Badger mumbled.

Badger had gone to the party for one reason alone: to fuck.

This wasn't unattainable. Badger fucked a lot of boys in his prime. A teenager charged with testosterone and a superiority complex, he put his dick into anything that'd let him. Like El. They did it. A lot. Messy and violent, they fucked in toilets, classrooms, and parking lots. Badger desired this. El's ruggedness and masculinity rivaled his.

No one (or at least very few) knew about them. Badger was confident in El's discretion. Worst case, he'd probably tell his friends. Badger was fine with that. Everyone needed a living diary to brag to. His was his best friend Si. Si had the same masculinity in spades, but the one time he and Si fucked in the showers after a glorious match, they ended up splattering water at each other's dicks. Si was a bro and bros before hos.

El behaved as Badger wanted. Brisk, direct, and fast. In and out. Kisses leading to foreplay leading to sex leading to clothes on and a goodbye. Uncomplicated. Neither was interested in anything more than physical. El claimed he had a purpose he couldn't achieve if tied down. Bunch of shit but Badger couldn't judge.

Badger never saw himself tied down with anyone, period. He didn't feel the need or even the desire to form partnerships. Romance was alien. He tried it a few times, dating, courtship, wooing. *Shudder*. Some people aren't built for love. And that's okay.

After high school, he lost touch with everyone. A political science major, he gravitated toward the fraternity culture of toga parties, hazing, and orgies. The house's devil-may-care views suited his hedonistic lifestyle. What he couldn't get in romance, he found in brotherhood with his frat brothers who were clones of himself.

He also had his fill of men. His stature gave him the privilege of choice. He wasn't interested in twinks or chubs. He wanted men. Men like him, who bench-pressed, played sports, and didn't wear nail polish. Fucking himself became the ultimate form of self-love.

He wouldn't have had his job at the foreign ministry if not for a fraternity brother. His job involved international policy and the management of key diplomatic roles. In truth, he was way over his head. Popularity, good looks, and charisma didn't help in the boardroom.

Working for the government came with conduct clauses that prevent controversial public behavior. No more clubbing, no more streaking. For the longest time, he couldn't get laid. The available men were too effeminate. *No.* He'd rather celibacy than fuck a flaming queen.

When Si told him about the party, his hormones woke up. Especially when he was told El was coming. Nostalgia did weird things. Even though Sugar was also on the invite, Badger took his chances. Nostalgia, indeed.

Seeing his classmates so catty and feminine made Badger choke. At the bar, Sugar, Ryan, and Long pumped their arms to their chests while bending up and down to the steps of a YouTube craze. *Pathetic.*

But masculine Zeke wasn't like that. The rage with which he punched that wall made Badger's throat wet.

"Sorry he stood you up. Try hitting on people in person. Way more fun."

"Alright, how?" Zeke asked. "I'm so…I'm bad at groups."

"First, spot someone you like. It's about eye contact. You got a drink, he's got a drink. You're sipping, he's sipping. Catch his eye. It'll take a few times unless he's also playing. Once he's spotted you, hold the look for three seconds. That's all you need, three seconds. Stare at his eyes for three seconds. Then smile."

"Smile?" Zeke asked. "I'm bad at this. Uh, how do I smile? Like this?"

Zeke put on a few smiles. First was a slight grin. ("That's a little girly.") Then he pursed his lips into a pout. ("Too girly.") Finally, he widened his mouth showing all his teeth. ("Okay that one's creepy. Never do that again.")

They laughed. Badger took another swig and handed the beer back. *This boy'll learn even if I have to teach him in private.* The doorbell rang. "Door!" Badger yelled.

"I have ears, swine." An irate Percy strutted across them. Focused on scoring, Badger disregarded Precious Percy.

"What next?" Zeke asked, as Percy walked back to the living room with the newly arrived bald guest.

"Next, you approach him, then you say hi. That's it. Hi. No stupid pickup lines or shit. Hi. If he's not interested, apologize, and back off. Don't chase. It's stupid. But if he's willing to play, game fucking on."

"Makes it seem so easy." Zeke emptied the beer.

"It is. Everything beautiful is always simple. Everything."

He wasn't lying. Badger didn't do complicated. No chasing, no weeks-long seduction. They either wanted to play with him or they didn't. And if they did, better drop their pants.

Zeke pulled out another can of beer, fiddling with the lid as Badger glanced at the bar. Percy put on a few tracks, and the boys danced to a disco beat. *Madonna? Cher? Who cares?*

"Maybe if I acted like that," Zeke said, following Badger's gaze. "Maybe I wouldn't be single."

"Be glad you don't," Badger replied. "That disease is an epidemic."

"And you're the cure?" Zeke's fingers brushed against his arm. *Score.* But the cure was some modicum of common sense. Gay men liked men. *Why would I fuck someone who acted like a bitch?*

Zeke's skin tickled Badger's arm hair. "Sure wish you were TigerClaws69."

"I'm not." Badger grinned. "But I'm Badger."

Zeke stretched his arm out for a handshake. Badger was so close. He could almost taste Zeke. Yet from the corner of his eye, he spotted Sugar headed their way. *Fuck. Foul!*

Sugar. Or Edgar back in high school. Badger noticed him a lot then. He ran with El's crowd and Badger fancied him.

He was everything Badger found attractive in El and more. He was as masculine and reserved, but unlike El, he was raw. Everything was manly, the color of his skin, the fall of his hair, even the lack of scent. Yet Badger never spoke to him as Sugar was never without his friends.

Once when Badger was banging El in the comfort rooms, he asked him about Sugar. El wasn't the type to gossip but when you are being fucked in a cubicle, lips get loose.

El told him Sugar came from a poor family, yet he hated being pitied. Compared to El, everyone was poor, but Sugar's family was impoverished. El'd been to all his friends' houses except Sugar's. He didn't want people over, and no one pushed.

What Badger found most intriguing was Sugar's gift. According to El, he was a natural with the piano, able to create magic with his fingers.

Badger felt the closest thing to an emotion. A longing for music that could heal his damage. *Was the piano too gay?* Badger didn't care. The thoughts escaped him as he and El came at the same time.

Yet he'd always think of Sugar. Once, he snuck into the music room to hear him play. El's description wasn't glorious enough. Badger knew squat about music, but Sugar's tune opened his emotions more than a championship trophy. It brought memories of childhood when he played kitchen with his sisters. Or that time he got elbowed on the court, and his other teammates ganged up on the offending player.

Weird thing, music. Badger didn't understand it. He was just a jock.

●

Years passed, and Badger accepted his brokenness as part of him. Bored at the ministry, he was browsing Facebook when he came upon Sugar.

He sent him a message asking if he wanted to go for coffee. Badger waited a week before a curt "Sure" came.

Arriving early at the coffee shop, his feet tapped the rhythm of Kobe's playbook from last week's play-offs. Badger hoped Sugar still played the piano.

What a surprise the person he was meeting wasn't Edgar but—

"Sugar. I'm Sugar. Edgar is my father." He crossed his legs, opening a pack of cigarettes.

Nothing about the Edgar he remembered was sitting there. Instead of the masculine boy, what sat across him was a blonde curly-haired twink in a tiny shirt, smoking long thin cigarettes. He cringed at Sugar's clutch bag. He cringed louder upon noticing traces of foundation on his face.

"So nice of you to contact me, sweetie," Sugar said. "I always wonder how my old high school classmates are. I asked El about you, but he had no clue."

Badger raised a brow. "You knew about us?"

"Oh, sweetie." Sugar flicked the ashes from his cigarette. "The entire school knew."

Appearance was one thing. The personality change was worse. Sugar spoke in an annoying high pitch. Gone was the silent lad, replaced by this gossip. As their drinks were delivered, Sugar showed him pictures of a chihuahua, ("Look at the itsy-bitsy doggie!") as he prattled on about their classmates.

Badger had no interest in Mickey's break-up. *The fuck*, half their class were strangers to him.

Sugar never brought up music. Badger's dreams of hearing the haunting melody were replaced by: "I was talking to Mickey, and, well he was always closer to Long, but that's another story. But like Mickey's really nice, though it's hard to find time to catch up with him. He's so busy! Do you know what his job is? Oh, my! But anyway, I was telling him, poor sweetie, that it'd be alright, he deserves better, you know. What else do you tell a friend who just broke up, right? It didn't really feel like my place, look at me, the single aunt friend. But, like, I couldn't keep my mouth shut, could I?"

Enough. Enough. Enough! "You really couldn't, could you?"

Sugar dabbed his face with a napkin, a look of guilt creeping on. "Oh, sweetie, I'm sorry. I prattle too much. Tell me how've you've—"

Badger's ears heated. If anyone heard him being called 'sweetie', well, *damn it, conduct clauses*! He tightened his grip on the mug. "Don't call me 'sweetie', Edgar."

"Well, don't call me 'Edgar', sweetie!" Sugar said, voice raised. A few tables tuned in.

"Okay, okay, sorry, Sugar." Badger emphasized the name. "I just…I'm in shock, like, no offense but when did you become so faggy?"

Badger regretted opening his mouth. He didn't mean to offend Sugar nor scandalize the surrounding patrons. He meant, *fuck*, he wasn't sure what he meant.

In contrast, Sugar took his time with his words. "Well, then, Badger. I apologize for being, as you say, faggy. I'm sorry I'm no longer the Edgar you remember, who you probably wanted to fuck! I'm sorry I'm more fabulous now. I'm sorry you don't want to fuck me now. I'm sorry you're not man enough to fuck me!"

Sugar was causing a scene. Waiters were whispering and Badger swore a couple of patrons had their phones out.

"Damn it, Edgar—Sugar, I didn't, obviously, I'm gay too, I didn't mean it that—and I didn't want to fuck—to do what you said I wanted—I was curious where you were—if you still played. The piano! If you played the piano! I didn't mean to call you a fag. I was—shocked—I mean—you were a guy—and now you're so—so damn feminine and—"

Sugar picked up a glass of water and threw it on his face before walking out. As he left, people clapped.

He stayed there, dazed, embarrassed, and guilty. *Will this go trending?* People'd lost their jobs over less. His shame would last longer when the waiter, a bald guy whose nameplate read CC, came to him:

"I assume you're paying for everything?"

Badger was locking eyes with Sugar. *One. Two. Three damn seconds!* He averted his gaze.

Zeke lowered his arm. "Seen a ghost?"

Badger didn't have time. He ran. "I have to piss!"

He was marching so fast Zeke's yell barely reached him. "That's not the right way!" Still. Away from Sugar was away from Sugar. This was a mistake. Stupid, stupid mistake. One night of meaningless sex was not worth another confrontation. He should've known better. He should've—

Wait. Did he come here not for El but for Sugar? But he never thought of Sugar since. *Take it out of your damn mind! You're Badger. No chubs, no femmes, no uglies. Get out! Leave.*

All the doors looked the same. He passed by Percy's family portrait twice. He wiggled the doors, but they were locked. *Damn fucking rich kids.*

And what would Sugar do? Would he humiliate him? Throw more water? *Jesus,* he was thankful no video of their coffee shop date (the word 'date' gave him shivers) went viral. *How bad would it be now?*

He turned back to the hall. Zeke and Sugar weren't there. Creeping, he spotted a door that looked like the closet he left his jacket in. He's gonna go, grab the jacket, then bounce. *That's it. Clear your head, that's all.*

He opened the door and there stood Sugar.

"Sweetie, you forget," said the boy he was fleeing from. "We've had so many sleepovers here that I can sleepwalk and still find you."

Oh, balls. Badger clutched his chest. "I was just looking for—"

"Me?"

Badger looked at Sugar, expecting to see anger. His breathing hadn't steadied yet. *Dammit,* he needed to get back in shape. He braced himself for what Sugar was dishing. Yet nothing. Nothing but the playful smile of someone who had moved on.

Badger steadied his knees. "Sugar, I'm really—"

Sugar waved him off, grabbing his arm. "Hush, sweetie. Come back to the party."

Dear Mr. President

EL HADN'T LAUGHED THIS HARD in a long time.

He had arrived early to help Percy prepare, forgetting that his childhood friend wasn't only a perfectionist but also neurotic. ("Sit and look pretty!") He whittled the time away getting people to sign his petition. Long and Vyn put their names in, but he doubted either was aware of what they were signing. Badger was *this* close, but he wandered off to god-knows-where.

The agrarian reforms campaign drifted from his mind as he sat around a table with Ryan, Percy, and Si. *Oh, and Vyn!* Vyn was so quiet in his chair they barely noticed him. El sniffed his gin and water. Tangy and bitter but gets the job done.

They were asking Ryan so many questions about his exhibit until he finally revealed the title: *Dama de Noche.*

"Queen of the Night?" Spanish was one of the twelve languages El spoke.

"There's this flower," Ryan said, "that smells good but only at night."

Percy leaned his head on Si's shoulder. "No more nude boys, just flowers?"

Ryan smirked. "Who said I'm painting flowers?"

Si whispered to Percy, and they both laughed. El's thoughts, however, were still on the flower. He studied botany a while back, but he had never heard of this. *Its scent came out at night. Most peculiar. Was a chemical in the night air reacting with the pollen?* He'll look it up later.

His musings were broken when Ryan asked him how he'd been. El hated open-ended questions. "Me? Busy with work."

This was a lie. All of them knew El didn't 'work', at least not in any conventional sense of a job. Even Percy had to attend med school to take over the family practice. El didn't need to do anything. Their family owned pretty much the entire city, including the hospital where Percy was working and the gallery where Ryan would be having his exhibit. Officially he was the VP although only in title. He only goes to the office when bored.

"It's so calm out." Ryan pointed toward the backyard. "Look at the moon! Is that a blue moon?"

El peered out. Ryan was incorrect, but the full moon was beautiful. At its most rotund, it nestled above the trees. If he were to squint, the moon seemed within arm's reach.

"Up for a walk?" Ryan offered. El looked toward Si and Percy, but they were locked in whispers, their fingers playing together. El chuckled. *Percy never learns, but then again neither do we.*

Standing, he tapped Vyn's shoulder. "Coming?"

Vyn shrugged, dragging his ass off the chair, and the three headed to the backyard.

The evening was perfect, save for a chill. El wished he had grabbed his coat. Ryan was impervious to the cold and Vyn huddled in his jacket. Shivering, El clung on to Ryan's arm. He missed the rowdiness of his friends. A secret part of him wished he could pay them salaries so they could hang out all the time.

They were all wonderful, weren't they? Even though Percy could learn to relax and Long could sober up occasionally. Back in the day, he had also wished Vyn would temper his scandalous mouth; but now that he's faced with an uncharacteristically silent Vyn, he missed the crassness.

But no one's been the same. He shuddered. *What was it like to be Vyn the night of the car crash? What a champ, Vyn, surviving after that.* El wondered if he would've handled it better. *No. Damn no.* He'd fly off to live in a ranch in Australia.

As the trio strolled, they passed Long finishing a cigarette. Ryan invited him to come with, but Long, signaling his drink was empty, headed inside. *Ah, Long. We keep worrying about Vyn but perhaps Long's the one we should be worried about.*

"You know the problem with you rich boys," Eyes had said once as they sat around El's new condo. It was their second year in university and the boys were starting to get occupied by books and boys. Fortunately, Percy had a free day and Vyn wasn't the type to spend hours poring over charts. Eyes was like El. He never studied but managed A's.

El was glad to have friends over to view his condo. He'd bought it recently on a whim. A bachelor pad near the university was convenient after all. With a few swipes of his credit card, the place came to life. New layer of paint, the most luxurious chairs, and the most cutting-edge electronics in the market.

Eyes sat snug in the armchair. "Nothing. Nothing's the problem with you."

"Thanks, I guess." El was busy passing bottles of beer. He wasn't used to serving people, but his friends' presence pressured him.

"No. Not *thanks*," Eyes replied. "*Nothing* is the problem with you. You have a problem with *nothing*. You don't understand *nothing*. Take Miss Percy over here, incapable of solitude, and you, my dear El, incapable of boredom."

By the 60-inch television, Percy threw a remote toward Eyes. "I don't have a problem with solitude, you hipster."

This prompted Vyn to hump the sofa while mimicking Percy's shrill voice. "Oh, Si, oh, Si, I love you, I need you so much, mwaaah. Si, never leave, Oh, Si!"

El laughed. Vyn made a great Percy.

"Children." Percy ignored El's beer. "I am friends with children." He stormed off to the bathroom.

"My dear, can I have a straw?" Eyes drawled. "I don't drink without a straw. It doesn't make sense to drink without a straw."

Host duties fulfilled, El plopped down on the sofa beside Vyn. *Aah!* So comfortable, El put his socked feet up on Vyn's lap. "I don't have straws. I threw them all out."

"What did straws ever do to you?" asked Eyes. Vyn pushed El's feet off and tackled him across the sofa. "My dear, straws will never leave you. Straws will always love you. They will never replace you with a younger, hotter, fitter model with a 12-inch cock."

El's hands were pinned down while his face was subjected to playful slaps. In between hits, El tried to respond. "Been dating this guy. Cut it out. He's an environmentalist. Forests or mountains or some shit. Get off! And I went to his meetings and, like, did y'know straws are not just useless but since they don't decay, the landfills…"

"My dear, it's a straw. One straw. I will not destroy a rainforest with a straw."

"I will destroy you!" Vyn punched El's shoulders.

Eyes stood up to grab a cup. "And speaking of the goddamn rainforests and save the whales and kumbaya, out of curiosity, and no shade at all, how much power does this pad consume?"

As Vyn looked up, El found his opening. With his opponent distracted, he gathered all his might to push him to the floor. "Not the point, Eyes. We all gotta do our part for—"

"I love your bathroom." Perfect timing for Percy to return. "You have to give me the name of your decorator. Automatic flushes, centralized heating, clap-on lights. You've outdone yourself."

El's moment of triumph was brief. Even regular sessions at the gym were powerless against a raging Vyn, who locked El's arms behind his back. "I have a feeling I'm about to lose."

Vyn pinched El's cheeks. "Me, I like environmentalists."

"You know what an environmentalist is?" As if no one were wrestling on the floor, Percy walked over them to get to the sofa.

Vyn kissed El's nose. "They love wood."

Eyes sauntered back to his cozy armchair, his drink now in a plastic cup. El was going to throw out the plastic cups with the straws, but they were more convenient than having to wash glasses. "You know, the problem with you rich kids," Eyes said, as Vyn refused to let El up. "Nothing. Absolutely nothing."

By the pool chairs, they sat down, Ryan reclining while El laid on the ground, his head on Ryan's lap. Vyn sat two pool chairs down.

So nice to cuddle with Ryan. Even with a belly forming, Ryan was a delight. *How did we get this far alone?* "How're you doing, Ryan? Seriously?"

Ryan was silent. El followed his friend's gaze toward the forming constellations. His astronomy was weak, but he could make out the Dippers, Orion's Belt, and his star sign Virgo.

Ryan put his hand on El's shoulder. "I need more alcohol to answer."

Climbing up the chair, El rested on Ryan's body. "I went to a couple of your exhibits, but I must've missed you. I met this odd fellow with emerald hair—said he was your friend."

Ryan sighed, shaking his head. "Should've told me. We could've grabbed a drink or something."

"Yeah, or something." A few feet away, Vyn lay down. El wanted to tell him to come closer, but a nagging voice told him to stop fixing other people when he was as fucked up as everyone.

"How about you?" Ryan asked. "What're you up to? Rarely see you on Facebook."

"Yeah, I guess, you know, just work," El repeated.

Ryan messed up El's hair. "You don't work, El."

El chuckled. "Campaigning on agrarian reforms lately. I got a sheet, collecting signatures, you'd sign, won't you?"

"New cause of the week?"

El hated that phrase. His friends mocked him about his various plights, but they were important. Making a difference in the world wasn't a joke. Granted he does take on a lot of these, mostly dependent on the trends. But that was irrelevant. He fought for justice as long as time allowed.

He stiffened. "Nah. The farmers haven't been granted their land and we're picketing His Excellency."

"Say no more."

No further grief? El handed Ryan his petition. *Oh, Ryan, how you've changed.* They all have. Tragedy does that.

"Here you go, mate." Ryan handed the paper back. "Anything to make you happy. You're happy, right?"

He gazed at the petition. Progress. But Ryan's question hung over him.

Whether he was happy was something he couldn't answer. He supposed he was content but whether contentment resulted in happiness is something time or distance would prove.

A few months ago, a bored El was browsing Grindr, when he chanced upon a set of six-pack abs he fancied. Bringing home guys wasn't a challenge. Very few could say no to El's classic looks—and even if they could, they would change their mind once they realize who El was. What a shock then when six-pack told him to "eat a bagful of dicks, you bourgeois trust fund oligarch."

No one had ever rejected him like that. El was Golden Boy. Instead of backing off, his interest was piqued. The boredom of solitude was replaced by a challenge. He asked for clarification, but the guy never responded. As this was Grindr, the guy had no face. All El knew was the guy had beautiful abs.

Marxist emojis dotted the guy's profile and his description referenced a local leftist chapter. Though he adored social causes, El was unfamiliar with the greater political climate. After looking up the group, El donned what he considered commoner disguise (it wasn't) and went to their meeting. Thankfully, the organization wasn't picky and accepted him.

Although not his intention, El found a sense of belongingness in this group, the same kind he got from his friends. Before, his idea of the activism were stock images of riots, gunfire, and rebellion. But this group was more interested in discussions, debates, and drinking sessions to tackle the blunders of their president.

Their stories bothered El. Some of them worked more than forty hours a week ("I work 6 a.m. to 8 p.m. Monday to Sunday!") yet barely made enough. One of them had a son who disappeared. She suspected military abduction, but nothing had surfaced in years. The trans activists, despite their own battles for gender recognition, stood valiantly with the workers.

Of course, rallies were par for the course. They marched down the national highway, arms linked, chanting the rhetoric of resignation or death. He was proud of his slogan. (His maid drew it. She graduated from fine arts.) It bore the words "Dear Mr. President, No One's Better Than Us."

Once, as an outreach activity, they went to the slums to integrate with the homeless. *Wow.* His whole body had perspired. His armpits and crotch were drenched. How could people live in these conditions?

He was ashamed. Ashamed of the full breakfast he ate, ashamed of the sports cars in his garage, ashamed of the zeros stocking up on his bank account. What could he tell these people?

Outside an Apple store, he spotted a pregnant woman lying on a cardboard box. Her hair was greasy, and her clothes smelled like they hadn't been washed in months. She cradled a wailing baby while two other kids lay down beside her. Their bodies were so fragile, one push could break their bones.

But what broke El's heart was the way she knelt to pray. El didn't believe in a divine, but he believed in the power of man. He fished out all his cash and dropped it inconspicuously beside the woman.

That night, though he lay on Egyptian cotton sheets, he couldn't sleep. Yet, he found fulfillment. The life of an activist was so hectic, he forgot about the six-packed guy from Grindr until he got a message saying: "Hey, rich kid. Guess you're alright."

He was stunned. He didn't want his personal information revealed. The El who was a corporate vice-president, who lounged at pools and shopped for exotic animals, the Golden Boy was separate from the El who marched with a mask down Central Avenue. If the media found out, his company would be ruined. If the group found out, he'd be kicked out. A collision would ruin everything he created on both fronts.

Facing a tough choice, he never went back to the association.

"I envy you, Eyes," El had confided to his friend a few years ago. They were young professionals now, their lives busier than ever. They didn't know it then, but this would be the last sleepover they would ever have.

At that moment, only he and Eyes were still awake. The hours after a party were never clean. Figuring out where people were headed was a chore for drunken minds. Percy'd gone home, unwillingly driving a drunk King, Vyn, and Sugar. Long was passed out on the sofa, and Ryan had commandeered El's bed.

El was watching Eyes kick his jeans off. "Ever since high school, you wanted to be a writer, and look where you are now."

"Underpaid, overworked, and under-appreciated?"

El laughed. Chalk it up to Eyes to make light of his problems. "Some days, I think I'm just another lonely boy."

"Can I tell you a secret, my dear?" Eyes yawned as he lay beside Long, putting the latter's arms around him. "Everyone's lonely. Every single bloody person on this planet. You rich kids, you rich kids once again think it's just you."

Eyes was known for riddles like this. Had he been more sober or had the hour been godlier, El would've quizzed Eyes. But even great minds turn off. "Good night, Eyes."

He brought empty glasses back to the kitchen for the maid to clean tomorrow.

"Hey," Eyes said, as El headed to the guestroom. "You're alright, El. Bit of a prick, but you're alright."

Eyes's soft snores mixed with Long's grunts. El grabbed a blanket and draped it over his two friends. He was alright.

"I am not Eyes," Ryan said, as he held El. "I'll never be Eyes. He talked a lot of shit, didn't he? He was wise, but you had to wade through a good amount of BS to get the point."

"Fucking Eyes." El cuddled closer.

"We'll never know when we're happy, El. We never really do. And it's not a matter of waking up jolly and fulfilled and enlightened. As if happiness were a gift from a sadistic god."

El laughed. "Please don't say happiness is a choice."

"Jesus, lord, sodomites, and bedwetters. Eyes would kill me." Ryan joined in the laughter. "It isn't though. I think happiness is deciding when you wake up every morning to fuck the day, fuck the police, fuck the problems, fuck everything! Today,

I'm gonna smile. But smiling is hard. It hurts the face. Is that what happy is? Painful smiles? I don't know, El. Wish I did."

They lay there. El invited Vyn to join, yet he declined. He was alright. The stars agreed. Maybe El wasn't destined for happiness. But that was alright. A lot of people weren't happy. And they had it worse.

Did that poor woman outside the Apple store give birth? El made a mental note to get his secretary to check. Maybe he'd send her a basket of fruit. That always made him feel better. Not happy, but better.

After a while, the air was too much, and they made their way back in.

So What

CLICK. BEFORE WALKING UP to the door, Mickey took a selfie. *Click.* Alright. *Hair's good, love the classic big glasses, you're a rock star.* Mickey blew himself a kiss.

His phone's shutter clicks were interrupted by constant vibrations. All messages from work: a client wanting to push her reservation, a florist running out of tulips, and his personal assistant clarifying if the wine was indeed white, even though they were serving pork. All idiots, especially the last one.

Mickey's fingers itched to reply, but he needed a night off work. Pocketing the phone, he headed up. Someone else was knocking on the door. *Was that—oh, no…*

"Wallace!" Mickey called out. "Didn't know you were coming!"

"Hey, my man, what's up?" Wallace stormed down the porch to give him a hug. To Mickey's horror, Wallace was wearing a buttoned shirt with a Mandarin collar, a pair of ripped jeans, and alligator shoes. *Oh, Wallace. No.*

Wallace wasn't the guy one invited to a party. Already insufferable in high school, he graduated to an obnoxious prat who loved boasting about his new job, his new car, and his newfound success. Mickey didn't mind though. Part of being an event organizer (*THE event organizer, thank you very much*) was dealing with egos too large for their bodies.

"Stroke of fortune! Didn't know about this shindig until Angelo brought it up at the office. Said you guys were having a party and I decided, hey, why not, right? Gotta stop working so hard, y'know, bit of fun doesn't hurt. Besides, Cuba's not the best this season. Ah! I can go maybe later this year."

With a smile reserved for the most difficult clients, Mickey nodded as Wallace began to explain the various investments he made. Mickey was saved when Percy answered the door.

After surveying the room, Mickey felt relieved he arrived at the right time. Not early enough for awkward conversations, but not too late that everyone was singing shanties. Wallace left to go chat with Angelo by the pool table.

Reprieved of Wallace, Mickey caught his bearings over a glass of champagne with Sugar and his friend.

"This is my roommate, Drew." Sugar pointed to his companion. "Boy's new so I figured let's introduce him to the little monsters!"

The new boy looked like he'd fit better at a rave. Mickey had just organized a gig for a touring rock band and the people at the mosh pit wore similar colorful shirts. Sugar, as usual, was lovely. It was impossible to dislike Sugar.

"I wouldn't call you a little monster, Sugar," Mickey said.

"Oh, sweetie." Sugar laughed. "Some people here would!"

"Well, some people here are monsters. Just not very little!"

After more banter, Mickey continued his rounds. He greeted El, reminding him about the studio he'd been trying to book. El told him to talk to his secretary, before getting him to sign a petition. To get on El's good side, Mickey signed it without much ado.

Si, Percy, and Badger were talking by the table. Mickey'd say hello to them later. While customary to compliment the host, Percy was so engrossed in their conversation he barely noticed Mickey passing by.

And then Mickey spotted him. There he was, the mousy-haired guy lurking by the cactus. *Zeke*.

Mickey had many reasons to come to this party. One, he was a party planner and being seen in the company of rich guys like Percy and El, artists like Ryan and Eyes, etc., would boost his credibility. Two, ironically, there was little opportunity for a party planner to party without worrying about a melting ice sculpture or a DJ too drunk to scratch. And third, was the mousy-haired guy.

Zeke and Mickey broke up not that long ago. Days are a blur to Mickey. It could've been a year now and he wouldn't be surprised. Most would consider it fortuitous his ex was at the same party, but Mickey always had a contingency.

They'd been together, *what, two, three years? Jesus, you'd think someone with an affinity for calendars would be more precise with his own life.* But the truth was that time had an odd way of slowing when he was with Zeke, a moment he craved after battling it out with stubborn suppliers or confused clients.

He had met Zeke at one such event ages ago. At that time, he was a staff member, working under a prominent organizer who commanded events like a general ordering around their troops. They were under pressure; the anniversary party was commissioned last minute, and everything, from the caterers to the guitar cable, had been on the fritz.

Mickey was doing damage control, making sure the waiters had served all the tables. One of the busboys had confessed that a fingernail accidentally fell into the lasagna, and Mickey was on standby, waiting for the lucky guest to discover it. No one so far. A jazz song played. His breath was baited when this mousy-haired guy in a nice suit approached him.

"Looks like you need a cigarette."

As Mickey was new, sneaking out for a cigarette wasn't *à propos*. Yet, not only had he been on his feet for close to seven hours now, (barely a moment to sit before the booming voice of his boss would yell) *but this mousy-haired boy was also kind of charming, wasn't he?*

He went out to the parking lot with Zeke. Zeke leaned against a pole while Mickey relaxed his feet on the steps. He didn't smoke, but sometimes everyone needed a drag to get through the night.

"What's a good-looking boy like you doing working so hard on a Friday night?" Zeke asked.

Mickey sighed. He'd forgotten what it felt to be flirted with. "Getting away from lines like that?"

The smoke was a welcome reprieve from work. He wished cigarettes lasted longer than six and a half minutes. Thankfully, Zeke took full advantage of that time. He talked about his job at an accounting firm, the thrill of crunching numbers, the bliss of seeing column A line up with column B. It was total satisfaction.

Mickey didn't care much for math, but Zeke was so passionate. "It's like sudoku. It's the unknown, it's the chaos. What we don't understand looms over the comforts of where we are. But when you complete the puzzle, and all rows, all columns, all squares are perfect, you get that moment. For that brief period, you regain control."

Chaos theory. Mickey wasn't much for metaphors, but he remembered El talk about chaos theory at length back when he was part of the group. Order in chaos, method in madness. Nothing is random, everything is destined.

Mickey shared that need for order. He wouldn't be a good organizer otherwise. Fascinating how different their jobs were and yet the core was the same. Whether it was caterers or spreadsheets; or place settings or ledgers, Mickey craved what they called the collapse: the moment the body fell from exhaustion at the end of a successful event.

They continued talking until both their cigarettes had become stubs. The night wind was enticing, but enough was enough. As he put out his cigarette, he mumbled, "Dangerous to your health, they say."

"Cigarettes or me?" Zeke moved his face to Mickey. *Damn. Damn the crescent moon and damn the lampposts for making Zeke so attractive.* The night won.

As they headed back in, Mickey was greeted by his boss. *Oh. Shit.* They took less than ten minutes. His arm hair stood. *Was I getting sacked?*

"Where were you! Is the video ready? I give you one simple task to—"

"That's okay, madame," Zeke cut in. "I needed Mickey's help outside."

Yup. Mickey would later be in hysterics when he learned the whole story. Zeke was the client who hired their company for his parents' anniversary. Watching his boss shrink by being openly questioned by her client was an image that would tattoo itself into his brain.

"Very well, very well, Mickey. Once you're done, please make sure the band's ready."

As she stormed off, Mickey and Zeke giggled.

"We could leave," Zeke whispered. "The parents are just happy they're out of the house. No matter how it goes, I'll give you a glowing review. I could also tell your boss I needed your help with something urgent. Something big and growing. Something in my pants."

Grr. Gorgeous boys came rarely, and always with danger. The night was calling, and the kiss was begging to be repeated.

But then a shriek emanated from the party. The fingernail was probably found.

He was tempted. Really tempted. His boss could deal with the fingernail fiasco. *But no.* This wasn't a gig for Mickey. This was his passion. He already had five ways to fix the situation, all ticking in his brain at the same time.

But Zeke was so pretty. "How about you save me for the after-party?"

So what if Zeke were here? Mickey shrugged off the nostalgia. It wasn't Zeke's night. It was his.

As he poured another glass of wine, he chatted with Ryan about his exhibit. His firm badly wanted to represent the up-coming *Dama de Noche.* Mickey asked Ryan for gallery details when Zeke passed by.

They caught each other's eyes, a flash of time not dissimilar with how they first met at Zeke's parents' anniversary. Mickey's eyes chased him until Zeke got pulled off by Percy and his crowd of jocks.

"So, yeah, it's my agent you'd have to talk to." Ryan's words drew Mickey back in. "I don't control most things, as much as I wish. But yeah, come over to my studio. I'll show you some samples to see if it's a match."

That was something off his checklist. Mickey wanted to talk more about the exhibit, but Ryan was two topics ahead. "Mickey, about Eyes."

He froze. This wasn't the direction he expected though he should've guessed from Ryan's invite. *What was he up to?*

"It was shitty what we did to you. We were—Jesus, lord, sodomites, and bedwetters. We were stupid. Immature."

Mickey eased up. "Thanks. We were young. And I'm sorry about Eyes. Damn."

"Damn." Ryan raised his glass to Mickey.

The sound of footsteps made Mickey turn around. A bald guy was coming their way. As soon as he arrived, Ryan disappeared. *Artists.* Mickey rolled his eyes.

"You ever notice," the bald guy asked, refilling his wineglass, "parties like this, it's impossible to talk to the one person you need?"

"No," Mickey replied. "I do this every day."

With a nod, he walked away. Ryan put him out of the mood to talk to strangers. One way or another, it'd end with a fight.

He had checked off almost everything on his agenda. El's studio, Ryan's exhibit. Percy? He needed to ask Percy about the club. *Dammit, Mickey. You're still working!*

Have fun. Enjoy. Turn your phone off.

Across the room, a loud thud was heard when a drunk Long stumbled while in the middle of a story. *Typical.*

Back in high school, Mickey used to run with Ryan, Eyes, and the rest. And he had some good times, though things got complicated when he'd started sleeping with Long. They were never officially together, but they shared enough to be complicated. Neither was what the other needed. Mickey, a rock star in his head, couldn't fit into Long's simple life. Even back then, his social calendar was always full of parties and galas, and he rolled his eyes at how basic Long's desire to stay in and cuddle was.

Once, they were having sex in Long's room and everything was loud, the cats were meowing, his sister was screaming, his brother's metal music was blaring. And Long couldn't get hard. "Gimme a moment, Mick—c'mon, get up! Get up! C'mon, don't let me down!"

Mickey had no time to waste—he still had to check-up on the homecoming committee. As he lay there with a decidedly limp Long, he swore he would never be involved in anything this messy.

Unfortunately, when a couple in a group broke up, sides were taken. He found himself invited less and less to their hangouts. He got ghosted, the outlier, the one they joked about. *Awful.* Every time he saw them, the pain reminded him of the boys he used to like.

Years later, Sugar would confess to him exactly what happened. Sugar wanted to keep both Long and Mickey, but the awkwardness split the group. While Percy said he didn't care ("I didn't give a fuck. If he stayed, if you stayed, if you both left."), Eyes felt strongly for Long. And when the self-appointed queen made up his mind, everyone else fell in line.

So what? We're more mature now. Back then, he thought Long was his longest mistake. Back then, he had yet to meet Zeke.

Looking at Mickey, one wouldn't guess he came from a break-up. Yes, he went through the clichés, dyeing his hair, re-inventing his wardrobe, getting back in shape. But these made him more attractive. Private life stayed under the sheets. When he was commanding events, his staff needn't know the emptiness in his life.

He went over to the sound system. "Hey Percy, can I change the jam?"

"I will literally murder you," Percy called back. "But, sure, go ahead."

In a city ruled by an independent music scene, Mickey was first to receive the latest tracks from publicists. The songs were pre-programmed in his iPod, which he connected to the sound system.

Let's start with this jazz band. The last time he booked them, the entire floor was on its feet. He had the most appropriate first song planned. The one that played when he and Zeke met.

Not one second after the song started, Long yelled, "I love this band!" *Of course, he did.* Mickey'd bet his next commission

Long couldn't identify the band's name. Regardless, Mickey proved to be the expert as people bounced to the beat.

"Let's have fun, guys!" Party planner in full force. "Show me your rock moves!"

After making sure the playlist was set for the night, he went back to the bar. On the way, he ran into Zeke.

"You okay?"

Mickey wasn't sure what hit him more. Talking to the person he was dying to avoid or that the only thing he could say was 'You okay?'

"I'm alright," Mickey replied. "I'm just fine."

Mickey turned to leave, but Zeke's hand clutched on his arm. "I worry for you."

Mickey wriggled his arm violently. Zeke had lost the privilege of touching him and telling him what to do. "You're a tool."

With that, Mickey got himself another drink. He wasn't sure where the vitriol stemmed from. He was lost without his Zeke, without the pillow he slept on after getting yelled at all day. *Why am I pushing him away?* He downed his wine and poured out another glass. No more work, he was gonna enjoy tonight. *So what?*

A doorbell introduced the arrival of King and the twins. *Alright.* He downed his wine again. *Now we're in trouble.*

With Zeke making his way through the dancing crowd, Mickey went back to the sofa. Percy and the jocks had vacated it to dance, and Wallace took over with Angelo and Reyes. The irony wasn't lost on Mickey that the only people who would stomach Wallace's boasts were the two boys with the least options.

"Having a blast?" Wallace greeted. "I was telling Reyes he should work on a stock portfolio. I made thousands on it. Thousands! I'm poised to take over the market."

"Absolutely." Mickey waved at the others. Angelo lifted his glass and Reyes nodded. Unlike the others, these guys were low maintenance. He unbuttoned his collar.

"I got more brochures with me, though some are in the car. It's very expensive, you know, and one day you can buy one too. How're you feeling?" Wallace didn't wait for a response. "Look at that! King's here! And the twins! Oh, we're in for it. So, investing. There's the high-risk high-reward if you're a go-getter, but there are also some fiduciary-backed low-risk ones."

Reyes whispered to Angelo causing the latter to snicker. "Enjoying yourselves?" Mickey asked. The two stood out worse than Wallace. Mickey couldn't remember a time when either attended a party. If not for Wallace, they'd be twirling their thumbs at the corner all night.

Wallace didn't give the two a chance to speak. "Where is Eyes, that old fucker? I haven't spoken to him in years. He still hangs out with this crowd, doesn't he?"

Mickey stared in disbelief. Angelo and Reyes had similar expressions on their faces. *How could he not…?*

"Wallace," Mickey said curtly. "Eyes is dead."

Who Knew

THERE WERE MULTIPLE REASONS why Eyes wasn't at the party. He didn't have clothes Percy would approve of. As a writer, events with more than ten people caused him to grow unpleasant. And, yes, he was dead.

Deader than dead, and even though Wallace didn't know (or didn't remember, perhaps? Surely, he's read about it somewhere), his presence or lack thereof was strong at the party.

Ryan once told him that he was the center of their little group. Eyes thought it balderdash. Yes, he knew everyone before they became a clique, yet everyone added something special. Sugar made everything sweeter (pun intended), Vyn turned up the volume at parties, Percy kept them on time, King started things up, El's pockets spelled opportunities, and Long could lift heavy tables.

"What about you and me?" Ryan asked. Eyes was visiting Ryan the day he sold his first painting, and they were sharing a cigarette at his balcony.

"My dear, you are our teenage angst." Eyes exhaled smoke all over, his ashes falling to the balcony of the apartment below. "And I, well, I bring the pretty."

Ryan was the newcomer. Back during the first day of freshman high school, Eyes spotted this meek hipster kid getting off his bike, trembling at the foot of the school stairs. *New meat. Delicious.* Eyes waltzed past him, chanting, "Beware, beware, the first of September."

During the first few weeks, Eyes always saw Ryan alone. Fumbling and awkward, the jocks of the school sniggered every time he walked past. But Eyes was fascinated, though he couldn't pinpoint why.

"What do you think of the new kid?" Mickey asked him, as they watched Ryan scramble to pick drawings off the floor. He'd been carrying a stack of papers when a stretched-out foot made him fall and drop the sketches.

Eyes pouted. "My dear, the last time I fell like that was because of gin."

Mickey laughed, and they went on their way. Before Eyes disappeared into a classroom, he turned to look at Ryan. There was a shared connection that Eyes almost got compelled to help Ryan pick up his stuff. Almost. He was Eyes. He didn't help people.

At the start of October, Eyes found himself in detention for failing to submit a science project. They were supposed to draw the insides of a frog, yet when Eyes was catching a frog in his backyard, he discovered a new species of worm. And worms were more interesting than frogs.

When Eyes entered the detention hall, the only other kid there was Ryan. "Oh, new kid." Eyes swung his bag down beside him. "Normally it's just me and the twins, what'd you do?"

Massaging his jaw, Ryan ignored his gaze. "Fighting."

Eyes couldn't read Ryan. He prided himself on the ability to see through people, but Ryan's shyness was his downfall. "My dear, this isn't prison. You don't go in on your first day and hit the toughest-looking kid. You can hit on him, but don't hit him."

"Just some jock." Ryan's voice cracked. "He called me a fag."

"What's so bad about being a fag?" Eyes laughed. "I am one."

Silent, Ryan stared at his fist. Perhaps Eyes crossed the line. It wouldn't be the first time Eyes inadvertently caused pain. Eyes took out his study books, letting the other kid take his time.

"I am one, too," Ryan whispered.

"And so are the jocks, if we were to be blunt, though they don't know it yet. Everyone is. We're all faggots here," said Eyes. "Here we are, my dear, two punk fairy queen faggots stuck in the horrid detention cell of this existential high school. What say we sue for discrimination?"

"I'm not really keen on the whole punk fairy faggot queen," Ryan replied. "Besides, it's not like everyone knows—"

"Oh, my dear, we've all seen how you sashay down the halls. Again, this is a high school, not a Victoria Secret runway," Eyes said, finally causing Ryan to laugh. Eyes smiled at the new kid's laughter. "If anyone thinks your sweet ass is heterosexual, they probably had a lobotomy."

Ryan shook his head. "Oh, Jesus, lord, sodomites."

"And bedwetters," Eyes finished. "Curse the bedwetters! You should add them to your list."

As a teacher could pop in at any time, they took out their study materials. Ryan flipped through his notebook, as Eyes snuck a peek at its contents, most of which were drawings. Though primarily the scribbles of a bored freshman, certain pages showed potential. There were superheroes, landscapes, monsters, and—

"You dirty, dirty boy!" Eyes couldn't control himself when he saw a sketch of a naked man chained to the bed. "Give that here!"

A red-faced Ryan shut his notebook. Eyes spent the rest of detention teasing Ryan about the erotic drawing. In between, he squeezed out more details about the new kid. Ryan moved from a town right outside the city when his mom got transferred. And he was pleased to leave. His dreams of being an artist were better situated in the city. But the most interesting thing Eyes learned was how Ryan had never been kissed.

Ryan blushed and diverted the topic by asking Eyes about his name. "It's not because you're cool as ice, are you? Because that's lame."

"E-Y-E-S," Eyes replied. "And I'm Eyes because I see everything."

Ryan thumped his desk. "That's even lamer!"

When the bell signaled the end of detention, Eyes watched Ryan pack his things. This was it. He couldn't resist. He grabbed Ryan's face and locked lips with him.

Ryan pushed him away. "You're Eyes, not Lips."

"My dear, since you've never been kissed, doesn't hurt to start with the best."

Despite the rumors, Ryan and Eyes never became a couple. Not because they didn't care for each other; on the contrary, both loved each other dearly. But their love wasn't romantic, but instead intimately platonic.

Yes, Ryan and Eyes took each other's virginity, a story they told with contrasting details. Occasionally, a drunken night or a depressing event would find them naked in bed together. But they preferred being cuddly and affectionate best friends.

Both were in search of elusive love as they looked toward a world both captured and free. As Ryan's skill in drawing grew, so did Eyes discover an affinity toward words. This became a collaboration the two would find beneficial.

One night, Eyes answered Ryan's knock, to find his best friend weeping. He'd just been broken up with ("My dear, you can cry over onions but never boys"). Yet, as the two boys lay in bed, Eyes was silent, content with caressing Ryan's hair.

He hated seeing his best friend cry, yet broken hearts and Ryan went hand in hand. Boys were stupid. They can't see the cornucopia of colors within Ryan.

"How about when we're forty," Eyes said, "and still single, maybe, what if the two of us be a couple or something?"

"That's what I am now?" Ryan buried into Eyes's shirt. "I'm a backup?"

"My dear, we're all just backups," Eyes said, holding him close. "All just backups."

It was here at Percy's mansion that Eyes had his last birthday party. Instead of a big bustling event like what was happening now, Eyes insisted on a more somber affair with only the eight friends present.

The birthday boy was lying on the sofa, his head on Long's lap. King was on the floor, rolling tobacco, his back reclining on Long's legs. El was cross-legged in the armchair, with Sugar sitting on his armrest. Vyn was annoying Percy by the patio doors.

Eyes yawned as Ryan balanced a tray of drinks from the bar. Everyone's drink was needlessly complicated, and it was Ryan's turn to fetch. "Need a hand, my dear?"

Ryan grunted. "I'm good, thanks."

"Oh, I was gonna offer Long, but, sure, you're welcome."

The drinks were parked at the coffee table. With his beer, Ryan sat on the floor opposite King. Sugar got up to get his grasshopper and El's old fashioned. "Okay, grab your drink. Time for your birthday toast, sweetie!"

"My dear." Burying his face in his hands, Eyes pretended to cry. "I'm ancient! Positively ancient!"

In between tickling Percy, Vyn chimed in, "Some boys are into old men now."

"You're five months younger than I," Eyes drawled.

"Yes, but you look forty and I look flirty!"

Percy slapped free from Vyn's fingers. He walked toward the table for his martini. "I think you mean filthy."

"What about my rum and coke?" Vyn demanded as Percy sat by Eyes's feet.

Percy gave him a harsh look. "You have legs."

Always willing to help, Sugar handed Vyn his drink and King his sex on the beach.

"Lemme just finish this," King mumbled. "I'll get tobacco all over."

Though Eyes was acting up, he was enjoying the evening. Long was a good pillow and kicking Percy was fun. "Oh, do make a mess, my dear, it'll make for an interesting evening: Percy taking the broom out of his ass to sweep."

Everyone, save Percy, laughed. "Did anything fun for your birthday?" El asked.

"Oh this and that," Eyes replied. He caught Ryan's look, who blushed. *He should after what they did earlier. All day.* "Been practicing my calligraphy, I suppose."

El perked up from his chair. "It's a dying art. Remind me, I have this book I can lend you."

"No. No silly books, my dear." Eyes still had a few volumes from Golden Boy's library. "Calligraphy is not learned from books but from the heart."

"What's calligraphy?" Long asked.

Eyes put his hands around Long's face. *So beautiful and so dumb.* "Oh, my dear, calligraphy is the art of letters."

"Lettering. And your penmanship's atrocious." Percy pushed Eyes's legs to the floor. "I could barely make out your note."

"Take note, a doctor's telling you your handwriting sucks!" Ryan added, the red gone from his face.

This was Vyn's cue. "I got something else you can suck." He grabbed Long's head and shoved it into his crotch. Long flailed his arms, trying to push Vyn away. Long was kidding, of course. If he wanted to push Vyn, he'd be sprawled on the floor by now.

"I suppose, might as well, get these shenanigans over with." Eyes sat up to get his margarita and Long's tequila sunrise. "Dearly beloved, we gather here today to pray for salvation. Jesus Amen!"

"Could've gone to the twins'," King said, his cigarette rolled. "Good ol' Timmy's been bugging me to host a game."

Eyes sighed, but Ryan was quicker to respond. "No way you'll convince any sane person to go to the twins'."

King was about to light his cigarette but a look from Percy made him tuck it in his jacket. "There are hot boys! Imagine strip poker with them."

Eyes lounged back, sniffing his drink. *Mmm.* "He's right. Hot boys are a commodity these days."

"Oh, sweetie, hot boys are a headache," Sugar said. "Besides, who needs hot boys when we have each other?"

There was a pause before everyone, absolutely everyone roared with laughter. They tried to contain it, but *who needs hot boys.*

"My dear," Eyes said, wiping tears from his eyes, "if I could trade you, all of you, for one night with the hottest guy in the world, I would do so in a flash. And I wouldn't even regret it."

"On that note," Ryan said, raising his glass. "Happy birthday. And fuck you."

They clinked their glasses. As everyone raised their glasses to their lips, Eyes caught Ryan's eye again. He tipped his glass slightly, which Ryan returned with a smile.

If Eyes were at this party, he'd probably be the least pleased. He loved mingling, but having too many people would make him bitchy. Well, bitchier than he already was.

Eyes did relish being the center of attention though. He'd be glad the party was in full swing. The arrival of King, one of the most creative hosts (Percy and Ryan would disagree), together with the twins could only raise the shenanigans. While the twins were considered trouble in certain places, trouble was what tonight needed.

The twins were drinking by themselves while King waded through the crowd. Of the remaining members of the gang, he was the outlier, the last guy the others'd stay in contact with.

Their loss. Yes, the gang ribbed on Vyn for his obnoxious antics and Long for being somewhat simple, but at least Vyn was funny and Long affectionate. King got the short end. He was friends with drug dealers and strippers and was more at home in dark alleys than museums. Even Sugar—*Sugar!*—had little patience for King.

Across, Percy and a drunk Long were dancing with the jocks from school. Eyes would've chuckled seeing Percy all over Si. High school indeed never ends.

Angelo and Reyes were there! Eyes would've loved that. Reyes was deep when needed and Angelo had a charm no one, not even him, was aware of. They were sitting with Wallace and Mickey. Eyes wasn't particularly fond of those two.

Sugar was also there and El too. El was taking people's signatures. *What else is new?* But Sugar? Eyes adored him, although it was impossible to dislike Sugar. During their graduation party, they had shared a joint as he convinced Sugar to pursue music. Sugar said, "Dreams are for rich kids like El and Percy. Boys like us, Eyes, boys like us have to live."

Poor Vyn was sitting by himself. *What happened to my little firecracker?* If only Eyes were here, he'd have Vyn dancing. But alas Eyes wasn't there. He had to trust his friends to take over for him.

Of course, the center of it all, Ryan. He was pouring drinks, yelling out to El for ice. Eyes was fond of Ryan: he was his first kiss, his first sex, his best friend, his partner in crime, his fellow believer, his chosen brother. Ryan's head was an open book and Eyes could tell him whether his plan for the night would succeed. *It wouldn't.*

Eyes didn't know Ryan blamed himself for not counting his blessings when he was alive. Eyes would've felt the same way had situations been reversed. Even with his bravado, Eyes would've been an emotional shell.

But Ryan wasn't gone. Eyes was, but he was very much here, locked up, unyielding to forgetfulness.

"What if I told you that five years from now I'll be a best-selling author in Europe, what'd you do?" Eyes had asked Ryan, as they walked their bikes home from school.

Ryan laughed. "The Europeans better be more vigilant."

They stopped at Ryan's house. "I'll always be around, my dear," Eyes said. "I might not always answer because I'm Eyes and I have ten thousand boys in bed, but I'll pick up. Eventually."

"So, are we like best friends?" Ryan asked.

Eyes wheeled his bike away, giving Ryan a condescending look. "My dear, you did not just ask me to be your best friend. That is so laaaame."

Who knew that when Eyes kissed Ryan it was to be the last? Certainly neither of them.

El was having a party at his cabin. Half the crew was already there, and Ryan was supposed to drive the other half. But the flu had other plans.

"Take my car," Ryan told Eyes. "You're the only one I trust. Probably the only sober one."

Eyes was bummed his best friend wasn't coming. "You know, my dear, Percy'll be there. He's pretty much a doctor, give or take a few years of med school? And Sugar too! He'll have herbs."

Ryan declined and Eyes wasn't one to push people, though maybe he should've that night. Who knew how things would've changed?

"Love you, my dear." Eyes kissed him on the cheek. "See you in forever."

As he got into Ryan's car, he spotted him waving from the window. Long and Vyn were already sitting inside. Drunk. *Fun times ahead.* He waved back at Ryan, thinking of all the stories he'd tell him when they got back.

A few hours later, he was being wheeled into the emergency room. Flitting in and out of consciousness, he barely made out the two stretchers beside him. Long was yelling, though Eyes would never know what it was. His brain couldn't adjust, and he passed out again.

In his last waking moment, footsteps rushed into the room. Through the darkness stood Ryan. Eyes tried to open his mouth, but he was too tired. The one time he had so much to say, he couldn't. He wanted to apologize for Ryan's car. He wanted to apologize for missing all of Ryan's future exhibits. He wanted to apologize for leaving.

Instead, he raised two fingers in a sign of acknowledgment, mustered up a scraggy smile, and then slumped down on the hospital bed.

Try

THROUGHOUT THE NIGHT, Si and Percy had been acting like a couple. They were giggling, holding hands, passing secrets. Si wasn't sure how he felt about it. Yes, it was good to have Percy beside him, their skin playing under the table. But he knew Percy wanted answers to countless questions. Si? He wanted to enjoy without asking why.

They were chatting with Long and Badger. Badger was trying to form an alumni basketball league, but most of their teammates were too busy to relive their days on the court.

"You're sturdy," Badger said to Long. "Wanna sign up?"

"Not my thing." In one gulp, Long drained his beer. "Too much running and too much, uhm, whistles."

Oof. As Badger continued convincing Long, Si leaned over to Percy. "How much has he had?"

"Clearly not enough," Percy whispered back.

As Long went on a tirade against basketball, Si surveyed the room. Most noteworthy was the arrival of King with the twins, Joule and Timmy. As soon as Percy let them in, Si sensed annoyance in Percy's face. He knew Percy loathed the twins. Si didn't mind them; they could be a refreshing (if controversial) addition to any party.

Across the room, Ryan called out to Percy. With a quick "excuse me", Percy untangled their fingers to join Ryan, El, and King.

As soon as Percy's back was turned, Badger stopped bickering with Long and turned accusingly toward Si. "You lost your balls? You seriously back with Precious Percy? Mental!"

'Precious Percy.' Been a while since Si heard that moniker. It had been coined by Badger after one basketball practice, when Percy waltzed into the men's locker room, took a sniff of the sweaty jockstraps, and marched out without a word.

His teammates were hard on anyone they dated—locker room talks about boys whipped by their partners. But Si had it the worst. Percy's flamboyance, extravagance, and queendom caused Si plenty of grief from the team, though none of them would dare use the name to Percy's face. They talked big but a vengeful Percy, backed by Eyes, El, and the rest, was an image too frightening even for jocks. All just big talk among little boys in the privacy of the locker room.

Answering Badger's question would ruin Si's plan. He was here to enjoy the night. This wasn't even planned. He had received Percy's invite just earlier today. He scratched his beard, rereading the message to make sure it was real.

Si didn't like parties. More comfortable with few people, Si's bliss was cuddling and watching Netflix on a Saturday night. Three people, he could tolerate, maybe even four. Even when he was the team captain, he'd rather play video games with Badger and Percy than have the entire team over.

Postponing his RSVP, he headed downstairs for breakfast. He kissed his girlfriend and told her about the party, carefully omitting it was at Percy's house. Si half-hoped his girlfriend would give him an excuse not to go. He didn't expect she'd be pleased to find out he had friends.

"Oh, do go, Si," she said. "It'll be good for you and I can have a few hours without your sweaty shirts."

She was kidding, of course—or at least Si hoped so. *Did I smell?* Must be an alluring musk because Si could name a few folks who enjoyed snuggling with him. That list included her. And Percy.

Now that his girlfriend had ironically decided for him, Si had to follow through. While apprehensive, a part of him missed Percy. Regardless of how it ended, regardless of where they were, there was a time Percy had played an important part in Si's life. And Si would like to believe he too was once important to Percy.

"What *now*?!" Percy screeched. Senior year, just a few months before graduation, and they were having a fight. Percy wanted to go to El's function at the fencing club, but Si thought the whole thing silly.

"You don't even know how to hold a bloody sword!" Si threw his hands up in exasperation.

"You don't understand." Percy paced around his bedroom. "It's not the goddamn fencing. When El throws a party, you go. You just go. You never know what you'll miss out when someone like him throws a party. You'll never understand, you Philistine who plays with balls to feel validated."

"La di da, I'm sorry I'm not sophisticated enough for Precious Percy!" The words spilled out of Si's mouth without a second thought. He wanted to change course, backtrack even, but the words involuntarily came out.

Si knew Percy had heard that name before though never directly. Percy once confided he found the name intimidating, like a badge of honor or a drag name. However, the moment Si yelled it out, the look of shock was clear.

"Percy, sorry, no." Si sat beside him. *Damn it*, he screwed it up. This was the boy he promised to take care of, no matter how ridiculous his caprices. Sometimes, he even found the pretentious clinging to a stratified social class rather cute. But now, he ruined it all. "Percy, I'm really sorry."

What followed surprised him. Si expected Percy to leave, slam the door, and refuse to speak to him. He was already planning on how he'd repair this fight, how he'd call him up all charming, hoping his charisma'd win Percy back. What he didn't expect was for Percy to put his head on his shoulder and say, "No, I'm sorry."

They stayed there as Si caressed Percy's hand. "I'm sorry I keep dragging you to these things," Percy said. "I know you don't like them, and I am sorry if I'm bossing you around."

"It's okay, baby." Si kissed him on the cheek.

"I want a boyfriend," Percy replied. "Not a sidekick."

Damn it, Percy. If only the world could see him the way Si did, without the façade or the layers one needs to survive. "I love you, Percy. So much. Now get up." Si stood up but Percy remained on the bed. "We'll be late for El's thing."

"We don't have to," Percy said. "We can stay."

Si looked at Percy, loving everything about the boy. There was a reason all the locker room teasing meant nothing to him. "I want to try."

Percy stood up and gave Si a kiss.

Si hugged him. "I know you hate the name, but I always call you Precious Percy in my head."

"Because I'm insufferable?"

"Because to me, you're precious."

"You are back." This time Long was speaking. "Sugar owes me five bucks."

No point in baiting. "We're friends. And we're both in relationships."

Long's stare belayed a hidden understanding. Si wasn't sure why Long was called the simple one in their group. He didn't share the lavish philosophies Eyes or Ryan were prone to, nor the wisdom in Sugar, but a quiet posterior did not equate to shallowness.

Shallowness might be better found in Badger, who seemed oblivious to Long and Si's stand-off. After scratching his nose, Badger ran off to talk to Sugar.

Though Si had his poker face up, Long said what was exactly on his mind: "Someone's gonna get burned."

Getting burned wasn't new to Si and Percy. Both had personal demons. For instance, neither was keen to discuss Percy's chronic pain. Yet even though Percy hid his grimace, Si knew whenever his boyfriend was in pain. And it pained him to be powerless.

For his part, sports wasn't his dream career. He joked about being a hustler, a remark Percy didn't find amusing. It was actually from Percy's friend, Ryan, that he got the idea to study design at an art school.

Whenever plates and illustrations caused him to grow drowsy, Percy'd bring him a cup of coffee and his brand of motivational speech. ("I will not be saddled with a mediocre partner!") After graduation, when he started freelancing as a graphic designer, it was Percy's turn to need encouragement. The rigors of med school took their toll on Percy. Yet, due to the inconsistency of freelance life, Si couldn't give Percy the same attention as Percy used to give him.

Si noticed a change in Percy. Initially, he dismissed this as regular med school stress. It wasn't until he found empty bottles of Vicodin that it became clear. Med school didn't change

Percy. Medicine did. And as Percy dove into a drug delusion, Si found his calling at work. His calling, and more.

It was a fateful night when Si admitted he cheated. Once again, Percy's reaction surprised him. Instead of anger or frustration, Percy shrugged and asked what was for dinner.

Si lost Percy. He couldn't get into Percy's head anymore. He yelled at Percy's Vicodin, asking what they could give that he couldn't. He wanted to try; he really did. But he was just a boy. All he could give was himself. Once the desire was gone, so was the flame.

The moment everything changed was the party at El's cabin. The ride there was pleasant. Percy was loose, jolly even, thanks to Sugar's presence. (It was impossible to dislike Sugar.) Si listened as Percy and Sugar discussed their plans for the party. Percy was haughty, demanding, and back to his old self.

They were the first to arrive. Sugar and Percy continued their chatter as they organized the place. Well, as Sugar and Si organized. Percy supervised. If only Percy's friends weren't so busy with their lives, maybe Percy'd be in better condition. Si vowed he'd get Sugar or Ryan to hang out with them more.

Later, Percy's headache made him nap on the sofa while Si shared a joint with Sugar at the balcony. As they smoked, Sugar asked about Percy's illness.

Si told him everything. Finally, someone who knew Percy more than he did. He talked about pain, suffering, and loneliness. And Sugar listened, occasionally suggesting herbal treatments. He had some drugs that'll ease pain without the nasty effects of Vicodin.

"The thing about Percy," Sugar said, "is he'll never ask for help. Sweetie, be there for him. He's a good guy. Promise you'll be there?"

Si didn't have time to answer. A scream came from inside. They rushed in to see Percy babbling on the floor, his Vicodin pills strewed around him. Si knelt beside Percy and all he could hear were babbles about an accident and a hospital they had to drive to.

He carried Percy to the car, Sugar right on his heels, and drove to the hospital. All the while, the calm and collected Percy was an absolute mess, hair out of place, tears and snot around his face. He leaned over to kiss him but, for the first time, Percy turned his head away.

After Eyes's death, an already distant Percy sheltered himself more. He found the solace of anatomy and pharmacy a worthwhile distraction. Si wished he could turn into a biology textbook. Maybe then, Percy'd give him attention.

But he stayed. He took care of Percy as much as Percy'd allow. He made good on what Sugar asked him. He held Percy every night, he cooked and cleaned, he drew charts and designs to help him in med school.

And all he needed was one sign, a sign things'd return to the old days. For even Si could get tired. Even he could get frustrated and impatient. A nagging thought was asking why he stayed with Percy even when it wasn't right.

"I want to try," Si confessed to Percy one particularly long day. They hadn't spoken in a week. "I want to try to make this work."

Percy couldn't give a straight answer. Si's flame died out.

Funny how the heart could deceive. Si had moved on, found a woman to love, pored himself into his work. Taking care of himself instead of another person was a reprieve. The happy-ever-after once dreamt with Percy was now a solo journey.

There were days he thought of Percy, and he'd look him up in social media. It made him sad. Sometimes, a memory had to be left the way it was. Untarnished. Beautiful. Over.

But Long was correct. *Someone will get burned.* If he were realistic, everyone will be burned. Si promised he wouldn't overthink, he'd let the moment live in the present. *Why am I thinking of tomorrow?*

The party was roaring. Mickey's beats and King's presence had everyone pumping. Long had left Si to his thoughts. Bodies jumping, colors mixing. *Beautiful.* And, as if on cue, Percy emerged from the crowd, drinks in hand.

"Thank you for inviting me." Si took the drink Percy offered. *Why did this have to be so hard?* He was prepared for fun but not guilt, confusion, or desire. "Maybe we should talk?"

Across, the twins were doing a keg stand, with King leading the crowd in yelling, "Chug! Chug! Chug!" Si laughed, stopping after hearing Percy's disgruntled noise.

"Let them be." Si wrapped his arm around Percy's shoulder. "It's good fun, your guests love it."

"My guests would love it if they could pee on the walls, but let's not go that far." Percy's arms slithered around Si's back. Moments passed, and they swayed side-to-side, in contrast to the rock anthem in the background. Everyone was jumping, yelling, moshing even, but not them. They swayed, their breaths syncing, their bodies closer.

"This is nice." Percy leaned his head against Si's chest. "This is nice."

Si agreed. This was nice. This was the Percy he fell in love with, the Percy that wanted to be loved. He kissed Percy on the cheek. As they continued dancing, Percy returned his kiss. He moved his head slightly, and they made out.

Percy's lips fit perfectly with Si. Like the old days, that kiss rendered Si's knees numb. This was his Percy, the boy he promised forever with. *But, no.* Tonight was not the night.

Si released the kiss. Thankfully, King had been juggling bottles by the bar, taking up everyone's attention. Between the applause, the music, and the yells, it was too loud for conversation.

Percy and Si went to the backyard where they reclined on the porch. Maybe it was the dance of moonlight on Percy's hair, the amount of alcohol Si drank, or even the memory of the kiss, but watching Percy lean on the railings made Si fall in love again.

He couldn't stop his emotions, but he could control his actions. "Babe. Someone's gonna get burned."

Percy stared into the trees. "No one dies from a little fire."

That was it. Si hugged Percy from behind as they looked at the stars. He forgot what it was to hold Percy like this, the smell of his designer cologne seeping through his clothes, and the taste of his neck as he licked it.

Percy's hands were moving around Si's body. He wrapped tighter against Percy, his muscles wishing this were forever. He broke the promise to always take care of Percy. *Maybe it's time to be a man of my word.*

They kissed again, this time, the privacy of the backyard showed a tender side. Si didn't want the kiss to be over, didn't want to remove his hands away from Percy. He let Percy go once. *Never ever again.*

Yet, the doorbell rang, and Percy untangled from Si's arms.

Cock! Every time he was this close to Percy, the doorbell rings. Not wanting him to leave, Si held on. "Let someone else answer it!"

But this was Percy. Si released Percy from his arms and watched him walk back into the house. He stayed outside, regaining his bearings. *Cock!* He didn't want to think tonight, but there were a hundred thoughts swirling in his brain.

He needed a drink. He was unsure where he wanted to wake up tomorrow, but he knew his fears were true. He still loved Percy.

He went inside to get a refill when he noticed who entered the party.

Naveen. Percy's current boyfriend, who was giving him a kiss.

Fuckin' Perfect

ANGELO WANTED TO GET EXCITED, though he wasn't sure he was having a good time. He didn't drink a lot, much less party, and poor Reyes looked miserable. *It's good to go out*, echoed the advice from the self-help forums. *Get out of your comfort zone, try something new, and be the best you that you could be.* These were pieces of advice he'd never understood. Angelo liked his comfort zone, *thank you for asking.*

But here he was, having a drink with the unlikeliest group: his best buddy Reyes, the loudmouth Wallace, and the superstar Mickey. For a half-hour, Wallace had been talking about investments, a topic Angelo didn't even want to discuss with him at work, let alone at a party where he had to fight the urge to correct Wallace's financial analysis.

Mickey, *god bless his soul*, knew how to read a conversation and would switch topics. Yet no matter where Mickey brought it, Wallace would compensate. Mickey loved Percy's wine, oh, hey, Wallace had been to vineyard county and had six barrels of mead aging in his cellar. Books? Wallace met a publisher who wanted to do his biography. Music? Oh, he won VIP tickets to an orchestra. It was endless.

Angelo was envious when Mickey excused himself to mingle. Had he not brought Reyes along, he would've done the same. Among all the people, he had the misfortune of entertaining Wallace.

Thankfully, El passed by. Wallace, seizing the opportunity to network with Golden Boy, ran after him without so much as a goodbye, *thanks for wasting our time*. Angelo turned toward Reyes, apologetic. The good-natured Reyes waved it off as one of those things that happen at parties.

Was it? Angelo didn't really know.

Back in high school, Angelo's large posterior, pimply face, and sweaty underarms caused him to be avoided. On the other hand, Reyes preferred lurking at the library, gaining the moniker of library ghost.

In time, the two became friends. The two most despised people getting together was expected, but their influence on each other was pronounced. Library ghost got a friend who didn't mind hiding with him, and fat boy met someone who didn't care how many pimples dotted his face. Insults didn't hurt that much when they were shared, and both would learn to laugh at the absurd world of their school.

"Vyn said my face looks like the moon," Angelo whined once about the state of his pimples at their library sanctuary.

Reyes opened a book of astronomy. "That's not too bad. You can tell him he's like the Kuiper Belt. Icy and small."

"Wish I could be a star," Angelo pouted.

Reyes's eyes peeked over the top of his book. "Why? So you can explode?"

Fat boy and library ghost had since changed. Fat boy was still fat but had lost the pimples and the unwanted body fluids.

He took his scars and put them at work in a finance company. Library ghost was still lurking at libraries. Though instead of at a high school library rife with countless coverless *Huckleberry Finn*'s, he did it at law school.

Their success stories would be irrelevant to their high school peers, whose image of the two was stuck as fat boy and library ghost. What a surprise Ryan called him about the party. Someone remembered him. *Could this be a prank?* Though Ryan wasn't the type. He acquiesced and convinced Reyes to come with.

And he was glad. He really was. The forum advice must be true. This wasn't his regular Saturday night. Chances were he wouldn't have another Saturday night like this. But, yes, getting out of his comfort zone was fulfilling.

As he and Reyes talked about the latest *Star Wars* movie, they were approached by a bald guy who introduced himself as CC. Sitting down beside Reyes, he joked about being out of place in a room where everyone knew each other. Angelo coughed. *You could know everyone and still not enjoy it.*

Reyes struck a rapport with the stranger who had controversial views about Anakin's parenthood. Angelo took the opportunity to get a refill. At the bar, people were queuing up to do body shots off one of the twins. He never found how to distinguish between Joule and Timmy. (Reyes had a foolproof method involving how far they parted their hair, but he couldn't recall it.) He had a laugh thinking how people'd react if he queued up for the body shots.

King licked the salt off the twin's chest, sucked gin out of the belly button, and bit the lime out of his mouth. The crowd clapped. *How does that feel?* Desired, sexualized, and hot. Salt licked off him. *Nah.* His body produced enough salt.

Maneuvering around the crowd, he poured drinks for him and Reyes. He was joined by Ryan, who hugged him and asked how he was.

"I'm not used to this!" Angelo shouted, but his words were drowned out by the screams.

Clearly used to noisy environments, Ryan's voice cut through the chatter. "Louder!"

"I said I'm not used to this!" Angelo yelled as loud as he could. "So, this is what I've been missing!"

"You didn't miss much, my friend!" Ryan raised a glass. *Ryan was alright*, probably the kindest in the group after Sugar—but it was impossible to dislike Sugar. "Thanks for com— oh, Jesus, lord, sodomites, and bedwetters, Long don't hump the speakers!—Anyway, yeah, nice to see you! Eyes would've appreciated it!"

There it was. Angelo cleared his throat but had no words. At that moment, Percy crept up to grab Ryan. Of course, this was Percy and he couldn't let anything pass. "Oh, you're still here."

"Percy…" Ryan pulled his friend away to avoid what could become a disastrous confrontation. He gave Angelo a meaningful   'I'm-sure-he-didn't-mean-what-he-was-about-to-say' look. *Yeah.* Percy meant every damn word.

To say that Angelo was used to insults would be incorrect. How does one ever get used to being an outcast? Certainly not overnight and certainly not at a drunken party.

Angelo had always struggled with his weight. When he was a kid playing with the neighbors, he learned what the word fat meant. It wasn't the number on the weighing scale, or the one on a measuring tape, or the one that dictates his clothing size. Fat meant ugly. Disgusting. Gross. Abnormal.

The word followed him throughout school. Never mind his grades, clubs, hobbies. They were meaningless. He was the fat one. That was all that mattered.

In retrospect, Angelo cursed the fact he wasn't even that fat then. But the constant reinforcement drove him to find satisfaction in food. As the insults grew, so did his eating habits. He grew fatter, and the insults'd get worse. It was a sadistic cycle.

Not that he didn't try to beat it. He and his mom did everything. They tried portioned meals, gym memberships, even fat camp. Nothing worked. His mother gave up and cooked whatever he wanted. But now that he was alone and had control over his diet—he could only blame himself.

All the way to adulthood, Angelo didn't know what a romantic relationship was. Dating was out of the question and Angelo resigned himself to jokes that he'd die single. He considered a cat, but that was too sad.

Once again, Reyes to the rescue. Reyes read about a subculture called chub chasers, boys who were into bigger men. *Huh. How could people desire the most repulsive thing about me?* He was a fetish, but, as Reyes said, we're all gonna die anyway, might as well have some sex.

So, he met with these chasers. They came over and played with his belly. They jiggled his thighs. One of them wanted to feed him ice cream all the time so he'd get bigger. Angelo finally felt another person's desire touch his body—although at the end, it was the same thing. Desired did not mean valued.

Through the app, he stumbled upon Eyes, whose profile picture was, appropriately, a pair of eyes. He knew Eyes by reputation—Eyes and his crew were straight out of a high school B-movie: everything in slow motion as the popular girls turned down the hallway. Eyes dead center as queen, flanked by Ryan and Percy (rumored to be plotting a coup), with El and Long not far behind. (Sugar, King, and Vyn used to walk at the back.)

Here was the most popular boy in school sending Angelo a date request in a bear heart emoji. Angelo had to breathe deeply before agreeing to meet at a coffee shop. At the very least, Eyes had promised the barista provided eye candy.

Angelo couldn't stop panicking. Reyes came over to help him pick out an outfit. His only black shirt was at the laundromat and he was torn as to what color would make him slim. Polka dots wouldn't help, and neither would these Charlie Brown squiggly lines. *Everything I own makes me look like a fucking ball!*

Reyes pursed his lips, saying that if Eyes were a chub chaser, why would he hide his fat?

Angelo sighed. His best friend was right. *How'd I ever function before Reyes? Oh, right.* He didn't.

He put on a bright yellow shirt, hoping it would make him seem brighter too. When he arrived, Eyes looked at him from head to toe. "You look like the sun."

Uh-oh. Angelo's entire back sweated. Taking off his sunglasses, Eyes followed up with, "The sun's hot."

Contrary to his fears, they had a good date. Eyes was cute, especially when he was going on about his passions. When he talked about the theatre, his arms waved. When discussing spoken word, his voice dropped to a whisper. And while recollecting an argument with his publisher, he used the cutlery as props.

That night, he made out with Eyes at his apartment. It was sweet how Eyes kissed him, playful how he held him. Angelo wasn't a number on the weighing scale. He was just another boy.

Drinks in hand, Angelo traced his route back to Reyes. He was careful not to spill. *Yeah, that's what I need, another reason for Percy to throw me out.*

"You!"

A finger pointed at him.

"You! Body shots, now." Taking Angelo's drinks, King pulled him toward the crowd.

Angelo had no plans to touch another boy. He heard someone yell, "He only eats at buffets!"

"Snip it, Badger." King glared at the offender, now visible amid the laughing crowd. "Or you're missing your turn."

The same twin from earlier was lying on the table. King magically reassembled the scene: the gin in the bellybutton, the salt on the chest, and the lime in the mouth.

Angelo searched wildly; Reyes was hidden by the crowd and *where did Percy drag Ryan? Crap.* Unlike earlier, the crowd was silent, their attention zeroed in on Angelo.

A panic attack coming, Angelo stared pleadingly at King, but he was busy talking up the crowd. *This was a bad idea. Reyes was right. They were invited here to be mocked. I'm a grown man, why can't they leave me alone?*

A hand laid down on his shoulder. Long stood behind him whispering, "Just do it and be quick." *Eww.* His breath reeked, but Angelo appreciated the support. "Do it once and you're done."

One more reassuring tap and Long joined the audience. King turned to him, a grin on his face. Even the twin was observing. Everyone waited for his move.

"Boyfriends exist so you don't go to restaurants alone." That was one of Eyes's famous quotes.

Angelo had been meditating on this remark as he and Eyes continued dating. For the first time, someone joined him at his favorite joints. (*Reyes was a love, but he could be basic in his palate.*) They'd tried out various restaurants, buffets, and food trucks. On one of their park dates, Angelo confessed.

"You know, I'm starting to really like you." They were on a blanket, surrounded by sandwiches, hotdogs, and beer. A sunny day, kids were flying drones behind them. Angelo'd been ducking down. He didn't want to show up on anyone's home video.

Crumbs spilling everywhere, Eyes munched on a sandwich. "I figured. Otherwise, why keep going out with me?"

Angelo picked up a hotdog, flicking off the approaching ants. "Do you kinda like me too?"

"Obviously." Eyes wiped his mouth. "Otherwise why'd I keep going out with you?"

The guys Angelo confesses to usually respond with 'Uhm, thank you?' or 'I'm not looking for love,' or 'Great! Well, bye!' Eyes's directness was refreshing and Angelo wanted to be relieved. Here it was, the admission that someone legitimately liked him. *Where were the goddamn butterflies?*

"How could you like a loser like me?"

Having eaten a sandwich in record time (even by Angelo's standards), Eyes reached out for another. "Whatever are you talking about, my dear?"

Angelo stared at his hotdog, unable to bite. *Stop talking, Angelo. Don't ruin this.* Yet, what his gut was suppressing, his mouth let loose. "Look at you. Look at me."

Eyes didn't respond for a while. He opened the basket and got another sandwich. Angelo worried he blew it. He lay down, helping Eyes unwrap the sandwich.

"So complicated." Eyes bit into the sandwich, chomping off more than half. "We're full of so much hatred."

"Again with your riddles!" A surge of fire welled in Angelo. He didn't care if Eyes were offended or if the other picnic-goers would turn their heads. "You never second-guess yourself. You never get underestimated. How could you? You're perfect!"

Eyes laughed so hard that bits of the sandwich fell on the grass. "My dear, I can introduce you to seven boys who'd disagree." Eyes reached for his fourth sandwich of the day. *Blimey, where do these carbs go?* "How can you be so mean when you talk about yourself?"

"Because I'm not perfect!" He'd never thought of perfection this way, but it aptly summed up the difference between them. The diva and the one chasing after him.

Eyes sat up, licking his fingers. "Fuck perfect." He reached out to grab another sandwich but hesitated. "Mmm, maybe that's enough. Know what you need?"

Instead of sandwiches, Eyes took out a couple of beers from their basket. He had the foresight to pick up a few cans before the date. Nothing beats ice-cold beer in the summer. Angelo's nerves were still all over, but the beer helped.

Eyes put his head on Angelo's lap. "When you're naked in the mirror, what do you see?"

If it weren't for the beer, Angelo wouldn't have answered. "I see fat. I see ugly. Unattractive. Unsexy."

"Can I tell you what my mirror shows? I see skinny. I see ugly. Unattractive. Unsexy." Eyes rolled over. He played with Angelo's collar. "I used to cut. Now you know. Not even my friends know this. Well, Ryan. At first, I did it because I hated the fag queen staring at the mirror. The mirror, she's a bitch, you know. Then I did it to feel alive. After a while, I just did it 'cause it's fun."

Eyes tossed his empty can before grabbing another. Angelo restrained himself from commenting on environmentalism.

"Ryan drew me a picture. A pair of eyes. He said it'd remind me of him. Seen it? It's the one above the bed. Those eyes see what I cannot. Because one of the eyes has a tear.

"I'm really sorry, Angelo, my dear. Sometimes I wish we could scratch the word 'perfect' out of the dictionary. But, please, pretty, pretty please, don't ever feel you're less than fucking perfect. Because fuck perfect, you're perfect to me."

Angelo and Eyes sat at the park for an hour longer, however few words passed between them. Later, back in Eyes's place, Angelo stared into the sketch of the eyes, as they cuddled all night.

Ryan had appeared beside Long, worry on his face. Yet this wasn't the reprieve Angelo needed as the body of the twin lay beckoningly. He wished Reyes would show up, but his friend could drone out anything.

With every bit of courage he could muster, he walked up. King gave him a crash course. "Salt. Shot. Lime. You can do it."

Angelo grabbed on to the twin's arms and lowered himself. He closed his eyes and licked the salt off the chest. Some chest hair came off but he didn't mind.

"Don't swallow! Shot!" King called out. Angelo crawled lower and feasted on the gin from the bellybutton.

His throat protested. He didn't know how his stomach would react. King held him, anticipating perhaps that he'd stumble. The twin sat up so that the lime was in line with Angelo's face.

"Just bite it!" Long called out.

Grabbing the twin's head, he swooped down crushing the lime from his mouth. There it was. The citric flavor made the gin go down better.

It wasn't half-bad. Wasn't half-bad at all. He survived it. There was a decent round of clapping, loudest from Long and Ryan. King patted him on the back and handed him back his drinks.

People were now cheering on Si's turn. Angelo passed by Ryan, still clapping for him. "Thanks for coming."

Angelo raised his glass. "Wouldn't have missed it."

One of the things Angelo had complained about was why they never hang out with Eyes's friends. Eyes had laughed. "Between Percy and Vyn, you're dead meat in ten seconds."

Angelo didn't push it, yet it was pleasant when Eyes brought Ryan along on one date.

"You remember Angelo from high school," Eyes said. "He's kind of, I guess he's kind of my boyfriend."

Boyfriend. It was the first time someone called him his boyfriend. He shook hands with Ryan, saying he was so thankful he could come. ("Please, he's just here to ogle the barista," Eyes commented.)

Angelo and Ryan hit it off. Listening to Ryan and Eyes argue about postmodernism, Angelo could see why Eyes adored him. Both competitive and artistic, they grounded each other. Ryan was to Eyes as Reyes was to him. That friend you don't always want but you need to survive.

"You should come with us to El's cabin," Ryan said. "Yeah, we used to be dicks, but we don't really fuck around that much."

Eyes coughed. "Except Vyn."

The two of them shared an inside giggle. Angelo agreed. He was nervous but he wanted to be part of Eyes's life. If that meant bearing a few insults masquerading as good-natured ribs, he was used to that anyway. At least, Ryan would be there.

On the day of the trip, Angelo found out that Ryan was stuck with the flu. Though he'd been making strides on his self-image, paranoia set in. Especially when he found out he'd be riding with a drunk Vyn. He told Eyes he wasn't coming.

Angelo would forever wonder what would happen if Eyes convinced him to come. *Would things have been different, would I be happy now?* But Eyes didn't push it. He kissed Angelo goodbye, whispering, "I'll be back soon, my heart."

This was to be their last kiss.

Please Don't Leave Me

WHEN ZEKE HAD RUNG The doorbell earlier this evening, he'd had no idea what he was signing up for. A guy from Grindr had asked to meet up here, but he was yet to show up. *What a gentleman.*

Oh, and Mickey was here because of course he was! Running into your ex at a party seemed highly suspicious, but he was suppressing thoughts of Mickey. The main priority was meeting TigerClaws69 and testing how sharp his talons were.

A few names were crossed off. He had a disappointing chat with Badger earlier. Percy frightened Zeke—if it were him, he seriously needed to reread their conversation. The others didn't have the right build.

Time for detective work!

Recalling a conversation with TigerClaws69 about their shared love of crime thrillers, Zeke approached a guy reading in the corner. Reyes was pleasant and reserved but he had no idea what Grindr was. He didn't even have a smartphone, proudly displaying one of the last remaining flip phones in the world.

Apologizing, Zeke continued his investigation. An imposing El wasn't TigerClaws69, but would Zeke mind signing his petition? Si too wasn't TigerClaws69. ("I'm more of a dog person.") There was also that silent boy staring at the wall—Zeke prayed to all the gods that wasn't him.

What about the loud-mouth guy who arrived with the twins? The twins were too slender, but the loud-mouth had the right fit. He approached loud-mouth, who was currently pouring a line of shots at the bar.

"Hey-yo!" loud-mouth yelled out. "Shots!"

"I wanted to ask—"

"Timmy! Joule!" The guy turned away from him.

"Excuse me—" Zeke tapped his shoulders.

"Get these into everyone, hurry!"

On cue, the twins descended and passed out shots. Loud-mouth handed one to Zeke.

"Hey there, are you—"

"We drink, then we talk!" the guy yelled to a chorus of cheers. Resigned, Zeke downed the shot and planted the glass rim down on the table.

"Are you TigerClaws69?" Zeke asked.

Loud-mouth downed his shot ferociously, spit landing on Zeke. "Baby, few more shots, I'll be the good ol' Queen!" Zeke was exasperated, but loud-mouth had already turned away to yell at the twins.

"What up, King?" one of them asked.

King told them to get out the 'real good' stuff. The twins looked hesitant, but a quick spank at the ass from King resolved that. Their heads soon sauntered off into the crowd.

"King, is this guy bothering you?" *Oh, that voice.* Mickey was returning his shot glass. "Tell him it's past his bedtime, and he'll naff off."

King tried giving Mickey a high-five, which the latter ignored. "Nah. He's cool. He's looking for——"

"Oh, Zeke, Zeke, Zeke," Mickey cut in. "Looking for someone else again?"

Zeke backed away. He had half a mind to leave. No one was worth a confrontation with Mickey. As much as he adored him, his ex could be unpleasant when provoked. Put a few shots in him, and he was the spitting image of satan.

No matter what Mickey said, Zeke truly loved him. They had met when Mickey was starting in the fast-paced world of event organizing. It didn't take many dates before Mickey moved his bags to Zeke's condo.

As for Zeke, he was an accountant in one of the country's top firms. He would wake up at 7:30 while Mickey was still snoring, take a three-minute shower, and then put on eggs or toast or sausages, depending on their meal plan. When breakfast was cooked, a sleepy-headed Mickey would stumble to the kitchen, and they'd sit down, discuss the news or the weather, followed by the unneeded "Don't forget your umbrella" or "I packed your gloves in your briefcase", before Zeke would give Mickey a peck on the forehead before heading for work.

A full eight hours for Zeke were spent on meetings, spreadsheets, and ledgers. He always started with a twenty-minute productivity meeting before settling in with a coffee and the daily balance report. His staff could only bug him between one and two while his boss had coffee with him every Thursday at three. Even emergencies had a time slot in his day. Nothing was left to chance.

At 5:30, Zeke would head home on the same pre-defined route. It was an odd day if Mickey was home before him. Normally he'd be alone and he'd do as much housework as possible before preparing dinner. He ate alone, but he'd leave something Mickey could heat up upon returning.

After dinner, he'd prop up on an armchair with the latest crime thriller (his one guilty pleasure, he'd admit) and read for an hour. When it got too late and Mickey wasn't home yet, he'd change into his pajamas and go to bed.

It was constancy Zeke sought, that one-second pause in the middle of the din, that reveal at the end of the novel, that moment of ecstasy after an orgasm. That was what Zeke prized above all else.

When did I become so obnoxious?

Zeke put his coat back on. *Awful idea to come.*

He hadn't seen Mickey since the break-up. He hadn't seen anyone socially, to be honest. TigerClaws69 would've been his first date in years.

Though anonymous, TigerClaws69 clicked with Zeke. They both shared the same thoughts on constancy and had predetermined daily routines. They even matched in the nonsense. TigerClaws69 had confessed he ironed socks and underwear, so they'd be nice and crisp in the drawer. He might've thought this silly, but Zeke's underwear was also folded meticulously.

TigerClaws69 was perfect for Zeke—they even wanted the same number of dogs! Yet, Zeke never knew what he looked like. Forming bonds with faceless profiles is rare, but Zeke wasn't here for mere attraction. He could get off by himself, *thank you very much.* Looks were important, for sure, but Zeke's needs were hinged on tomorrow and not tonight.

Multiple times, Zeke had asked TigerClaws69 to meet up, but he was elusive. He claimed he had just gotten out of a relationship and wanted to take things slow, glacial even. "The problem these days," he wrote, "is we throw each other away like nothing."

Zeke respected that. People in dating apps don't often want anything more than a shag. He too was out of a relationship, and, while eager to get back in a routine, he needed to be wary of who he let in. The wrong person would mess up his schedule, but the wrong person masquerading as the right one would throw the whole thing out the window.

In one of their more sensitive conversations, TigerClaws69 had asked Zeke about Mickey. Zeke was hesitant. He respected Mickey enough not to slander his memory. And yet, as TigerClaws69 put it, talking about things can spool problems into neat little categories.

He was right, of course. Zeke typed back, "When we're broken, we're capable of anything."

He had heard that statement a long time ago when he and Mickey were watching a social experiment on YouTube. It was a test on how far someone can be pushed before they can hurt their loved ones. Zeke found it nihilistic. How could a person hurt what they loved most? The answer was simple yet painful. It happened not in an instant but like sand trickling down an hourglass.

For as Mickey climbed up his job, his home presence became less and less frequent. Zeke would find days, even weeks at length, of waking up alone, of going to bed alone, and receiving nothing more than a "Stuck at work" text from his partner.

This messed up Zeke's day. Without Mickey, Zeke had no one to talk to at breakfast. He'd end up arriving late for work, causing their productivity meeting to shift up the schedule. A five-minute tardiness led to an hour's delay. Everything was off.

At first, he was afraid Mickey was having an affair. Mickey's job involved getting together with the city's most eligible bachelors. To be more successful, Mickey pretended to be single. *It's an act to land the top clients*, Mickey convinced Zeke.

But when a tabloid printed a photo of a celebrity getting off a limo with Mickey hanging on to his arm, Zeke found it harder to believe. If he were to just think it through, it was nothing more than shallow jealousy, but as sand trickled, the hourglass tipped over.

In the sparse moments they were together, he would hold his tongue. When Mickey would kiss him or even when they were fucking, he held his tongue. He held his tongue, even when more tabloids were printed. He held his tongue when his colleagues asked him if he were okay. He held his tongue at family gatherings when his mother gave him a sad look.

But what was unsaid was not necessarily unfelt. He took his frustration out at work by yelling at his subordinates. He once threw his keyboard out the window when his word processor froze. At home, he had to buy a set of new dishes as he kept breaking plates whenever Mickey would come late. Mickey complained he was banging doors too loud at night. *Wow, so he has the nerve to complain?*

Still, he held his tongue until he couldn't.

It was the anniversary of their third year living together. For more than a month, Zeke had begged Mickey to take a couple of days off to celebrate properly. Mickey agreed, saying about time they did something extraordinary. That was enough for Zeke. He negotiated time off with his boss, promising to come in on the weekend. Working weekends wasn't in his routine, but anniversaries came but once a year.

With that taken care of, Zeke channeled Mickey's party planner mode. He listed down Mickey's favorite things, his go-to menu with the fanciest clients, where he booked those extravagant flowers, what the most current band was. He enlisted the help of Mickey's assistant to ensure every aspect met Mickey's highest standard. Their itinerary made, Zeke was pleased.

The night before the anniversary, they had sex to commemorate three full years. They hadn't made love in months and Zeke forgot what it was to see that beautiful face below him, to kiss those lips for the first time, and to feel his lover's breath on his neck. And as Zeke lay with Mickey snug in his arms, he'd never been happier. The hourglass cracked.

On the anniversary, he arrived early at the gazebo. Mickey's assistant was there, and the two of them set off preparing for a magical night.

Past midnight, four hours later than Mickey agreed to show up, the waiters and the band were getting restless. The duck was cold. Zeke kept promising to up everyone's pay, yet eventually he told Mickey's assistant to let everyone go.

Around 2 a.m. was the worst fight Zeke and Mickey ever had. Zeke never hurt Mickey before, letting his rage manifest through punching a wall or kicking pillows. However, in front of a tearful Mickey, he threw plates, he knocked down vases, he ripped paintings off the wall, yelling profanities and hatred, cursing that Mickey ever came into his life, cursing he allowed himself to be played like this.

Mickey tried restraining him, holding him back, apologizing that he couldn't get out of an emergency. But Zeke had enough. They were flailing when Zeke accidentally (or perhaps subconsciously) punched Mickey in the face.

He slept alone that night. He woke up dejected, morose, guilty, and, yet, glad to release all his tension. Unfortunately, he also woke up single.

For the first time, he took sick days from work. He didn't answer the telephone, no matter who it was. He slept during the day and spent the night heating frozen dinners. He thought Mickey fucked up his routine. Losing Mickey fucked him up.

After a week, he resolved to pull himself together. His boss sent him to their corporate-sponsored counselor who told him he had anger issues. He was put on a program. He replaced everything that was broken. But Mickey could never be replaced. He faced the sober truth of his own life. For him, it was all just a contest where the one who wins was the one who hit the hardest.

He texted Mickey, "Please don't leave me." He never got a reply.

"TigerClaws69?"

The bald guy putting on his jacket beside Zeke looked up in confusion. Zeke sighed, shaking his head, focusing on zipping up his coat.

"Leaving?" the bald guy asked. "It's just getting interesting."

Zeke checked his phone for any message from Tiger-Claws69. Nothing. "I'm done with interesting."

"About to have a smoke," the guy said. "Come join?"

Though hesitant, Zeke found himself sitting at the front patio. The bald guy, who introduced himself as CC, smoked beside him. Zeke had quit smoking a year after he started dating Mickey (it was in exchange for Mickey having to text him when he's late) and continued the habit even after they broke up.

CC blew out a puff. "You went to their school?"

"They all went to the same school?" This was the first Zeke heard this.

CC laughed. "Guess not. And, yeah, that's why they're all bat-shit in there."

"It's never fun to crash a reunion." Zeke stretched his legs. "How do you know who's slept with whom and who has issues with whom and who's in love with whom!"

"Trust me," CC said. "I've dated one of those loons long enough to stop caring."

The smell of CC's cigarette was tempting. It'd been two years since one of those nasty things was in his mouth, but Zeke resisted. CC blew the smoke in the opposite direction, but even the way the smoke danced brought back times when problems were solved with the flick of a lighter.

Zeke slapped himself. *No. No smoking.* "This was supposed to be a Grindr date. How'd I get dragged into this mess?"

CC flicked ashes away, careful not to get any on his clothes. "I think no one gets dragged into things they don't want."

"It always comes back to this."

"Yeah, it always comes right back to this." CC put out his cigarette. "Trust me. Sure you don't want one for the night? You look like you need one."

Zeke politely declined, watching CC light another cigarette. Even in his day, he didn't smoke two sticks in a row. "How hard is it to say sorry?"

"It depends," CC replied.

"On?"

"On how much you can live without him."

Zeke wanted to ponder on what the bald guy was intimating but destiny took a different turn. His phone vibrated. Grindr. One notification. TigerClaws69: 'Meet me by the pool.'

A few minutes ago, he was ready to leave, but now his feet were bringing him back in. As Zeke stood up, CC chuckled. "It always comes back to this, doesn't it?"

By the door conveniently left ajar, Zeke turned to him. "It always does."

As Zeke made his way past the living room, the guests in a wild state of intoxication, jumping to the beats only his ex-boyfriend could've put on, he pondered on CC's words. Every guy he spoke to led to the same person. It was all a pattern and, really, it shouldn't have taken him this long. For someone who lived for routine, for someone who read detective fiction, it should've been plain. He knew exactly who he was meeting by the pool.

And he wasn't wrong. For standing by the pool was Mickey.

The lighting was soft and, once the patio doors were shut, the music became a faded soundtrack from an old movie.

It couldn't be this easy. But then again, who else would know exactly what Zeke wanted enough to create an alternate persona that mirrored him in every single way? Who else could've known him this intimately? *No one.* No one was capable of such a thing, except the beautiful boy standing a few feet from him.

He should've expected this. A move patented Mickey. CC's words drummed into him still. No one ever gets dragged into things they don't want to.

As Mickey stood defiant, Zeke recalled how in their final months, he never said out loud how beautiful Mickey was. Or how much he appreciated all the little moments of waking up and kissing and breakfast. Or how he never said I love you, how he never fought for what they were and should have been.

Zeke opened his mouth, but Mickey shushed him, gesturing to his phone. Zeke opened the app to see a message from TigerClaws69: "Hi."

He couldn't hold anything back. He was crying, remembering the anger and hatred spilled between them. This gentle boy. His gentle love. He typed back: "I'm sorry."

"I am lost without you." Zeke looked up to see that Mickey too was in tears.

Zeke typed his final message and put his phone back into his pocket. He walked closer toward Mickey, who was reading his last text. "I am just lost."

Zeke's legs went limp as he wept uncontrollably. Mickey's arms tucked around him. He let his head rest on Mickey's chest, lovers reconnecting in sorrow, in pain, and in necessity.

U + Ur Hand

REYES SQUINTED. He was the only one sitting. Everyone was dancing, drinking or taking some form of cocaine or ecstasy. Two people were making out at the backyard. A little bit of everything for everyone. Except him.

Where's Angelo in this madness? He had gotten up for drinks, but that was ages ago. *Oh, well.* The bar's full of people queueing for drinks. He thought he saw Angelo's bright orange shirt walking with Ryan, but he blinked, and both were gone.

From the get-go, he'd known he'd be uncomfortable here. Now that the party'd cranked up, his fears were fully realized. The music hurt his ears, the drug use offended him, and the display of lust made him edgy. If he weren't afraid of what'd happen to Angelo, he would've gone home hours ago.

Aside from being out of place, Reyes had readings to attend to. Any law student worth their salt would attest that a social life is a privilege none could afford, save sparingly and in the face of utter failure. While everyone was preoccupied with drink, Reyes's mind was on the six-inch stack of cases to peruse for Monday's recitation.

"It'll be good for us, you especially," Angelo had said earlier. "You barely leave your apartment, you haven't had a haircut in a year, and your classmates don't talk about anything other than Russell v. Sullivan."

Angelo was right on all those counts. Reyes had begrudgingly agreed. Everyone, even the loneliest souls, could do with the occasional socializing.

If only he could slap some sense into his past self. *Never ever go against your better judgment.* He played with his straw, wondering what time was appropriate to ask Angelo to leave.

His contemplation was broken by two guys stopping by his corner. Reyes smiled at Sugar and got introduced to Sugar's roommate, Drew.

"Here's a little quieter." Sugar sat opposite Reyes. "That conga line! Whew!"

Reyes liked Sugar—though it was impossible to dislike Sugar. Between his genuine nature and the tragic stories surrounding his childhood, Sugar remained pleasant and bubbly but never to the point of overexertion. Drew seemed like a decent chap, but the psychedelic shirt was difficult to look at.

"All by yourself?" Drew asked, as he sat beside Sugar.

"Oh, don't bother him, sweetie." Sugar diverted the attention like a pro. "Reyes here's a law student. A law student! You know how hard law is? I don't, but I hear it's rather tough."

Reyes stopped himself from laughing. Rather tough was an understatement in law school. *God bless Sugar.* Reyes had been answering that question all night. *What the hell's wrong with being by yourself?*

Drew got the hint and busied himself with rolling a joint, Sugar occasionally supervising. They were alright. Reyes figured if someone else came by, Sugar'd lead the conversation away from him. An awkwardness bouncer, if you will.

The quietness would be brief as across the room King and Long were challenging each other on the beer pong table.

Drew looked at Sugar. "Up for some beer pong then?"

"Oh, no, no, not for me, thanks, sweetie." Sugar chuckled. "Grind those, they're too big."

The beer pong proved too much a distraction for Drew, as he'd been pinching the same stalk over and over. "Think Long'd win?"

Without a hint of exasperation, Sugar took over the rolling process. "Oh, I wouldn't say that. I'd say it's pretty even. Long's the better shot, sure, but the poor dear's had too much. King handles his liquor like a champ, but please never ask him to play a sport."

"How 'bout a bet then?" Drew helped Sugar pack the joint. "Me money's on Long."

Sugar laughed, swatting the idea off with his hand. "Oh, sweetie, even if I had the money, I know these boys too well."

This conversation fascinated Reyes more than anything here. "I'll take you on that."

Sugar looked up from the table. "Oh, sweetie, you don't have to—"

"It's fine." Reyes extended his arm to Drew. "You're on."

People assumed someone like Reyes, who went unnoticed the entire time in school, would know nothing about the human condition. They would be wrong.

Lurking gave Reyes the opportunity to observe. He predicted the fall of the jocks, as well as the irresistible rise of Sugar and company. He watched people hold hands at the parking lot, watched the same people cheat, and then watched them break up loudly in the hallways. It was his propensity to observe that propelled him to enter law.

It was this same propensity that gave him full confidence King would win the beer pong challenge.

A year ago, Reyes had his worst day in law school. He scrambled to class after dozing off on his textbooks. Twenty minutes late, his misfortunes piled on. All his professors called him for recitation and he forgot the difference between malum prohibitum and malum in se.

Wanting to forget the day, he went to a pub. Reyes didn't enjoy drinking, but it was fun to observe people getting into messy situations. This was why he went to law school.

He didn't plan on staying long. One drink for the nerves, and back to the apartment to catch up on two days' worth of readings. Yet as he was paying his bill, the bar doors flung open and in came Sugar, King, and Long. Instead of their usual bravado, they seemed tense as they occupied the farthest table. Already drunk, Long needed Sugar to help him sit.

Even though his gut told him to leave, Reyes's ears perked up when Sugar said, "They're not coming, are they?"

King's drones contrasted with Sugar's musical voice. "Ryan's still not leaving his place. El's abroad to, how'd he put it, reflect." The way King said that last word dripped with sarcasm. Sugar ordered a round while King continued. "And good ol' Percy—well, to be honest, I didn't bother, but y'know. Precious Percy."

Reyes could feel Sugar holding back against King's tone. "And poor Vyn?"

"Still in shock." This time, King's tone matched the gravitas of Sugar's. Their drinks were delivered. Long's glass was empty in less than two minutes.

"Oh, poor Vyn," Sugar said. "And no one's heard from Ueliton?"

King banged his glass on the table. "What happened to us? We used to be fucking royalty! Now, I'm stuck with you two."

Long's eyebrows narrowed and his lips curled into a snarl. "Well, I'm sorry it's just us. You should've been there, you fuc—"

Always the peacemaker, Sugar had his hand on Long's arm before the drunken lad could say more. But Sugar had a few words for King. He was whispering and Reyes had to strain his ear to catch the end of the sentence, "…so fucking cut it out."

King was on the aggressive. "Yeah, I get it, we're sad and shit, but come the fuck on. We gotta move on. How long's it been since, fuck, since Eyes—"

"Not long enough," said Long.

"You weren't in the car, sweetie." Annoyance was clear in Sugar's voice. "Stop forcing—"

"Yeah, yeah, I get it. I'm the bad guy." King chugged down the rest of his drink.

Sugar scanned the room and spotted Reyes. His demeanor changed, as he nudged King and Long to tone down. "It's Reyes! Join us, sweetie!"

Reyes had no desire to join a heated conversation, however, with no prepared excuse, he dragged his feet to the table. They sat awkwardly, Sugar trying to ease the mood by asking Reyes about law school. Knowing his presence was a formality, Reyes replied appropriately. No one else seemed interested in the daily life of a law student, so Reyes offered his condolences to which the group mumbled thanks.

King called for shots. Reyes hated hard liquor, but King was hard to say no to. Two shots later and Long forgot how to construct sentences. He tried putting his shot glass on the table, but it ended up as sharp fragments on the floor. King laughed and Sugar walked the drunk boy off to the bathrooms.

Maybe shots aren't so bad. But how on earth can King still be sober? Sugar's speech was slurred, even Reyes's mind was foggy, yet King maintained his composure. Well as perfect a composure as King ever had.

Reyes flicked an olive toward King. Catching it with his mouth, King flashed him a grin. Reyes blamed the alcohol for his behavior. King was a silly boy, always getting into scrapes. *I really want to ram my lips into his.*

"This is nice, you know," King said. "I don't drink enough anymore. We don't drink enough anymore. We don't even hang out, not after, shit."

Reyes clutched on to King's hand. King didn't move away. "Again, I'm sorry about the—"

"Please, Reyes." King moved his fingers up and down Reyes's hand. "Good ol' Sugar talks like we're in therapy. But dammit. This isn't Eyes. This goddamn charade of burying his memory has to stop. He would've hated this. He would've hated this so much."

With his free hand, King took another shot. Reyes badly wanted to touch his face. "You didn't know him that well, did you? Yeah, figured. Fucking Eyes. If you had to know one thing about him, one damn thing about that motherfucker. He'd yell at Sugar and order another drink."

King succumbed to a fit of laughter, before continuing. "CliffNotes version of my life. Enjoying your drink?"

"It's alright." Reyes withdrew his hand, a glimpse of clarity returning to his head. "I normally don't go out drinking, but it's alright."

"Yeah, well, what's your number? These pussies can continue their support group, but I sure could use a drinking buddy."

Reyes was divided on giving his personal details, but the drunk part of him won. He wrote down his phone number. After a while, Sugar and Long stumbled back and King proclaimed the night over.

Passing by a dartboard on the way out, King threw three darts in succession. Turning, he winked at Reyes. *Ooh.* His gut tingled as he settled his tab.

Before leaving, he checked the dartboard. Three perfect bullseyes.

King had seven cups remaining; Long was down to one. Long's shot. With a shaking hand, he threw the ping-pong ball. It flew one inch before falling straight down into his own solitary cup.

With the crowd's applause, King marched around, giving Long a pat on the back.

"Guess I owe you." Though laughing, Drew handed Reyes his winnings.

Sugar finished rolling the joint and soon he and Drew went out to the patio. Left by himself, Reyes took out his binder full of case files. *Might as well squeeze in a little study.*

Yet, his vision was blurry. He hadn't drunk a lot, yet the atmosphere, the music, and the chatter prevented him from reading past the opening statement. "It proved that the constitutional right to privacy scores higher than the preconceived notion of security. It proved that the constitutional…" *What the heck was the right to privacy? Was this constitutional?* "…scores higher than…." *Oh, god, whose laughter is that?*

He felt a pair of hands massaging his shoulder. He didn't hear anyone sneak behind him. He shrugged them off, but they clasped on.

Resigned and pissed off, he turned to confront the unwanted masseur. One of the twins. *Of course.* He only needed a second to determine it was Timmy. (Timmy worked out more and was huskier than the toned, but lean, Joule.)

"Mr. Lawyer." Timmy leaned into Reyes's ears. His breath reeked of beer, liquor, and weed. "Mr. Legally Brown, how 'bout we do something illegal?"

Reyes shut his binder. "How 'bout you back up and don't touch me."

"Let's have fun tonight." Timmy's whisper stabbed at his ears, as his hands crept down Reyes's back.

Reyes flinched. *Not again. Never again.* He balled his hands into fists.

◂

Because he'd given King his number, he got invited to countless parties. He declined all. King was a fantasy and lawyers live outside fantasies. However, after a nasty midterm, he found himself meeting King and the twins.

King said their group was officially over. "But don't feel bad 'cause I got the twins wrapped around my finger!" King laughed.

Reyes didn't remember what bar they were going to. King went to whatever party was lit, and the naïve Reyes tagged along. After arriving, his gut wanted to withdraw. Reyes couldn't place the feeling, but every bit of him warned him to leave.

Yet, King was insistent. The two beers turned to four and then six and then gin and vodka and Reyes experienced drunkenness as he had never before. He walked around, danced, laughed, joked, as if he were invited. All those years of studying the popular kids paid off. Reyes was resplendent.

King offered to call Reyes a cab home. *What time was it? Only three a.m.? Round of drinks!* He was laughing so much he ignored King. He didn't notice when King and the twins left.

Even though there wasn't a karaoke machine, Reyes belted a pirate shanty. Someone passed him a drink. It proved one too many. He reached the stage of drunken awareness, where every body part revolted and his mind cleared briefly to remind him of his inebriation. *Fuck.* He should've left with King. *How am I going home?*

He stumbled worse than an experienced Long. Drinks spilled on him. The laughter drilled into him, the music garbled. That was it, that was enough fun for the night. He shuffled outside the bar when a pair of arms wrapped around him, dragging him down the street. He didn't want to go with Mr. Stranger. His mother always told him to not speak with strangers, much less go home with one. He wanted to squeeze out and run back to the apartment and hide under the comforter Angelo got him for Christmas. But even if the stranger's hold weren't firm, he was too exhausted to resist or even yell out. He blacked out.

The next thing he remembered was being slumped on an unfamiliar bed, his pants being taken off. He tried to scream but the only thing coming out of him was sick. He struggled, rolling around side-to-side, but his underwear got pulled off and a pair of sticky lips plastered itself on his mouth. He mustered the energy to push the guy, but his efforts were futile. His arms were pinned down.

Reyes didn't know how it felt to be penetrated until then. He kept blacking out. There was nothing left to see but the darkness of the room, yet he felt everything. The pain. The vomit. The humiliation. The struggle. All too real and all too raw.

His next memory was waking up on a park bench covered with newspapers. The sun was at about 8 o'clock. He missed class again. He could run home, change, and make the next one, but his legs didn't want to move. He lay on the park bench, the stories of the newspapers his only attraction.

Reyes didn't have the words to talk about what happened. He was fine, perfectly fine, before he went out last night. *Trust your damn gut, Reyes. It got you this far, but because of your indiscretion, your stupidity, your inability to handle liquor, because of these, you were fucked.*

As usual, Angelo came by that night. He asked Reyes how the party went. Reyes considered revealing everything, yet *would Angelo believe me? Me, Reyes, the life of the party? Who would believe a drunken faggot?*

He knew it was over before it began.

"You don't wanna mess with me tonight." Reyes's fists were dying for a fight as Timmy's breath ran down him.

Timmy licked the back of his neck. "I'm drunk, babe."

Just take a second. Through his squinted eyes, he saw Joule and King snickering at them. King gave Joule a high-five.

Reyes got infuriated. It wasn't enough that Timmy was humping him, his hands circling through his nipples, but now he was the butt of the joke. His gut *once again, thank you very much for being right.* And King. *Fucking King.* He couldn't believe he once fantasized about kissing him.

Where was Angelo? Please come save me. His eyes were watery, not from sadness but from anger. His gut was wrong. Fuck his gut. He had every right to enjoy himself, to enjoy a drink with his friends, to meet new people. He had the right to all of that and not be made the laughingstock of the party. And he definitely had the right to not have his dick touched, *thank you very much.*

Enraged, Reyes elbowed Timmy right in the ribs, before picking up his thick binder and slamming it across Timmy's face. "I'm not your entertainment!"

His scream cut through the entire room. As if on cue, the music stopped. All of a sudden Reyes was the center of the party. The once invisible watcher was being observed. And he liked it.

"Bitch." Timmy clutched both his ribs and face. "They said you were an easy lay."

Reyes put his binder back in his bag. He took his time, knowing everyone was waiting for a response. With a smile, he turned toward Timmy. "It''ll just be you plus your hand tonight."

The room applauded.

Trouble

THAT HURT. FUCKING BITCH.

Timmy stormed off to the backyard where his twin brother Joule was collapsing with laughter. Behind him, King, Angelo, Sugar, and Ryan were restraining an agitated Reyes.

"Shut it," Timmy growled at Joule.

Joule snickered. "Want an ice pack?"

Timmy clutched the red spot on his face. "Wouldn't hurt."

"Oh, poor Timmy needs his twinnie to take care of him." The mockery in Joule's tone was clear. "Get one yourself."

Grunting, Timmy sat beside Joule.

"You're the reason people don't invite us to parties, y'know." Joule took out a bundle of pills from his jacket. Popping one, he tossed another to Timmy.

"And I thought your winning charisma cost us those invites." After scrutinizing the pill, Timmy swallowed it. "This Sugar's stash? Not bad. What you doing out here anyway?"

Joule pocked the pills. "If I go in, they might mistake me for your dumb ass. I don't want a book flying at me."

Fair. Few people could tell them apart. *Amateurs.* Joule didn't have his hustle while Timmy hated how his finesse wasn't at Joule's level. Joule pointed toward the bushes. "Two guys making out there."

Standing up, Timmy stared toward the direction Joule was pointing. The bushes were rustling, but the darkness masked their identity. Timmy looked at Joule.

Twin telepathy. Joule didn't need Timmy to ask. "It's that retard Mickey."

"You're the retard," Timmy replied. "This party's lame. Shall we bounce?"

Joule shrugged. "It's alright. You're lame. Anywhere we go'd be lame 'cause of you."

Timmy sat back beside his twin, resting his head on Joule's shoulder. Joule wrapped his arm around Timmy. "You have no subtlety."

Timmy scoffed, "You're gonna lecture me on subtlety? Spring Break 20—"

"What I recall, you were so into it." Joule's voice dropped to a whisper. "You slut."

There were a few things Timmy could throw back at Joule. His memory of that Spring Break was different. Joule would blush if a certain story came out. He should be grateful they were interrupted by the opening of the patio door. They turned to see a yawning El walk toward them.

Timmy felt Joule stiffen up. And for good reason. The two were competing on the number of boys they could fuck that night. El was a prime target. But Joule could have Golden Boy. Timmy had lost his appetite, though he wouldn't make Joule's win easy.

"Alright?" El sauntered in front of them. Timmy avoided El's stare. *The fuck was wrong with him? Boys'd been punched for less.*

"Mostly his pride though that needed a sore beating." Joule's voice was seductive, as he handed El a pill. "If it were you, you'd probably let Timmy slobber all over your shirt."

El laughed, taking the drug. "I've never been with twins. Thought about it, sure, but in the words of the bard, 'to thine own self be true'."

Timmy rolled his eyes. *Nerd.* Joule was more accommodating. "Oh, just him, not me. I'm more high maintenance. Boys need to get me a drink first. Which reminds me, my glass is empty."

"Shall we?" El offered his arms to the twins. Joule plopped to his feet, but Timmy shook his head. The honor of being with both Trouble Twins was reserved to a select few.

As El turned, Joule whispered one last time, "I win. I always win. And you know what losers have to do." Joule kissed him condescendingly on the cheek, before biting his ear. *Ouch! Slut!*

That cheeky look Joule had was familiar. They were always playing, and something was always at stake. In that area, they were very similar—twin-like even.

Joule disappeared back into the house. There went half of the Trouble Twins. And sitting alone, his face stinging, his ego wounded, was the other half.

The moniker of 'Trouble Twins' followed Timmy and Joule since childhood.

They had come from a religious family. Their parents forced them into their Sunday Best for church, even when Timmy was dying from the flu. He and Joule even became altar servers. However, in their second year of service, their mom ran away with the vicar, causing their dad to plummet into a self-destructive spiral.

From their father, the twins learned how to take drugs, how to drink, and how to be men. Blaming the church for the loss of his wife, their dad made them quit service. Every religious item in their house was broken. Timmy didn't care. He hated sitting still every Sunday.

In time, the system took them away from their father. They went into a series of foster homes incapable of handling them. Used to having free reign, the twins found the confines of foster care restrictive. They rebelled, harmlessly at first. They stayed out past curfew, switched sugar with salt, and let the cat out.

Then the childhood pranks escalated. Their names got equated with trouble. And trouble always came in pairs: one to restrain the kid, the other to beat him. One to be decoy, the other to throw rocks. One to nick the pawnshop, another to keep watch. *Y'know. The drill.*

High school was worse. In and out of detention hall, juvenile centers, foster homes. When the only thing constant in their life was each other, an unbreakable bond was formed, a bond that surpassed even a blood relation. Timmy and Joule against the world. Or, more apt, the world against Timmy and Joule.

One time, Timmy was in detention after annoying the coach with ball jokes. After detention passed, he went to the back of the bleachers where he and Joule had agreed to meet only to find no one. He lit a joint and waited a few minutes. Joule wasn't known for being late. When the joint became a blunt, the worry started.

He ran around. Not at the halls, not at the track field, not at the theatre. *Joule!* Timmy wasn't going to give up. And as he rounded the back of the gymnasium, he heard yelps.

His instincts sharpening, he hid behind a dumpster to see his twin getting beat up by four seniors. Joule was lying on the ground, trying to protect his face while the boys kicked and punched him from all angles.

The adrenaline in Timmy's blood rose, but he had to be careful. *What did Joule do now?* Two of the boys stood close to each other, opposite a rat-faced guy currently kicking Joule. Off to the side stood what looked like the leader of the gang—a big, muscled guy who flunked senior year three times.

Use your environment. There was chicken wiring around the fence, but it was too far. Some boxes were strewn near Joule, but they seemed empty. *Ah-ha!* The metal garbage can in front of him.

He sneaked toward the can, grabbed it, and tossed it toward the pair standing close to each other. Hit on the head, they fell right away. The rat-faced guy and the leader turned toward Timmy. Though he no longer had the element of surprise, it was still a two-versus-one fight. They hadn't counted on those odds being very much in Timmy's favor.

The rat-faced guy rushed him. *Easy.* Timmy sidestepped and elbowed him in the spine. As the guy reeled, Timmy ran toward the leader, hitting him square on the face. This had no effect on the big guy. Timmy followed with two more punches, hoping the guy'd tire out. He was preoccupied putting the leader down he didn't notice the rat-faced guy creeping up.

Had things been different, the fight would've been a loss for the Trouble Twins. Yet Joule managed to get up. As the rat-faced guy was about to hit Timmy from behind, Joule delivered a roundhouse kick to the guy's groin, causing him to fall in pain.

This was the momentary distraction Timmy was waiting for. He and Joule slugged the leader straight on the face. The leader swayed around. He still had some fight in him, but a push from Joule made him trip over his friends. The next thing Timmy and Joule were looking at was four passed-out boys.

Timmy looked at Joule. He was bloody all over. "What the fuck did you do?"

Joule spit out blood. "Asked them to blow me."

"Why'd you do that?" Timmy rolled the boys over to one side.

Joule shrugged. "Dunno. A laugh?"

They took off the bullies' pants and threw them in a dumpster far from the school. Everyone in the fight got suspended the next morning. Timmy and Joule didn't mind. During the day, Timmy nursed Joule's broken arm and black eye, while at night, they held each other through suppressed tears.

The effects of Sugar's drug were taking over. He could feel every blood vessel drip throughout his body. He wanted to yell, to dance naked in the backyard, to gnash his teeth and prowl the city as a werewolf. But he also didn't want to stand up.

Mickey and his boy passed by. Timmy gave them a knowing grin, holding out a high-five for Mickey. Mickey gave him a dirty look, ignored his hand, and walked back in.

"What's the big deal!" Timmy yelled at the retreating back of Mickey. "You fingered your boy's asshole and now you're too good for a high-five! Don't worry, I won't steal his ugly mug from you, ya prick!"

The walls surrounding Percy's mansion weren't so tall now. A dangerous voice inside Timmy's head egged him to leap over it. *Wasn't that tall, was it?* He'd definitely jumped higher than that before. He can jump over the moon at this point. And those fences didn't go as high as the moon. *Or did they?*

He looked at his hands. Funny, he didn't wear jewelry that night. He never wore jewelry at all! But now, his fingers were decked with diamonds and sapphire and gold. It weighed down his hands so much he fell on all fours, cackling.

The rings on his fingers transformed into Reyes's haunting face. He wasn't sure if this were his hand or Reyes's or even if it were a hand or a face, but it was slapping him again and again. He yelled *stop*, he yelled for help, but it never stopped. It was so absurd, he couldn't stop laughing.

After what felt like hours, another voice joined in. His hands were being restrained. He pulled away. *I want to be slapped!* But

Ryan's face came into his view, struggling to control him yet also trying not to laugh.

Timmy didn't know Ryan well. He and Joule were only here thanks to King's uncontrollable tongue. Ryan was a bit of a dick though Timmy couldn't say why. *It's the stupid drawings.*

Timmy and Joule did know Eyes. They were often in detention together. Unlike the twins who frequented the hall for attitude problems, Eyes was sent there for refusing to submit homework, follow instructions, or obey the teacher. "Insubordination. It's ridiculous, my dears," Eyes said. "When she corrects my grammar, she's teaching, but when I do it, I'm 'difficult'."

Timmy took an initial dislike to Eyes. He was too much, just plain too much. However, the monotony of being locked up with Joule led the twins to befriend Eyes. Eyes regaled them with stories or humdrum philosophies. The twins thought his larger-than-life musings nothing more than a laugh, though they did grow fond of Eyes.

"It's ridiculous, this idea of a soulmate," Eyes had once said. "People are obsessed with a soulmate. They don't know we are all born with two souls. You know where they're found? At the bottom of our feet."

The twins laughed.

Eyes gave them a haughty look. "You laugh but I'm perfectly serious. We have a left soul and a right soul. And we search for soulmates because our feet never meet. They keep going forward."

Ridiculous moments indeed, but it made perfect sense to Timmy. For once, the twins found someone who didn't talk down to them.

"Why don't you two kiss?" Eyes asked on another occasion. "Just for fun."

Timmy had a few comebacks, but Joule beat him to it. "What makes you think we don't?"

Eyes perked up. "Talk is cheap, my dears. What about doing it now?"

Timmy looked at Joule. They had kissed before. People spread rumors, but a kiss is just a kiss. A little fun though would hurt no one.

He was about to grab Joule's hair and plant a sloppy kiss on him, but once again Joule was faster. Timmy felt his twin's lips lock into his.

After Joule let him go, Timmy turned to Eyes with a grin. He expected lust to be registered on his face. This was what everyone wanted. But Eyes kept his stare blank. "That was hot, my dear. Oh, if Ryan could only draw that."

Later, Timmy and Joule were dragged to Eyes's bedroom. Timmy and Joule had never opened their playtime to others. They weren't prone to sharing, however, Eyes was an experience they devoured together.

A few days later, Eyes showed them a picture Ryan drew of the twins. Timmy expected a sketch of them kissing, but Eyes once again surprised him. Instead, it was them holding each other, staring at opposite directions, the loneliness etched perfectly as if every stroke described a sad moment in their lives.

How did Eyes know that every night we hold each other like this? He never brought it up and he would bet his left nut Joule wouldn't either. But it didn't matter. He liked the drawing. They even had it framed for their new apartment.

As much as Timmy and Joule wished to continue hanging out with Eyes, they drifted apart. Eyes went to university and was tighter than ever with his friends. On the other hand, the twins were preoccupied with building a life of their own, recreating a future once denied.

Timmy had heard about Eyes's death from Joule one night. It'd been a while since they thought of Eyes. They snuggled and looked at the sketch Ryan had made of them.

"The service is tomorrow," Joule said. "Shall we go?"

Timmy smoothened the curls on Joule's head. "I can't."

"I know." Joule rolled around. "Neither can I."

Timmy turned to face Joule. He wiped off the tears forming on Joule's face. "We'll go the day after, okay? Just us two."

"Timmy, Timmy, Timmy." Ryan shook his body. "Jesus, lord, sodomites, and bedwetters."

The drug was waning off. Timmy pushed Ryan away. "I'm not a fool, Ryan, get off."

"You're disturbing the whole party." Ryan offered Timmy a hand which he ignored. "Everyone could hear your screams."

Timmy rolled to a squat. "Tell them to wank each other off."

Ryan stood in front of him. Timmy expected a lecture or at least a look of disdain. Maybe Ryan was gonna ask him to leave. In that case, *he should've brought one of the jocks because I don't leave without a fight.*

And yet, Ryan was just observing him. *Why aren't you afraid?*

Eyes didn't talk much about Ryan back in the day. Though Timmy knew how devoted the two were, he never understood what Eyes was doing with a snob like Ryan. Joule explained it to him once, "Look at us. We're exactly alike and we destroy each other."

Finally, he understood what Joule meant. Ryan wasn't Eyes's twin. They didn't have twin telepathy, but they had conversation. They didn't always agree, but that created dialogue.

The whole thing made Timmy bitter. "You were wrong."

"Excuse me?" Ryan asked.

"That drawing. Remember? That drawing you made of me and Joule where we were sad and shit. As if we're nothing but pity. You're wrong. Dead fucking wrong. We've a life now. It ain't much. It ain't as fancy as this fucking mansion. But we're happy now."

"Then why do you pretend not to be?"

Timmy squinted. *I will not cry.* So much of Eyes had rubbed into Ryan. "Sorry for wrecking your party. I'm trouble." This was a first. The Trouble Twins never apologize. Rule one.

Ryan rubbed Timmy's back. "I'm not the one you should apologize to."

Timmy chuckled, wiping his face. "Shit. Figure Joule could do it for me? Reyes'd never know."

Ryan returned the laugh. "You're wearing different clothes."

"Oh, that's simple. I could strip Timmy and leave him in the garden butt naked while I pretend to be him." Timmy turned to see Joule behind them handing an icepack over. "Remember Mardi gras? Here ya go, mate. Twinnie saves the day again."

Timmy looked at a haughty Joule. "Thanks, twinnie."

Probably expecting a comeback, Joule got milder. "Well, I guess, you're welcome, you silly goose."

Icepack on his cheek, Timmy looked at Ryan. "Will you come with me? With Reyes? I don't need a bodyguard or shit, but he might be more comfortable with you there."

Ryan nodded, once again offering his hand to Timmy. This time, Timmy took it and jumped to his feet. He turned toward Joule. "Stay out. Two of our faces might be too much."

Joule pouted. "Few people can resist twice our dashing good looks." He winked at Ryan. "But yeah I've no interest in fixing your shit."

The three of them went back inside. Joule disappeared into the crowd and Timmy, assisted by Ryan, went to find Reyes.

Slut Like You

AS FOND OF TIMMY as he was, Joule never hesitated expressing pleasure at his twin's discomfort. Some people would call it sadistic, he called it brotherly love.

Joule watched Timmy and Ryan head over to Reyes. His brother had no concept of subtlety. Joule smirked. When they were embryos, he must've absorbed all of Timmy's seduction skills. It worked for him. Take tonight. The wager was simple: as many boys as possible before the party ended. The score stood: Timmy 0, Joule 1.

Joule got his first point from El. He gave him a good tumble in Percy's bedroom. Yet the disappointment on El's face was clear. He had been expecting both twins to go down on him. *Golden Boy could keep dreaming.* With just Joule, El needed five minutes to regain functionality in his legs. He would've been bedridden if Timmy were involved too.

To compensate, Joule had signed the stupid petition El'd been carrying. He signed it with a fake name, but it was the thought that counted.

Joule scanned the remaining boys. Percy already had two boys hovering over him. Sugar's blonde hair was peeping over somewhere—would've been interesting, yet as King said, there were Barbie dolls more sexual than him. Long was too drunk it wasn't fair. *Mickey?* Mickey was a wildcard, but he was googly-eyed at the mousy-haired lad. There was also the bald guy Joule hadn't met. He was hot as fuck, but he kept disappearing.

His eyes darted to the corner. *Vyn!* Vyn was a barrel of laughs. A bit loud for Joule's taste (though Vyn was a bit loud for everyone's tastes). If rumors were to be believed, he was animalistic in bed. But those rumors were probably started by Vyn himself.

Joule sat on the sofa beside Vyn, flashing the smile that rendered grown men weak. Vyn barely registered it. Joule offered him a pill, only to have Vyn shake his head.

What the fuck is wrong with him? Vyn wasn't even looking his way, preferring to stare at the wall. He'd been this way since Joule had first come in.

Joule had to escalate. He put his hand on Vyn's knees. A tender touch that led to a massage up and down his thigh. All the while, he was waiting for any sign to proceed further. He dug his fingers and grabbed Vyn's crotch.

Without a single word, Vyn flicked Joule's hand away. That was enough. Unlike his twin, he didn't go for guys who weren't interested.

◐

Everyone here thought he and Timmy were sluts. Joule didn't care.

Even in high school, their reputation preceded them. Ironic given how their mother took their names from the bible. Timothy and Joseph. Timmy and Joey. Tim and Joe.

So, why 'Joule'?

He and a classmate were being frisky during chemistry class (at one point, Joule's hand was playing with the guy's zipper) when their teacher slammed a book on his desk. "What is the SI unit for energy?"

Joule didn't even know what SI meant. "I measure energy by the condoms in the trash can."

The class laughed while the teacher shook her head. This wasn't the first either twin gave a smart lip. "Detention. And the answer is Joe, Joule. I mean, Joe, Joule. Joule, Joe."

This confusion caused the class to roar harder as the teacher struggled to get her class in control. That detention was worth it. People started calling him "Joule Joe" and eventually just "Joule." Joule liked it. He liked being the standard to measure energy.

Alright, who's next? Passing by the bar, Joule handed King a pill. Without hesitating, King drowned it with a shot of gin.

King was a possibility, but that would be cheating. Joule and Timmy had both slept with King. He used to be Timmy's fuck buddy, but once as a prank, Joule pretended to be Timmy and crawled on him in bed. King's reaction was priceless. He looked so puzzled that both twins decided to jump on him afterward.

Regardless, Joule was glad King was spending more time with them. Ever since his gang had a falling out, he'd be over at their pad almost daily. People called them his lackeys, following King around like puppies. *What a laugh.* They ran with King because he was an initiator. He was the master of games, the convener of schemes, and the keeper of the social calendars. But them, his cronies? *Ha.* If they wanted, King would kneel before them.

Across from King were Badger and Si. *A jock delivers in a pinch.* Swaggering over, he offered them pills. Just like King,

Badger took it without a second thought though a hesitant Si needed some coaxing.

Drugs were supposed to make people interesting. Yet Badger and Si arguing about an alumni basketball team made Joule feel invisible. As Badger went on about jersey design, Joule noticed how Si's eyes strayed way, way over to the foyer where Percy was entertaining his newly arrived boyfriend. Si was too emotionally preoccupied for Joule's needs, *but Badger?* Badger was simpler.

After Si made a clumsy excuse to walk over to Percy, Joule put his game plan on. Unfortunately, every pick-up line Joule used flew over Badger's head. Maybe it was the alcohol, maybe the drugs, or maybe he was just a dumb jock.

"The thing I love most about sports? Hanging out at the locker room after a sweaty match. Everyone's naked and playful and showering. Let's have the after-party in the locker room, shall we? For old times' sake." Out of options, Joule was being as direct as he could.

Yet, this was Badger. "Nah, we'd probably go to a bar or something, you know, so we can talk and shit. Hey, did you wanna join the team? You and Timmy would be…"

Joule had had it with buffoons. Before Badger could make the mistake of inviting the twins to the team, Joule walked away. He could keep Badger in his back pocket in case the night got lonely, but he left the former athlete mumbling basketball terms to himself.

Forgoing their history of foster homes, the twins did their best to make a life for themselves. They tried acting but the most they got were bit parts in a community theatre production of *Amphitryon*. There was a market in porn for twins, but they refused to do hardcore sex. Joule was walking past a strip club when he got a brilliant idea. In today's world of fetishized beauty, they had one vast audience to tap: The Internet.

Joule and Timmy created a YouTube channel, a venture they found profitable. They started off filming vlogs, before branching off into prank videos. It wasn't an overnight success, but their twin cuteness brought a steady following that they could live off ad revenues and sponsorships.

For the patrons willing to donate highest, they did delicate things on camera. Sometimes, it was mundane stuff like smelling each other's armpits or tickling each other through long, white socks. The farthest they went was to kiss. And they only kissed when they needed to invest in new recording equipment.

Though they had a huge online following, it did little to change their real-life reputation. One time, Joule was sipping martinis by himself at a pub when a stranger ran toward him. With his finger wagging, he accused Joule of sleeping with his husband. "You want him? You want me out? Tell that wanker to return my hard drive and you can have him! Wanna fight! Come at me, you slut! I know you, you're the whore of the city!"

Joule gulped the rest of his martini before slugging the stranger in the jaw. The man crawled across the floor. "Sit down, oaf." Joule signaled the waiter for another martini.

As the guy struggled up, Joule sipped his fresh martini. "One. I didn't know he was married. Two. Your marriage isn't working. You're welcome. Three. You're perfectly capable of getting your hard drive back. You might want to delete some videos. And four. Scared of losing him to someone younger and fitter? Well, you should. But not me. You can have him. Consider it an early Christmas. Hanukkah. Whichever."

He drained the martini as quickly as the first. "Check, please." He was out the door.

Who can I fuck? His luck was never this bad. He didn't want to just win, he wanted to win with a margin so high he could strip his twin of his dignity. Among other things, of course.

Speaking of stripping, King had said a stripper was coming. He could bang the stripper; that'll show Timmy. There was always Wallace. Joule physically shuddered as he saw his old classmate chatting up Badger. *Ew. Ew. Ew.* Timmy would mock him for days.

By the pool table, Sugar was talking to a guy in a psychedelic shirt. *New blood.* Joule walked over and got introduced to Drew. His charm was instant. He offered them both pills. Sugar, the original supplier, pocketed his for later while Drew declined, saying he only smokes weed. *Amateur.*

Sugar was lovely—and it was impossible to dislike Sugar—but Joule needed Drew alone. Fate intervened in the form of a doorbell. Ueliton and Lee. Joule knew them from school, though they were a couple of years older. Sugar seemed to be friends with them as he hurried to meet the couple.

With Sugar gone, Joule started unpacking Drew. "I moved in with Sugar a while back." Drew was lining up a shot at the table. "I'm glad he invited me, I'm drove mad at home with my thoughts."

Joule picked up the eight ball. "We can always exchange dirty thoughts."

"You play?" Drew took the ball from Joule's hand.

"No, but I gamble."

"Oh, I lost me cash on the beer pong," Drew replied.

Joule bit his lip. "I had something more exotic to wager. How 'bout when I shoot my balls, I get to shoot off yours?"

If Joule's previous flirtations weren't apparent enough, this had to be. Drew could no longer pretend it wasn't there. "I'm not looking for sex."

Three busts in a row! What's happening?

Joule now shared Timmy's desire to leave while he still had one point over his twin. Although if Timmy miraculously got game, he might be screwing Reyes right now. *That'll never happen. Probably. Hopefully.*

He was looking around for his twin when someone yelled at him.

"You!" Joule turned to come face-to-face with a mad Angelo. "Apologize to my friend right now!"

Joule wiped the spit off his face. "Twin brother."

Joule watched as the furious red on Angelo's cheeks turned to an embarrassed crimson. *What a cute guy.* He didn't know Angelo well, but he did allow him to take a shot off his body earlier.

"I'm sorry," Angelo stammered. "Get that a lot, I s'pose."

Joule noticed the sweat forming on Angelo's forehead. "My brother can't keep his hands off pretty boys. Me? Pretty boys can't keep their hands off me."

Angelo coughed. "Must be the drink. I should know the difference between you."

"Differences?" Few could tell them apart. There were distinct physical and personality traits but only a handful took the interest to notice.

"I guess." Angelo shuffled his feet. "Well, Timmy is more I'm gonna fuck you up outside—"

Joule couldn't help laughing. "And I'm more I'm gonna fuck you outside."

"That wasn't what I was gonna say!" There was a hurriedness in Angelo's voice. "What I meant was, shit, I dunno, words are hard!"

Angelo took a swig out of his beer. They'd been heading toward the hallway. Joule sat down by the stairs while Angelo leaned against the banister. "No offense, but Timmy's always fighting, yeah? But it's like you're the one he's fighting for."

Joule mulled over it. It was off by so, so much, but it was perfect. With Angelo relaxed, (his charming presence?) Joule pried, "You look like you're not having fun." Of everyone, Angelo and Reyes stood out worse than a straight person at this party.

Angelo's response was too quick. "Oh, I am! I am, I really am." Joule gave him an unconvinced stare. "Okay, I'm not."

"Welcome to the scene!" Joule said.

"This is the scene?" Angelo asked. "Everyone tells me about the scene and, woah, it's just this!" They laughed. "Guess I'm just, well, you know I'm not like you, I'm not…"

"A slut?"

"That's, no, not what I meant!" Angelo plopped down beside Joule. "Sorry, this is like strike two now."

"Well, strike three actually." Joule counted with his fingers. "Strike one was thinking I was Timmy. Strike two was saying I fuck people outdoors. And strike three is I'm a slut!" Joule laughed. "Don't worry, I love love."

Now sitting beside him, Joule could smell Angelo's strong perfume. Classic and piney. Something a guy who doesn't go out would find appropriate. Joule couldn't resist imagining how his ear tasted.

Is this what attraction feels like? He was used to going out, getting the hottest guy, and waking up alone, with nothing more than a wham-bam-thank-you-ma'am. Yet this boy droning on about his party mishaps was drawing him in. *Maybe I've had too much to drink?* Joule wanted to reach out and bite him.

"Do you wanna fuck?" He cut Angelo off in the middle of a story about a mix-up in the liquor store about gin and wine.

Angelo's jaw dropped. Clearly, he'd never been propositioned like this. Another first broken. "Ah, ah, me? I mean, here? I mean, me?"

Joule put his arm around Angelo, letting his free hand play all over Angelo's shirt. Angelo's breath rose. The boy was feeling it. He went for his signature kill—a bite on the ear. "A little taste test," he whispered.

Angelo pushed him away. "Why me?"

Joule backed off. *Again, don't be Timmy.* He sat observing Angelo drink his beer.

"You're Joule." Angelo wasn't looking at him. "You're the Trouble Twins. You get all the hottest guys. Even I know that. And this party's not lacking." He kicked the beer can to the floor. "Why me?"

Joule couldn't answer. Noting the silence, Angelo continued. "That's not it, is it? You don't just wanna get some. You wanna get with the weirdos. You and your fucking twin. You're no different. You think, here are the weirdos, let's fuck with them. Ain't that some shit."

Was Angelo right? He and Timmy were just playing a game. He was just a slut, a body that enjoyed the company of other bodies. He mocked Timmy for a destructive habit, but maybe Angelo was right. Maybe he was no different.

"Go. Go get with the pretty boys," Angelo delivered his killing blow.

Joule's instincts were to bolt. *Find the next hot guy. Rub my face on their six-pack. Drown in brandy until the night was over. Wake up alone. Hate yourself. Repeat.* But Joule was done following his instincts.

He swooped in and kissed Angelo on the lips. Joule was so used to passionate kisses, hickeys, and biting that the tender kiss they were sharing was new. He held Angelo gently and felt the boy kissing him back.

Angelo's hands were moving on his body. First by his nipples, then his thighs, almost teasing the crotch. Joule broke the kiss to look at Angelo. It was more than lust, more than desire. It was a connection—a connection once thought impossible.

"Look where your hand is." Joule pointed to Angelo's hand on his crotch.

Angelo sighed. "I guess I am a slut like you."

Glitter In The Air

WHAT A NIGHT! A bit of drama, a bit of romance, a bit of sex, *excuse me*, and it was barely midnight. Sugar missed parties like this. They were more common back in the days of no timecards, the nights of laughter and poetry, and clocks that never ticked forward.

Since Ueliton and Lee's arrival, Sugar'd been swapping anecdotes with them by the piano. The two had a peculiar contrast. Ueliton's crisp platinum hair, baggy shirt, and sweatpants clashed with Lee's polo shirts and slacks. Sugar'd never seen a couple more mismatched, although he'd admit he wasn't the expert on romantic pairing.

Apologizing for their lateness, Lee said it was his fault they had to swing by the office where he and Ueliton both worked. Sugar brushed it off, asking them how work was. *Same old time-in time-out*, Lee joked. Sugar was all too familiar.

A few laughs later, Ryan swooped in to greet the couple, El not far behind him. This was Sugar's cue to excuse himself.

Not that he didn't like Ueliton and Lee, (he adored them!) but Ryan'd also want time with Eyes's brother and he didn't want to get in the way.

Sugar appreciated this breath in the party. They weren't the restless teens or hungry young adults of old. Now, they had responsibilities. He played with that word in his head, making it longer and more ominous. *Reeesponsibilityyyyy*. He himself had work tomorrow ("On a Sunday?" El was incredulous). Thankfully his shifts started past noon. Although his roommate, Drew, would start work earlier. *Maybe he wants to head home?*

Oh, but Sugar, enjoy yourself. He still had Joule's pill as well as other drugs he brought. *Might as well.* Headed to the bathroom, he saw King trying to get Long to do another shot.

"Oh, but sweetie, don't you think he's had enough?" Sugar asked.

King poured a shot for himself. "He's fine."

"I'm fiine." Long struggled to stay upright.

"See." King poured a third shot. "For you, Sugar."

Sugar took the shot with no further debate. Any argument with King would be drawn out and he wasn't in the mood for King's antics.

"To Long!" King raised his shot glass. Sugar toasted to that; however, Long could hardly muster the energy to lift his glass that King had to pour it down him.

As he walked away, Sugar wondered how much alcohol was safe to mix with hard drugs. There were enough doctors here that everyone could get as wasted as a Greek orgy. Although, Sugar wasn't sure Percy would resuscitate a drunken King. He'd probably let him suffer, at least for a while.

His mind drifted back to Drew. *Should I ask him if he wanted more weed?* Sugar felt bad he kept leaving Drew alone. *Oh!* There he was talking to Mickey and Zeke by the sound system. Confident his roommate was enjoying himself, Sugar decided not to bother him.

Mickey looks ravishing! He'd been through so much Sugar was glad he's back with Zeke. He was rooting for them, to the point of helping Mickey create the TigerClaws69 scheme. Even though Mickey'd been kicked from their group, Sugar stayed in touch. He didn't believe in taking sides, especially when both parties were his friends.

The bathroom was at the hall across the stairs. As he entered, his mind shifted to Reyes. *Should I check up on the poor boy?* He and Ryan sat with him earlier to calm him down, their efforts almost null as King's presence removed any sense of propriety. Ryan had to escort a cackling King out before Reyes had a complete meltdown.

Sugar made up his mind. He'll check up on Reyes. And then Drew. And, *oh, yes,* poor Vyn. As he locked the bathroom door behind him, he could imagine Eyes mocking him. "For the love of everything unholy, my dear, you are not our mother. Stop taking care of the drunks. Heaven knows some folks are more tolerable in that state."

And yet, taking care of people was precisely what Sugar was best at.

It was their high school graduation party at El's manor. El spared no expense for their last hurrah as adolescents. High school was enjoyable, years they'll all miss, but thank god they were done.

At the center of the madness, Vyn and King were having an arm-wrestling contest, with the winner set to challenge the undefeated Long. Everyone gathered in a circle to watch. True, Long would beat either of them, but it was fun seeing people fail.

Sugar—who, up to that point, still answered to Edgar— was having a drink with Eyes and Ryan. Arm-wrestling was too crude for him, and he'd rather gossip with friends.

"Eat Wallace's cum, shithead!" A burst of strength from Vyn overturned the table. Down went glasses, bottles, even an antique hourglass El was bragging about earlier. Several cracking noises punctuated the mess of glass, blood, and booze on the floor.

Without a hesitation, Sugar was in motion, escorting the drunk Vyn and King away before picking up shards from the floor.

"El, sweetie, do you have a broom?" The glass was piercing his hands. Blood poured out but Sugar couldn't stop cleaning. Around him, people were yelling, but Sugar zoned them out.

It wasn't until a pair of hands pulled him away that Sugar's palms seared in pain. "My dear, presence of mind. Look at your hands."

El, not knowing where the broom was, was calling out for the maid. Sugar wanted to shush him. The poor woman was asleep (it was close to 2 a.m.), but Eyes had taken him outside.

"Poor King, he needs to be attended to." Sugar fought against Eyes's grip.

Not letting go, Eyes took bandages from Percy. "The King has gotten himself into worse. Your hands, my dear!"

"Oh, don't mind me." Sugar was used to scratches. With both Eyes and Ryan holding him down, he consented to let Eyes bandage him, amused at how haphazard they were thrown around his hands.

Clearly, Eyes had never bandaged someone before. "My dear, if you rush out cleaning after everyone without nary a thought to yourself, look what happens."

Ryan handed him a glass of whiskey. "Jesus, lord, sodomites, and bedwetters. He's just sweet."

"You are so sweet sometimes, my dear." Eyes was done bandaging him. "We have to start calling you Sugar."

Sugar looked at the tourniquet crisscrossed in different directions. "That's so nice, thank you."

"My dear, it wasn't a compliment." Eyes backed up to admire his handiwork. "Too much sugar kills you."

The party was over at that point. El did wake up his maid who got the mess cleared by the time they came back. Sugar felt guilty they had to wake her up but kept his mouth shut as Eyes announced his new name. Everyone agreed it was fitting. Sugar didn't mind. Regardless of how Eyes framed it, it was an endearing name. It was impossible to dislike anyone named Sugar.

With the night at a close and everyone too drunk to leave, most passed out on a bed, a couch, or in Long's case, a soft spot on the floor.

Sugar was going to join, however, his bleeding hands made sleep evasive. Smoking a joint, he sat at the outdoor swing. Moments later, he was joined by Eyes.

"Does it still hurt?" Eyes asked.

"Oh, no, sweetie, it's fine." Sugar gave him a pained smile. *No point in troubling Eyes.*

"Don't lie to me," Eyes replied.

Sugar lit up his joint and took a long deep breath before passing it to Eyes. "Happy graduation." The weed helped numb the pain, and now, close to the croak of dawn, did he find a peace. High school was over. They were adults. Tomorrow was a different problem but for now, let tranquility take over.

Eyes handed the joint back after a long draw. "What're you gonna do now, my dear?"

Sugar sighed. As a group, they were splintering for college. Percy was going to a pre-med program across the city, El was taking a year off abroad, Long had a scholarship to a community college, and Eyes, Ryan, and Vyn were accepted into the state university. Even King, who had no interest in higher education, had plans to work at his father's garage while saving up for his much talked about entertainment business.

That left poor Sugar. Getting through high school was hard enough. His dad had died in a hit-and-run, leaving him alone with his mom. His mom, a college dropout, worked two jobs, to get them through life. Sugar even took on a part-time job to help out.

He wasn't the most gifted in school. He struggled with mathematics, the sciences, even in English. The only subject he showed a modicum of talent with was music. He loved the piano. He listened to the classics, to jazz, to opera and he could replicate it on the school's piano. As they couldn't afford a keyboard, Sugar relished every minute of music class. He had been invited to the marching band, the choir, the theatre program. He declined them all. Between work, studies, and friends, he had no time for extracurricular activities.

A few months before graduation, his music teacher called him into her office. She told him how proud she was. He had the whole package, an ear for pitch, fingers that dance, and a heart bursting for release. She talked about a music program at a conservatory a few cities away. Sugar'd heard of it, of course. It was where all the best classical musicians trained. Now, his teacher was willing to write him a letter of recommendation for a scholarship.

It broke Sugar's heart to decline it. He didn't hesitate, for if he dwelt on it longer, he would've accepted. But he couldn't. He really couldn't. Dreams were for rich kids. Boys like Sugar are the ones meant to exist.

He never told anyone about it. Not his mother, not even his friends. He didn't go out with them for a few weeks. He didn't even touch the piano, hating every single tune he could hear. But that one gesture, that one glimpse into a future that could've been touched him so gently he had to cry.

All that was the baggage that flashed in Sugar's mind in between puffs. Leaning back, he looked at Eyes and told him no, he had no idea what was next. Sugar expected Eyes to push back, to lecture him, to give unsolicited advice about life. (Eyes was prone to that, especially the last.) Instead, Eyes cuddled with him, not a word said.

Even though Sugar didn't know what tomorrow was, he had a rough idea. While his friends went off living their dreams—of which he will be proud of—he would be left behind. He would be working minimum wage, maybe at a restaurant or a hotel, and eventually (*and hopefully not too soon*) his friends would move on with their lives. One day, when they're all rich and famous, they'd meet-up at a downtown high-rise and jokingly say "Remember our friend Sugar? Whatever happened to him?" and Sugar would enter the boardroom as a maintenance worker, and they'd look at him, they'd be dumbfounded, and they'd cry and laugh and—

Sugar wiped off a tear. His friends talk about how lucky they were Sugar was always taking care of them. They didn't know how lucky he felt that he had one good thing in his life. He shouldn't worry about them. He cuddled deeper into Eyes, staring at the starry sky. The moon was special tonight, bigger and rounder, as if calling out to be lassoed and stored in a vault like a precious little diamond thing. Ridiculous, Sugar mused. *Tonight, let's wish for an endless night.*

Sugar checked Joule's pill. *Nice.* He popped it in. He checked his stash and chose two other pills that complemented it. There was a special herb separated from the rest. His supplier gave it to him as a personal treat for selling so much. Salvia, he was told. Highly potent and should only be used in extreme cases. *Maybe later.*

He stared at the mirror. He couldn't believe the transformation. Before he looked like a regular bloke, gaunt and pasty, yes, but not a boy someone'd take a second glance at. Now, with his blonde curly hair and rosy complexion, he was fabulous.

Surprisingly, life had been good to Sugar since high school. He landed a job at a call center. Shitty shifts and horrible customers, but the pay wasn't half-bad. The late shifts also gave him time to pursue a part-time gig selling drugs. It wasn't the best nor the safest side-line, but no one would ever suspect him.

Sugar saved enough to move out of his mom's place (though he'd still send her part of his check). He got a dingy flat close to work and, after interviewing potential roommates, struck gold with Drew. They've been cohabiting harmoniously for some time now.

With the solo life, Sugar shook up elements of his personality. He remained the kind and gentle Sugar everyone loved, but he got more comfortable pushing his boundaries. No longer caring about people's opinions, he had a perm, he had his nails done, he wore skirts and shawls. Music now out of his life, he found escape in fucking up gender roles.

His supplier chalked it up to too many drugs, but Sugar knew better. Sugar was finding himself.

His drugs taken, Sugar left the bathroom focused. *Alright, game plan.* Reyes, Drew, then Vyn. He walked across to the siderooms where they had brought Reyes. He peered in but no one was there. He walked across the hallway, wondering if Reyes left, but nothing.

Odd. Where could he've gone? Sugar saw Angelo exiting one of the rooms, his shirt untucked. He jumped when Sugar asked if Reyes were with him. Shaking his head, Angelo disappeared back into the room he came from.

If Angelo wasn't worried, then perhaps Sugar should move on. He'll circle back to the both of them later. For now, Drew.

Back at the living room, all the couples, Mickey and Zeke; Percy and Naveen; and Ueliton and Lee were playing a game facilitated by King. One of those "How well do you know your partner" games where the host asks a question and both parties will raise an answer.

King's latest question was "Who is the better kisser?" Ueliton and Lee answered each other. Mickey and Zeke answered themselves, causing some chuckles. Yet, it was Percy and Naveen, with both their boards reading 'Percy' that made the crowd go wild.

Drew was cheering with the audience. No need for Sugar to bother him for now. He should stop worrying about Drew. *He's a grown-ass man.*

King's game wasn't Sugar's thing. He was both a virgin and perpetually single—two things he had no problem with. Whenever his friends rambled on about boys, he'd lend a sympathetic ear, but he'd be confused about their need for romantic relationships. Whenever they talked about how horny they got, Sugar'd draw a blank.

Romance bored him. Sex disgusted him. Sugar's idea of fun was glamour and music and ecstasy. Which made the whole affair with Badger more gratifying. Sugar didn't hold grudges, no matter how horrible the scars.

Oh, Sugar keep on track, who's next? Oh, dear. The one person who needed help the most: Vyn.

Vyn had been alone on the sofa all evening, *poor lad.* Sitting beside him, Sugar put a kind hand on his shoulder. He asked if everything was fine. Vyn'd been so non-responsive Sugar would've been happy with a shrug. Thankfully, Vyn turned, smiled, and nodded, even letting out a soft "Yeah, just tired."

Yet, the look on his face was familiar to Sugar.

It was only a few years ago. El was having a party at his cabin because, well, because why not, he was El and he could throw parties whenever he fancied. Since the gang couldn't fit in one car—and some of them refused to be in confined spaces with others—they planned to convoy over.

On the day itself, emergencies sprung up. They couldn't leave at the same time. A plan was hatched. El would drive first with King to set up. Percy would follow suit, bringing Sugar and Si. Later that evening, Ryan would arrive last with Eyes, Long, and Vyn.

Sugar was thrilled Percy asked him to drive down with him. Percy didn't let just anyone in his car. He and Percy gossiped throughout the drive as if Si weren't there.

Arriving after a few hours, they were surprised they beat El and King. Sugar called them up. El apologized—they were delayed at a local town. "Go ahead, use the spare key and get comfortable."

Since the place had been uninhabited for months, they began cleaning. Walking around with a feather duster, Sugar spotted a box of glitter. The trio laughed as they imagined what possible use El could have for so much glitter. Sugar scooped a fistful and threw it in the air.

Floating down, the glitter was magical. Happiness bloomed inside Sugar. His friends were making waves and chasing their dreams, yet they found time to hang out. Granted, not as often as before, but moments like this were moments to be cherished. The glitter flew all around them, and they fell on the floor laughing.

Later, Sugar was having a joint at the balcony with Si. Si was asking for advice on pain relievers when they heard Percy shriek. They rushed in. Inside, Percy was lying prostrate, his phone beside him and the specks of glitter that once rained so elegantly now struck a foreboding gleam. It was half-past the point of oblivion.

On the way to the hospital, Sugar tried contacting everyone: El, King, the families of Long, Vyn, and Eyes. Late at night, no one was answering. At the hospital, a broken-down Ryan was weeping hysterically. While Percy embraced him, Sugar stared at his phone, wishing for a reply from anyone out there. No one, save for Eyes's brother Ueliton, called back.

It was never pleasant to relay news like this, and after a few words, Ueliton hung up. Ryan yelled out, "Call Angelo, call Angelo, please!" Dialing, Sugar handed the phone to Ryan. Speechless now, he held both Percy and Ryan, staring into the surgery room, into the blankness, the tip of the iceberg, the sun before the burn, the thunder before the lightning.

He cradled Vyn in his arms as Vyn held on for dear life. Sugar hugged him tighter. He felt that way before.

Poor Vyn. Poor, poor Vyn.

His thoughts were interrupted when the front door was kicked open. The stripper had arrived.

Lady Marmalade

CHASE RELISHED THE MOMENT. That moment all eyes undressed him. And he hadn't even begun.

Boombox in hand, he marched into the room. Whenever he entered a room, every single goddamn person had to want to fuck him. Regardless of who they were, whether they're straight, whether they're celibate, every person had to ravish your body with their eyes.

And it was all the look. That one-second look that told a person *you are wanted, you are desired, you are a body, and I am the flesh that will cover you*. It was a look Chase had perfected throughout the years. He only had precious seconds before clothes fly off. But if the audience couldn't fantasize, even for a minute, how sweaty he'd make their bed, their wallets wouldn't get slimmer.

He slammed his boombox by the bar and pranced around. This was the act, the moment of tease. However, his routine was cut short by Ryan.

Could he please wait for folks to settle? Everyone was scattered and there was no stage. Chase suggested dancing on top of the bar, an idea Percy absolutely put down. They compromised by dragging chairs out of storage so he could do his routine by the sofa.

The boys rushed to move furniture. *Well, there went the desire. Dammit. They call in the professional, but these amateurs kill the vibe.*

There were around twenty people. If he played the next few minutes right, he'd have two months' rent. Although he and Ryan negotiated an appearance fee, any stripper worth their salt knew the real money came from gratuity. And, of course, the after-party.

Tick, tock! Finally, the chairs were set up. Ryan, the only person Chase knew, sat front and center. A bald guy tried making his way beside Ryan, however, Percy scooped up the seat to his right and a blonde curly-haired boy sat on the other side. The rest found their own available space.

Once everyone had settled, (time wasted by numerous "There's a spot here!" and "Wait! Can I run to the toilets?" and "I wanna be at the front!") Chase bent down to let the entire room marvel at his glutes and turned on the music.

Whenever people talked about sex workers, the tone was always sympathetic. And while Chase hated pity, pretending to be an underdog drew more money.

He'd been stripping for a few years now. He started when he was sixteen with a fake ID. The manager would tell him years later he knew Chase was lying, but it was worth having a guy so beautiful to attract both the desperate and the broken.

And Chase was beautiful. He'd tell it himself. The years of vodka and sex and sleeplessness had roughened some of his finer qualities but even now, he commanded a legion of eyes. With his mocha-colored skin, haunting purple eyes, and plump lips, *who'd dare turn away?*

In his first few shows, he got surprised when he raked in a fraction of what the other boys got. He was just as beautiful as them—more beautiful than most. *What was wrong?*

His manager laughed. People don't buy the beautiful that lies behind a museum exhibit. People buy the beauty of the streets. The unattainable was out, in was the guy everybody could fantasize about. *All they had to do was spend one dollar more, just one measly dollar, and they would have you.*

With that advice in hand, he catapulted to fame—well, as famous as strippers can get. He was no longer the mythical Apollo, but rather the Everyman blessed with divine looks yet forced to sell them. A tragedy indeed, but as with all classical works, it sold.

The strip club's headlining act was a group routine by its four best boys. First was Ricardo. He used to be a laborer before the strike. With no resolution to the labor dispute, he used his ripped body to strip. On busy nights, he'd walk down to the audience and carry one of them onstage.

Next came Ion, a boy Chase mentored. He entered the industry to save up for university, however, he found that strutting down the catwalk with killer heels gave him more money than any profession.

The penultimate was Viper. Viper'd been working there for years but even the manager knew little about his personal life. That was irrelevant. True to his name, his package was thick and biting. Even with a thong, its outline prepared the crowd for the final act.

The coup de grace, Chase closed the show. If anyone wasn't swayed by the previous three, no way they'd resist the Chase. The moment he burst out of the curtains, they were on their feet. While the other boys relied on dancing, Chase's weapon of choice was his look. With just his eyes, he slept with the crowd.

When the four boys are onstage together, dancing, touching, even licking (*Dammit Ion!*) in an orgy of the imagination, the crowd would hand over their last mortgage payment.

One slow Tuesday evening, Chase met Eyes and Ryan. He didn't need to chat up the guests as socializing was relegated to the newer boys. However, weeknights were slim, and the lack of tips forced Chase to mingle.

He stopped at Eyes's table where he was greeted with a "My dear, aren't you the most absolutely beautiful thing! I could gobble you up like last night's leftovers."

Chase smiled. "Why, hello, handsome. How lucky am I to be talking to the cutest guy here?"

That line worked with every guy Chase picked up. He didn't even need to speak to some of them. Yet Eyes snorted, his drink coming out of his nose. "That was, that was bad, my dear. Please. Dance, don't talk. You're too pretty for words."

He tried getting in a couple more lines, but Eyes waved him away. This was new to Chase, a guy who was used to being chased. As he walked away, another bout of laughter rose while Eyes mimicked his walk.

Never in his life had Chase felt like an object.

When you're dancing onstage, you are not the object. That was Chase's philosophy. It didn't matter if it were the stage at the club or the living room at a party. He wasn't the object. He was the subject. He was in control. The audience thought that just because he was getting naked, they controlled desire. That's why magicians, con artists, and fortune tellers existed: people believed what made sense.

With the music turned up, Chase was unbuttoning his shirt. Shrieks came from the back. He cast his eye there and gave a wink. This elicited more shrieking as he slithered toward the audience. Licking his lips, he knelt in front of Ryan.

Holding Ryan's shoulders, he wormed his body up. He grabbed one of Ryan's hands and put it inside his shirt, letting the boy feel his nipples harden. After registering Ryan's desire, he took the hand out, wagged his finger, and slid back.

Shirt unbuttoned halfway, the hair on his chest was saying hello. He scanned everyone's faces. Might've been a genius move to sit the audience like this. Easier to seduce. In every eye was lust.

He ripped the last two buttons off and leaned back so everyone could admire his torso, taut and glistening. He crawled forward, peeling off one side of his shirt to reveal a Mickey Mouse tattoo. Taking the hands of the boys beside Ryan, Chase allowed them to wander all over him.

Exploration was key. He needed to bring them to the peak of desire. As soon as those hands were on him, more came from all sides. One played with his ear, another pressed against his lips.

This was the life. This was his life. He unbuckled his belt.

"What a lovely boudoir you have, my dear. How utterly quaint."

Chase would be lying if he said he didn't find Eyes intriguing. He and Ryan had kept returning. Even on a packed night, Chase would slink off to their table, a new pick-up line in store. And, on cue, Eyes would mock it.

What an odd predicament. For once, he was the one chasing and not the one sought. He did everything, even getting them free beer—which Eyes promptly sent back because "beer is for boors, my dear, real men drink magnolia wine."

On another slow night, a frustrated Chase asked Eyes point-blank if he wanted to be brought to the backroom. Scoffing, Eyes said, "No silly backrooms, my dear. Backrooms are for brooms, mops, and undiagnosed depression."

Chase offered his place. He tried negotiating a price, but Eyes rejected it even after a substantial discount. Chase's annoyance was only matched by his libido. *Fucking shit!* Chase wanted it done and over with. *It was just sex!* He put his head in his hands and said he'd have sex with Eyes for free.

Eyes lit up. Raising his martini glass, he turned to Ryan with a smirk. "Lesson learned, my dear."

So, Chase finally had Eyes in his bedroom, *excuse me*, boudoir. Chase had no idea what a boudoir was, but he was afraid he'd be met with mockery if he asked.

Nonetheless, Chase hadn't had sex for free in years. As he and Eyes tussled in the bed, he tried remembering when it was. *Was it four, five years now?* It didn't matter. Years at the club robbed him of sentimentality.

But with Eyes, Chase could let his guard down. He wasn't pleasing a client, he wasn't here for the payment, or the hustle, or the necessity. He was here because he wanted to be.

And Eyes complemented that desire. What Chase considered aloofness was veiled lust. Chase grabbed on to his sweat-soaked satin sheets in bouts of ecstasy as he felt what he'd given all his clients—the satisfaction of the chase.

Afterward, they cuddled when Chase surprised himself by kissing Eyes. "First whore. How does it feel?"

Eyes poked him on the nose. "My dear, what makes you think you're my first?"

Chase snuggled closer, draping his head on Eye's chest. For a minute—and exactly one minute—he envisioned a life away from the club, maybe with a boyfriend, working the gray flannel life, a nine-to-five, punching holes into documents.

His fantasies were broken by Eyes. "My dear, you remind me of the Lady Marmalade."

Chase was drowsy. "Who's she?"

"He was a harlot. A well-known harlot of the Harlem years. He slept with everyone—politicians, bankers, artists, window-cleaners. His bed was a goddamn national attraction.

Everyone could get him. But no one could win his heart. Oh, many tried. Many gave him gifts. Many promised him a future on the stage. But he gave his heart to no man. That's all he did. He broke men's hearts."

"Have I broken yours?" Chase looked deeply into Eyes.

Eyes laughed. "My dear, I do not have a heart left to break."

Chase yawned. "What happened to the Lady Marmalade?"

"He died. Reportedly alone from an overdose. His cats ate his flesh."

After that night, Chase took a couple of days off work. He lay in bed, contemplating on normalcy and the Lady Marmalade. *Someday. Someday, but not today.* When he went back onstage, he became more driven, more passionate.

Eyes never returned to the strip club.

"Gitchie, gitchie, yaya, dada!"

Yelling out gibberish was a trick to seem more youthful. And as he waved his belt like a lasso, people looking at his armpits, he'd never been more on fire.

He kicked off his shoes and slid off his socks. Now the pants. The trickiest part was always the jeans. Unless they were strip-off, taking jeans off was never sexy.

Thankfully, he had a plan. He dragged one of the boys up front. Getting the boy to kneel in front of him, he grabbed his hands and put them on either side of the jeans. He then pushed the boy's hands down, revealing little by little the tight white briefs that covered his hairy legs.

The crowd cheered as the volunteer stripped him of his jeans. As the volunteer stood, holding his jeans like a trophy, Chase sneaked up and gave him a kiss.

Riot. Some were jumping, yelling "Me!", "I want a go!", and "Fuck you, Wallace!" *Perfect.* They were at their breaking point. All that was left to drive these animals to insanity was a pair of tight white briefs.

He looked forward, scanning the eyes of the boys. Glee. Bliss. Lust. Yet, one pair showed nothing but dejection. *What the fuck was wrong with Ryan?*

A few days ago, he saw Ryan smoking outside the strip club. After placing the boy's face, Chase joined him for a smoke. Right after a shift, he usually crashed into bed, but for old time's sake, he made an exception.

There was a party, Ryan said, *would he like to perform?* Chase didn't say no to a job, especially one with rich kids. After the necessary negotiation, they shook on a price.

That should be it. All business. Until Chase asked if Eyes would be there.

A long sigh came from Ryan. He told Chase what had happened. The accident. Why Eyes never returned. Chase was taken aback. It was as if Eyes were everything he'd been chasing for, the elusive (and illusive) fantasy of being human, as if normalcy could be pinned down and qualified. He didn't know how to say that or even if his thoughts would make sense, so he simply conveyed his condolences.

They stood leaning against the wall, their cigarettes running out. Ryan said goodbye and walked away. Looking at his back, Chase was hit with regret, as if he were watching someone walk away from him again. Maybe it was the night, the exhaustion, or the news about Eyes, but Ryan walking away was like every memory and promise Chase made was leaving. There goes his one connection to innocence. He couldn't just watch Ryan walk off.

Throwing his cigarette butt, he yelled out, "D'you wanna sleep with me tonight?"

Chase almost hit himself. This guy doesn't belong in his world. That kind of proposition would make him uncomfortable. And he wasn't even Eyes. True enough, Ryan awkwardly turned to him. "Jesus, lord, sodomites, and bedwetters. I already have a complicated relationship with someone I can't have."

With those words, Ryan slipped into the night, his shape getting smaller and smaller. Later, Chase had trouble sleeping, and even in his dreams, the memories of Eyes crept in more, more, and more.

Chase's fingers were inside the garter of his underpants. He was teasing it, pulling it down one side before pulling it back up. The groans were delicious. Chase wanted to eat their libido and regurgitate it in a spellbound stream of cum.

But his eyes couldn't move from Ryan's. Ryan was Eyes's best friend, *could he see through me?* His feet got out of tempo, causing him to slip on a move.

You're losing the crowd. He gyrated side-to-side, playing with the garter of his briefs. Yet when he looked at the faces of the crowd, all he could see was Eyes's face, that mystical gleam of what he had almost achieved.

His heart beating rapidly, his eyes chased across the room. *What's going on?* Sweat dripped down him, and not the fake kind he used to make his body glisten, but real damn sweat.

And then his eyes were back on Ryan. He was staring at him, concerned. In fact, everyone looked concerned. *Shit, fuck! Focus!*

He lowered his underwear. Everything went black.

What About Us

"I'M A DOCTOR," NAVEEN YELLED from the front row. They've been cheering on this young boy who, for Naveen, had too big an opinion about himself. Now, he was rushing forward as the stripper fainted.

His boyfriend Percy was also a doctor, although they had varying opinions on the Hippocratic Oath. Naveen swore by it while Percy considered it optional, like tomato on a sandwich.

He checked for a pulse at the carotid artery. *Steady but weak.* Around him, everyone was forming a circle. Naveen realized Chase's briefs were lowered, revealing his genitals. *Not bad, but focus.* He hitched the underwear back up.

He moved his ear against Chase's nose. *Positive for breathing and pulse.* He checked the head for signs of trauma. *None.* He propped the boy up on the sofa, elevating his legs in Trendelenburg position. *This'd do for now.* Later he'd move the boy to a more private room.

A few minutes later, he could hear grunts coming from the boy. He turned to the crowd "Alright. Nothing to see here, back to your regularly scheduled program."

There was a collective sigh. "Imagine dealing with a dead stripper," someone joked. Naveen didn't appreciate remarks like that.

After propping Chase up on the sofa, Naveen gave him a glass of water. Chase declined, however, Naveen made him drink a few sips. A little water went a long way.

"Man, that was weird." Water dripped out of Chase's mouth. *Motor skills are still waking up.*

Naveen wiped his face with a napkin. "Anything like this ever happen?" The boy shook his head. Naveen then fluffed a pillow behind Chase. "Take it easy. Lie down but don't sleep, okay?"

Naveen scanned the area, but he couldn't find the stripper's clothes. He took off his jacket and draped it over the half-naked Chase. He did find the boy's socks, so he put those on his feet.

At least, Chase looked comfortable. "Thanks, Doc. I'll return the favor someday."

Naveen had no idea what a stripper could do for him, so he patted the boy on the head before turning away. Percy, Ryan, and Sugar were the only ones left behind him. Ryan and Sugar looked concerned. Percy looked pissed.

"Just let him rest," Naveen said.

Sugar clasped his hands together. "Thank god, we have a doctor here!"

"I'm a doctor." Percy gave him a dirty look.

Ryan snickered. "Yeah, but you're Percy."

To avoid any further altercation, Naveen put his arm around Percy and nudged him away to the bar, where he poured out wine for them. As he handed Percy a glass, he could see a frown pronounced on Percy's face. Naveen felt guilty. After all, he wasn't invited. When he found out Percy was throwing a party, he had dropped hints for an invite, but Percy said he'd just be bored with his high school crowd.

He respected Percy's choice, but he also wanted a glimpse into Percy's past. He cut a conference short and drove back to see the mysterious side of Percy.

And he was glad he came. He acted decisively when Chase fainted. If he were honest, he wasn't sure what Percy would've done if he weren't here. A sneaky suspicion inside him believed Percy would dump him in the cold.

Attempting to cheer Percy up, he leaned to kiss him, but Percy turned away. *Yikes.* Naveen fiddled with his pockets, a habit to alleviate awkward situations (and he'd been fiddling all night). *Phone. Wallet. Keys. Beep—Beeper! Where is the beeper!?*

With his constant fidgeting, he must've put his pager in his jacket, which was now on Chase. He excused himself to go back to the boy. Back at the sofa, Chase's eyes were half-closed. Naveen nudged him, reminding him of the dangers of sleeping. He fished his beeper out of the pocket, relieved no urgent beeps had come up.

Beeper now in his pocket, Naveen went back to a deserted bar. He walked around, calling out for Percy. By the piano, he heard his boyfriend's familiar laugh. There stood Percy, dusting off the shoulders of his ex-boyfriend.

Naveen's grip on the wine glass tightened.

The life of a doctor was rushed. Taking a break to contemplate on stillness was a luxury they never had. When Percy joined the hospital staff, Naveen had been a senior resident for five years. He enjoyed having new residents and interns. The white walls were frightening for patients, but monotonous to those who worked there. Naveen had fun showing the new folks around, sharing tricks of the trade, and just getting to know the people who were now part of their little ER.

Most of the newcomers came with wide-open eyes, eager to heal the world (or at least a few broken bones). Naveen empathized. He was in their crocs once. But Percy was different. Strutting in as if he owned the place, Percy showed no interest in the operational function of the ER, as he lay around the doctor's lounge with the latest Elle.

A lot of people found this nonchalance a sign of brilliance. *Here was a new kid who found the whole industry beneath him. He's probably a medical genius!* Even Naveen had fallen for it, selecting him for surgery prep.

That whole thing was, to use the proper medical term, a clusterfuck. Percy was dropping scissors, sanitizing the wrong gloves, even mixing up the drugs. Naveen was speechless. Thank god the operation was a success, yet the new kid needed to start respecting the process.

"The fuck was that in there?" Naveen stormed in the doctor's lounge, where Percy was once again lying down with Town and Country. The other staff dashed out. "You could've killed him!"

Percy barely looked up from his magazine. "Have you seen his cholesterol? Dead in a year. Ten bucks."

"That is the most arrogant, narcissistic, ridiculous, stupid, asinine, absolute fucking dumbest thing I've ever heard!" Naveen wasn't letting Percy off. "You'd be lucky, damn fucking lucky, if you don't get fired, much less have your license revoked. I'm gonna report this, you know. Fuck you, do you think you're a medical prodigy? That you don't need to learn? Well, I got a word for you. Respect! You're dealing with a human life. The least you could give is some damn respect!"

As Naveen collected his breath, Percy continued flipping through his magazine. "You done?"

Naveen paced around, wanting to punch the vending machine. "No, not quite."

"Good." Percy threw his magazine to the floor. "You can either continue yelling at me until your vocal cords are fried, or you can bring me to the supply closet and bang me."

And that's when it started. Furious at Percy, Naveen roughly fucked the younger boy inside a storage room. Naveen had never been this unprofessional, yet the adrenaline, the anger, and even the desire all burst all over the closet.

Though it started as illicit acts in between surgeries, Naveen fell for the arrogant young man. They publicly became a couple after a few dates. Even with a distasteful beginning, Naveen was pleased he had a positive impact on Percy, who started putting in actual effort when on duty.

All for the best. Naveen hoped.

"Oh, Si, this is my boyfriend, Naveen." Naveen could barely hear Percy's introduction when he descended on the pair. "Naveen, this is my, uhm, this is Si."

Si extended his hand. Naveen wasn't the type to fake pleasantries, yet a glare from Percy made him shake Si's hand. It wasn't a friendly shake. He gripped the younger Si's hand firmly, crushing his tender bones. The same tension was returned as Naveen fought a wince. The two men were locked eye-to-eye, throwing as much shade as they could muster.

"Dunno who you were talking about. He doesn't look that old, babe, I mean, Percy." Si's smirk was hard to miss.

Naveen's lips curled. Age was a sensitive topic. Though Percy never talked about his past, the ever-persistent Naveen had gone through enough old pictures to recognize exactly who Si was. In a show of triumph, he put his arm around Percy's shoulder, which caused Si's eyes to narrow.

"Funny." Naveen faked a laugh. "I thought Percy used to date a stud. Wonder if he's here."

Percy slid off from Naveen's hug. This was a now-or-never for Naveen. Si put his drink on top of the piano and flexed his fingers. "Yeah. I was also told Percy's dating a total dweeb. I wonder if he's here. Oh, right, he is."

Naveen curled his hands into fists. A few people turned their way. "I dunno, dude, better a dweeb than a wash-up."

Si laughed as Naveen's face got hotter. Walking around, Si worked the crowd. "Y'know Percy always loved antiquing. And miniatures."

That was the tipping point. Naveen had had enough. With a growl, he rushed forward. He almost shoved Si had Percy not pulled him backward.

"That is quite enough!" Percy's tone was deliberate. "You are not children."

Naveen wiped his face. From the crowd, one of Percy's friends (it must've been King) led a chant of "fight, fight, fight, fight."

Si was retreating toward the patio, a challenging gleam in his eye. Frustration at its peak, Naveen wanted to beat the smug expression off Si's face.

"For fuck's sake!" Percy was exasperated. Naveen paused. *Give it up and go back to Percy. Think, goddamit!* However, Si's challenge was too much to ignore. He stepped out to the backyard.

But as he walked outdoors, the logical side of him began tinkering. *Am I mad at this douchebag?* Certainly appeared so. But it was a few words, *a few damn words, how could I get so riled up?*

Outside, people were having a smoke. Naveen recognized Ryan and Sugar right away. They were talking to the couple who had arrived even later than he did. He didn't catch their names, but they were a fun pair earlier during the couple games. When the foursome noted something was going down, they hurried indoors.

Ryan did hesitate by the door, glancing back at Naveen and Si. A good part of Naveen wished Ryan would say something, anything, to knock them back to their senses. However, with a sigh, Ryan disappeared inside.

Si jumped around, pumping himself for the fight. Naveen had no choice. He braced himself.

○

Unlike most of the younger boys, Naveen was of the age where the hangover mattered more than the party. Most of his friends were older, had spouses, families, the goddamn white picket fence that signaled a broken happily ever after.

Naveen was aware of the risks of dating a younger guy. Percy was a loose cannon, but he committed to that. He would persevere until Percy became more serious. Once, Naveen brought up the subject of marriage. How Percy laughed. Trying to save his dignity, Naveen passed it off as a joke, but the damage was done. Percy'd mercilessly mock him about his housewife fantasies.

He could only blame himself. Being a doctor, free time was a luxury, let alone a social life. He didn't have the opportunity to play the dating field. It wasn't like his favorite romcoms where two people had a chance encounter that would change their lives. He approached his feelings methodically, ensuring he didn't read more into Percy's every action.

For he thought Percy's eyes held the key to his happiness. That a future with Percy was the plan that wouldn't end in disaster. That their story would end neatly, and the audience would walk out in tears. But it might've just been Naveen's instincts to fix everyone around him.

And, boy, did he have a handful. Though Percy never mentioned it, Naveen knew his family had run into money problems. It was only beginning and no one except those with inside knowledge of business knew, but Percy stood to lose everything over their bad investments.

Accustomed to a certain lifestyle, Percy would be loath to change. Even with a decent job, his way of life would eat his paycheck. *Just look at this mansion.* Naveen wondered how long before Percy's world would get repossessed.

And the Vicodin! Percy'd been keeping it from him, but he knew exactly who'd been taking the pills from the nurses' station. He just zipped his mouth when the pharmacists went frantic about the missing medicine.

Money and drugs aside, Percy's biggest complication was himself. Naveen saw a deep brokenness he needed to heal. But unlike wounds created by sticks and stones, a splintered soul needed more than a doctor's prescription. It needed something Naveen was afraid he couldn't give.

But dammit if I wasn't gonna give Percy a chance. He loved Percy. Rom-coms taught him love conquers all. Yes, he may be getting sold down the river, but he wanted to give foolishness a chance.

But it ended tonight. Naveen was tired of being in control. *Time to let go.*

⏩

"Yo, shitface!" Naveen looked up to see another figure running out. "You wanna get to Si, you go through me!"

The newcomer put himself directly between Naveen and Si. Naveen had second thoughts. This new guy was bigger. He wasn't sure he could take down two of them. *Dammit,* he wasn't even sure he could take out Si! His greatest edge was knowing which body parts caused the most pain, but he wasn't ready to betray his oath.

"Go back inside, Badger." Si put a hand on Badger's shoulder. "I got enough in me for Doctor Quack-Quack."

After shaking a menacing fist, Badger backed away.

Though Si had his fists up, Naveen was surprised his own hands were no longer balled into fists. He didn't want to fight. *I'm a doctor, goddammit.* He healed, not hurt.

Instead of attacking, Naveen sat on the patio steps. This must've taken Si by surprise for he too put down his fists. "Yo, we fighting or what?"

Naveen shrugged. Si dithered for a while before joining him.

Looking at Si, Naveen could see why Percy was attracted to him. The jock and the prep. The queen and her guard. The princess and the pauper.

Naveen loved Percy and, in his own way, he knew Percy loved him too. But sometimes, that just wasn't enough. Naveen could give Percy a home, a life, a future. *But what did that mean to someone who had everything and wanted more?* Naveen's dreams weren't Percy's. Maybe Si's were.

The realization sickened him. He had an urge to run inside, shake Percy, and yell, "What about us, Percy? What about us!"

Yet Naveen would never do that. He loved Percy way too much. "You and Percy do make a cute couple," he said.

Whatever Si was expecting, Naveen bet this was the last. Si sat silent beside him.

"You should be with him," Naveen continued. "He loves you, and I know you love him."

Si drummed his fingers. "How unlucky we both fell in love with Percy."

They laughed, though it pained Naveen. He was making the right move. Si could take care of Percy. Percy would be happy. They could make it work. *Dammit, now I'm rooting for them?*

Si patted him on the back. "You two are kinda cute too. In a father-son kinda way. Okay, I'm joking. I'm sorry."

Looking at Si, Naveen felt a shared connection. A mutual burden. He leaned forward and kissed him. A sweet kiss that soon involved tongue. He'll take care of Percy. Naveen trusted him. He needed to.

Afterward, they sat uncomfortably. Naveen was ready to head home when Si held him back. "If you love him, like really love him. Then stay with him."

Now, Naveen was surprised. A million images flashed in his brain. "You sure?"

"No. Not really." Si bit his lips. "Better act now before I change my mind."

This night was taking all sorts of weird turns. "But you still love him."

"Yes," Si replied, "but you know that saying 'love conquers all'? That's BS, right?"

They had more in common than he thought. "BS indeed."

They sat for a few minutes, twin souls beating amid a billion beautiful hearts. Naveen looked at Si and smiled before they headed inside.

Family Portrait

UELITON WAS COLD. He and Lee had been having a lovely chat with some of his brother's friends outside when the chilly air and the possibility of a fight brought them back in.

So far, the conversations weren't of any importance. Ryan had an exhibit, Sugar got a promotion. *Wonderful.* But everyone was hesitant to discuss Eyes. *Fuck.* That's why Ueliton was here. *No worries.* With more time (and alcohol), they'd be more prone to talk about Eyes.

After the commotion, Ryan and Sugar disappeared. Ueliton was left with Lee, who, as always, was clinging on his arm. *Lovely.* When Ryan invited him, he planned to go solo. Though he and Lee were inseparable and, *yes, it was endearing*, some demons he had to face on his own.

There were so many questions about the night Eyes died. Ueliton never heard the full story. He'd been putting it off, but trauma can only be postponed for so long. He wasn't sure he wanted to share any new information with the too-happy-to-be-here Lee.

There were few secrets between him and his boyfriend. The two of them had been together since high school and they'd been living together since their second year of university. *Christ,* almost a decade now. Now, they even work in the same video game company. (Ueliton was a programmer while Lee an animator.) Oh, and the pets. *The damn pets.* They had a Husky who loved to whine and a couple of Siamese cats who loved to make the dog whine. Lee referred to them as their children.

Ueliton shuddered every time. They were the poster child for gay love.

When Ueliton and Eyes were growing up, they had a huge family portrait hanging above the dining room table. Ueliton was around seven, and Eyes was five. In the painting, Eyes was oblivious, playing with a toy train on the floor, while Ueliton clung on to his mother's dress. Their mother was resplendent, glorious even, as she lounged back on the sofa. Completing the picture was their father, smoking a pipe as he stood at attention behind them all.

The portrait had been commissioned back when the family had luxury. Their father was the CEO of a major company and their mother spent her days with yarn and wine.

If kid Ueliton were asked what true love was, he'd point toward his parents. Nothing beats the traditional family. The powerful commanding father, the magnanimous stay-at-home mother, and the two well-mannered intelligent boys.

Ueliton was eleven when the perfect picture faded. He didn't know the full details then, but later he found out his father got involved in insider trading.

The family's everyday veered off-course. Their father would no longer kiss their mother before work. Their mother gave up knitting and spent her days staring outside the window crying.

Her one glass of wine became three, then a full bottle. Ueliton would be ordered to go to the corner store to buy more wine. "Just tell 'em you're eighteen. Jesus, you got your dad's ugly mug, they'll buy it."

Growing up, Ueliton and Eyes shared a room and a bunk bed. As Ueliton was older, he claimed the top bunk. All the kids would tell you, the top bunk was the cool one. Whenever he needed to escape his parents, all he did was climb and nothing could follow him.

Nothing except the shouts. The walls echoed his father yelling at his mother for drinking all day. Their mother would blame his absence for turning their sons gay. Their father would call their mother an entitled bitch, while their mother called him a useless criminal. "I should've listened to my ma and not married a snake oil merchant!"

Ueliton pretended those were demons of the night. When he gazed down at Eyes, the same sleeplessness stared back at him. Sometimes, he'd climb down and cuddle his younger brother to sleep. Screams aren't as painful when you share the hurt.

It was a Saturday breakfast when World War III broke out. They were having cereal and Ueliton asked his father to *please, sir, kindly pass the milk.* Busy reading the newspaper (they mentioned him daily now), his father picked up the milk carton and handed it without looking, not knowing he was about to drop it on the floor.

Being a clumsy kid, Ueliton did his best to catch it, yet the carton grazed his hand before spilling all over. Eyes laughed and their father joined in, but their mother was beyond words.

She screamed at him for being a klutz, punctuating her yells by smashing plates. In turn, their father shouted back to *please stop screeching like a bitch before coffee.* She shoved him, slapping him with their cutlery. Backed into a corner, their father punched her in the face. *WHAM!* She sprawled all over the milk.

It was the first Ueliton saw his parents become violent. He cowered into the corner with Eyes. From the floor, their mother cackled. In a low voice, she ordered their father to *fucking move out* or she would call the cops and tell them he raped their children. Their father marched out.

And that was the last time Ueliton and Eyes saw him. They later learned he was living across the country. Ueliton looked him up on social media once. He looked happy in his pictures with his new family. His new wife was plump but homey, and their three daughters were as lovely as pictures could be.

If separation improved their father's life, the opposite happened to their mother. Almost immediately, she changed her last name. She'd been brought up as a society girl, taught to rely on husbands for stability. Now, she had to join the workforce. Unfortunately, not only did she lack marketable skills, her years of drinking gave her a few bad habits.

It was difficult for her to hold down even a minimum wage job before getting sacked. This did little to stop her alcoholism, which evolved into violent outbursts. Eyes once suggested calling social services. After all, they had the bruises to prove it. Yet Ueliton couldn't betray their only remaining parent.

This loyalty to his mother dissipated when she, tired of working, went on a husband hunt. After the first five men, Ueliton didn't bother remembering their names. They were all the same, big husky men who beat her and her kids before storming out. No matter how he pleaded, their mother sided with them.

Fed up, Ueliton once ran away. He was a sophomore then, Eyes in junior high. His mother had said goodbye to yet another man and was in a particularly vile mood. She called Ueliton *a faggot, just like your father*, right before she smacked him across the face with a spatula.

With no relatives or friends, there was only one person Ueliton could go to. He ran to the train station, hoping his savings were enough for a ticket cross-country to his father. It wasn't.

Though he begged, there was nothing the attendants could do. When the station closed, he roamed the drizzling streets.

With no canopy in sight, he lay on a bench, drenched and crying. As the city hid from the rain, the family portrait still hanging at their dining room came to mind. Their mother, in a drunken fit, tried to pry it off, but it was bolted so firmly that even her adrenaline-pumped state couldn't inch it. She settled by covering it with a blanket.

Ueliton pictured his life as a homeless youth. Home was no longer an option. Maybe there was a shelter for troubled teens like him. There had to be. They wouldn't let a young boy like him cruise the city for alms. Though that life was more appetizing than dealing with his mother.

Fortunately, Eyes had been looking for him across the city. Ueliton was covering himself with newspapers at the bench when Eyes rolled by on his bike. They hugged each other tightly. Eyes promised everything will work out as long as they had each other. Just like when they were kids holding each other through their parents' fights, pain shared was pain relieved.

Ueliton took him at his word. Even though both boys received a beating later that night, Ueliton treated Eyes as the only real family he had. Even after they both moved out, they stayed in touch. They went to different scenes, pursued different interests, and forged different lives, yet Ueliton found a few minutes each week to see how Eyes was doing.

But now he was gone. Ueliton had to make a family of his own.

That's enough chitchat.
With Lee in hand, Ueliton walked toward Sugar, who was showing King and El photos on his phone. Though two years younger, Eyes talked about his friends enough for Ueliton to match a face with a name. Interrupting their laughter, he asked if they had a moment.

The three boys fidgeted, yet Ueliton was on a mission. Their discomfort was irrelevant. He had to broach the topic. They had to talk about Eyes.

But none of them were there at the accident! Sugar was with Percy, and they had rushed to the hospital after they found out. Ueliton believed him. It was Sugar who called him that night to break the news.

King and El also had an excuse. They claimed they got stranded on the way, only hearing about the accident hours after.

"We're so sorry, sweetie." Sugar held Ueliton's hand. "I wish we could do more."

Though disappointed, Ueliton was grateful for Sugar's gesture—and it was impossible to dislike Sugar. "Thanks, but who exactly was there?"

"Well," El said, after a prodding from King. "Vyn and Long. But I doubt either's up for a chat."

Ueliton asked why. Apparently, Long was too fucked up with alcohol and Vyn was, in King's words, "too fucked up, period."

"Ask Ryan," El said, after Ueliton conveyed his annoyance.

Sugar agreed, "Best talk to Ryan, sweetie. He was the last one who saw your brother alive."

Frustrated, Ueliton thanked them. He declined King's offer of a drink and Sugar's offer to talk more. El had a petition circulating, *would they mind signing?* It was the last thing Ueliton wanted, but Lee swooped in to put down both their names.

As Ueliton walked off to find Ryan, Lee rushed to catch up. "You okay, babe?" Ueliton could hear the disapproval. *Let it go,* Lee said earlier, *it's the past, be an Elsa and let it go.* Lee didn't understand. People like Ueliton cannot let go. The past was all he had.

"I told you to stay home."

When part of a couple, it was easy to lose individuality to an image others created.

Ever since he and Lee became a thing, they were always referred to as Ueliton and Lee. Never just Ueliton anymore, Ueliton and Lee. Ueliton and Lee, the powerhouse couple who created video games. Ueliton and Lee, the proud parents of a majestic dog and two bitchy cats. Ueliton and Lee, the happy couple down the street.

Ueliton would lie if he claimed he didn't find peace in being Ueliton and Lee. He did. Especially since Eyes was gone. Once again, he had a family, one with three more animals than he wanted, but a family, nonetheless. He found love, he found safety, he found goddamn family.

And Ueliton didn't hate that, no. *How could I?* He couldn't hate Lee. Lee was...*considerate*. Very considerate. He set the thermostat per Ueliton's comfort levels, he created meals that fit his caprice, he even sent him little heart emojis throughout the day.

No, Lee was perfect. The picture-perfect boyfriend. His friends told him how lucky he was to stay in a committed relationship. That's cause for celebration, *apparently*.

But if Ueliton didn't hate Lee, then *why did home feel so lonely?* Fearing the worst, he got professional counseling. Yet his shrink was a quack, prescribing "friends" and "meditation" and "journaling". Things learned in kindergarten.

Even his therapist was dumbfounded when Ueliton told him about the new family portrait. For their anniversary a few weeks ago, Lee surprised Ueliton by having a painter come over. Though taken aback, Ueliton acquiesced. In a suit he hated, and a tie knotted too tightly, he posed with Lee by the fireplace. Their Husky sat in front of them while the two cats posed on the mantlepiece, one on each side. Symmetrical. *Perfect.*

Ueliton was out when the portrait had been delivered. The first time he walked into their dining room, a cold sweat came upon him. There it was in all its majesty.

Yet he couldn't turn away. Whenever he passed by, he'd stare at it. In particular, he marveled at how the painter drew his face. In his eyes, there was contentment, ease, serenity, grace. Ueliton had to stop his hands from ripping the painting every time. It was a lie to masquerade loneliness.

But it was beautiful. On occasion, he'd sit for hours staring at it, oblivious to the fighting animals or Lee calling out dinner. He wished he could trade places with portrait Ueliton. Portrait Ueliton would love his life, while he didn't mind getting frozen for all time. Perhaps as a portrait, he could forget the grief.

He thought about his mother. *Was this how she felt, staring at their portrait as she struggled to smile?* His fingers wanted to pick up the phone but what could he tell the woman they abandoned years ago? Was she still back home staring at her smiling portrait?

Ueliton loved Lee. He did. Deeply. He didn't hate Lee. He also didn't hate himself. Ueliton hated Ueliton and Lee. He hated what they were together, their persona, them. And he hated the fact there was no real reason for hatred, except that he did. Worst of all, Ueliton hated pretending to be happy.

Over by the bar, Ueliton found Ryan struggling to get a glass of water inside Long. "Come on, mate. You'll feel better."

While his sympathies went toward the drunk boy fighting against Ryan, Ueliton was on a roll. "A word?"

After trying a couple more times, Ryan gave up. "Stay put. I'll be back."

As Ryan led him to the hall, Ueliton considered having Long join them. One glance back proved that to be a terrible idea. Long was slumped across the counter, half-conscious. *Never mind.* Ueliton could talk to him when he sobers up. *And Vyn too!*

Ryan opened a room across from the toilets. "I knew you wanted to talk." He closed the door behind them. "That's why I invited you."

Lee grabbed on to Ueliton's arm. "Babe, you sure you're ready? It might be too much—"

Exasperation spewed out of Ueliton. "Get out!" He never wanted Lee to come and he had no need for second-guessing.

Though looking like he was about to argue, Lee left. *Finally, some breathing room.* His knees overwhelmed, Ueliton sat down on a stool.

Ryan leaned by the door. "I loved Eyes. Loved him so much. He was like a brother to me too. I probably knew him most. Well, aside from you, of course. This one time back in college, I got so depressed, 'cause of like boys and school and shit. And I wanted to die. Yeah. Your brother was the first person I called. You know what he did? He came over and showed me a Power-Point presentation he made. Goddamn PowerPoint. Why You Shouldn't Kill Yourself, a PowerPoint Presentation by Eyes. It had animations, it had music, it was cheesy as fuck."

"He spoke very highly of you." Ueliton spoke the truth. The bond between Eyes and Ryan was famous. On their weekly calls, Eyes spent a good ten minutes ranting about Ryan.

With a whimper, Ryan's body slid down to the floor. "I miss the fucker. You know I still have that PowerPoint. Even when he's gone, he still helps me. The *Dama de Noche?* That exhibit I'm having? You can thank him for that. Jesus, lord, sodomites, and bedwetters. I just wish he were still here.

"It was my car. It was my car. I was supposed to drive them, but I was being a bitch, so, so I asked Eyes if he could drive Long and Vyn. But he wasn't, dammit, he wasn't insured to drive my car and, so, after the accident, the police found my registration and they, they called me…"

Ueliton was kneeling beside Ryan, his arms around him. Ueliton's eyes were teary, but it didn't compare to the downpour in Ryan's. "You should know—you should know it really was an accident…"

Ueliton was harboring all the grief without seeing he wasn't the only one hurting. Holding Ryan so tightly echoed how he held Eyes when their parents yelled. How Eyes held him when he found him soaking wet the day he ran away. Pain connected people. Pain built families. And pain shared was pain relieved.

He didn't come here to burden people. Maybe Lee was right, maybe he was clinging on to a perfect portrait. Maybe there are no perfect portraits, only people who pretend they're no longer hurting. He patted Ryan's back. "Hush. Hush now. Let's have a drink."

After cleaning his face, Ryan nodded. Ueliton helped him up. They were about to leave when Lee came back in. *Sigh. Now this.* Needing a moment, Ueliton told Ryan to go ahead and he'll meet him later.

Holding Ueliton's chin, Lee wiped his tears off. Ueliton waved his arms away. "Babe, I don't want to pretend anymore."

"What do you mean, babe?" *Did he always have to be so charming and so cute and so lovable?*

"I don't want to keep asking myself if we can work it out. If we can be pretty normal. Or even just pretty. I don't want to keep promising it'll be better. I don't want to keep thinking I haven't done everything right." Ueliton was never this direct. Maybe he was channeling Eyes's energy. *Stop being superstitious.*

"Oh, baby." Lee's voice rose. "It's an emotional evening. Let's go home and talk. Please."

My god, this guy was perfect. He couldn't even make it easy for Ueliton to break up with him. Ueliton pulled away from Lee. He really did love him. And he would miss him terribly. He gave his love a kiss.

"Baby, I don't want love to destroy me like my family."

Funhouse

"LET'S GO FOR A SWIM!"

Sleep was settling in on Vyn when King suggested everyone go outside for a dip. Percy was vetoing the idea ("I just had it cleaned!") yet the idea had gained enough traction for everyone to run outside.

No one brought swimming trunks, so they had to swim in their underwear. King called for skinny dipping, but people weren't keen yet to take everything off. Emphasis on "yet".

Vyn had no interest in a swim. However, the prospect of being left behind made him consent to be dragged out by El. He sat at a poolside chair, watching people strip. In the olden days, Vyn would be the first naked wet boy in the pool.

Beside him, King dropped a passed-out Long. Thankfully, even King had the sense not to let the intoxicated guy into the pool.

The change of setting soothed Vyn. The living room was drowning in music and laughter that he had to zone the party out. At least the night air made him return to the gathering at hand.

One of the twins was first to strip and jump in. King was hot in pursuit, struggling to take a sock off. The other twin was pulling Angelo into the pool. Even though Angelo had taken his pants and shoes off, he was still wearing his shirt. That didn't stop the twin from pushing him in, before cannon-balling right behind him.

What fun. Half the boys were in the pool, the other half in the process of jumping in. Even the stripper, who spent the evening in his briefs, was splashing water toward Naveen. Aside from Vyn, the only ones who weren't diving in were Long and another guy across the pool. Vyn squinted. Bald head. *CC!*

Vyn didn't know CC was here. Though the pope could've been here and Vyn wouldn't have noticed. He didn't care who had arrived. They were just boys. They were just bodies. And those were meaningless to Vyn now.

Beside him, Long coughed. He never handled liquor well. A smirk almost played on Vyn's face. Almost. Even back in their prime (what a shuddering thought to be well past your prime), Vyn would outdrink Long and still be doing laps in the pool.

Vyn was trying to remember Eyes's quote about aging, but it was hard to think. Nonetheless, nowadays he and Long were the ones at the poolside. The presence of his friend calmed him. As much as Vyn refused to socialize the past few years, he missed the fuzzy feeling of familiarity.

Long's unkempt hair couldn't hide how some were turning white. *Must be the drinking. Maybe the stress.* Vyn was too familiar.

They're looking at you.

There it was again. Vyn tightened his grip on the chair.

They're looking at you, Vinnie. The voice hissed an inch away from Vyn's ear. Vyn closed his eyes. Most times, this made the voice leave. Slithering around him, the voice cackled.

Open your eyes, Vinnie. There's no escape.

Go away! Vyn droned out the voice with a hum. *Not now!*

But when, little Vinnie? Open your eyes. They're all looking at you. They see your guilt. They all blame you.

It was an accident! It wasn't our fault!

They don't care, my little one. You are guilty.

Remember happier times. You aren't here. Relax and let go.

Halloween, oh so many years ago at an outdoor rock festival.

Vyn was last to arrive. His costume couldn't fit in the bus and two taxi drivers rejected him before a sympathetic Uber driver let him in. His friends waited for him outside the concert grounds. Vyn looked at everyone's costumes. *Ha!* His was best.

In a fur coat and powdered wig, Eyes stood as a perfect copy of Cruella de Ville, blowing smoke into El's face. El was Iron Man though, so all he had to do was close his mask. On the other side, Sugar had to flap his angel wings to get away from the smoke.

Percy was stunning in his handmade Cleopatra outfit, though the cellphone he was using to yell at Si was anachronistic. Si's Caesar was supposed to match with him. Now Cleopatra had to untangle his braids from Long's wrench, part of his construction worker costume.

To everyone's disgust, King came only in a pair of golden bikinis, claiming to be Rocky Horror. (His similarities with Peter Hinwood ended at wardrobe.) Best in effort was Ryan. He had spent half the day painting himself as a Picasso artwork. The result was mismatched eyes, a mouth all the way to the left of his face, and ears where there shouldn't be ears. It was freaky but brilliant.

With his cigarette holder (in character for both Cruella and himself), Eyes blew smoke all over Vyn. "My dear, which porn star are you supposed to be?"

An untrained eye would think Vyn wasn't in costume. Black wife-beater with a checkered shirt on top. Faded black jeans.

White sneakers. Baseball cap turned around with the word "Kewl!". Gold chains. Leather watch. Wristband.

But what pulled the outfit together was a box he was carrying. He picked it up outside a grocery store the other day. Nothing special about it. It was a standard delivery box with a sticker in front that read "Fragile Top" and an arrow pointing upwards.

On second thoughts, perhaps it wasn't that funny. After a few guesses, Ryan got it. "You came as a fuckboy top."

Vyn set down the box and revealed its contents. "Anal beads anyone?"

That Halloween concert was a memory Vyn recalled fondly. When his favorite band came onstage, he lost it. He led a perverse conga line where everyone was grinding on the dance floor.

This was Vyn, so it had to be complemented with his classiest lines. "Hey, Percy, maybe I can be the snake that bites you!" "You may be Iron Man but is it hard where it counts?" "King, show us your pelvic thrust!"

Lost in the music, Vyn ended up in front of the stage alone. Moshing and surfing and banging. *Extreme!* Sugar and El had to drag him out at the end of the night.

The gang was stumbling through the alleys in search of a coffee shop. As usual, King was leading the way with Percy nagging behind him. Long was so drunk El and Si had to lift him, and Ryan and Sugar argued about the best band award. Vyn brought up the rear, with Eyes's heavy arm around him.

"I'm curious, my dear." Eyes blew smoke all over. "You will tell me what goes on in that beautiful head of yours."

"Many have tried." Vyn wasn't joking. As a child, he'd seen one too many shrinks. Frustrated by the lack of answers, Vyn refused to see one these days. *Why pay for a laundry list of medical terms that won't shut the voices up?*

Eyes had to stop to puke. "It's like a funhouse there, isn't it?"

Vyn wasn't sure what Eyes meant. His head was simply his head. Whether it was fun depended on the voices.

Maybe it was the useless doctors or the company of sardonic friends, but Vyn lost trust in modern psychology. He'd had multiple diagnoses: ADHD, psychosis, bipolar disorder. However they put it was irrelevant. All Vyn cared about was that there were voices in his head.

When he was a boy, the voices were his friends. The middle child among five, he lost out on their parent's elation with the first two, nor did he have the cuteness of the younger ones. He found a social life in the voices no one else could hear.

Some of them reaffirmed him. They told him it was okay to cut classes for a movie. Others were more daring. They commanded him to nick a few bills from his mother's purse. When his mother found out, he confessed about the voices. As expected, they freaked out and sent him to a doctor.

As he grew up, the voices merged into one persona. One voice that made him test his limits, drink one more shot, wager a higher bet, fuck someone bareback, *why not, right?*

Even when his isolation was broken by a steady group of friends, the voice never left. With the failure of medicine, he read about exorcism. That was a laugh. It wasn't that bad. The voice had never gotten him into that much trouble.

In fact, the voice made him more popular. His reckless behavior challenged his friends. They fell victim to his lewd jokes, rough manners, and daredevil antics. Maybe it was the draw of the peculiar that led them to accept him, unknowing of the voice.

Once at the prodding of the voice, he told Eyes, who dismissed it with a "My dear, all the best geniuses hear at least six voices." Maybe Eyes was right. Maybe he was a genius.

Beach balls were thrown, Marco-Polo's were yelled, bodies swam laps. Vyn slipped in and out of consciousness, as the voice lingered around him. *When did it become so vindictive?*

Why ask questions you know the answer to?

Timmy and King gained access to the pool house, and soon, mats floated around. *Percy'll love this.*

Percy would love that. Just as much as he'd love to hold your head underwater.

Mickey and Zeke made out in the middle of the pool, as everyone clapped. *Good for Mickey.* It was a shame he stopped hanging out with them. He liked Mickey.

But no one likes you. And you'll never find love like those two have.

Vyn sighed. It'd been like this all night.

Vyn knew exactly when the voice turned from mischievous into sinister. The night of the accident.

He'd been pumped to party. As Ryan was driving them in the evening, he'd been hanging out with Long and Eyes at a park since lunch.

The voice prodded Vyn to get them all to a bar. Ryan was driving anyway. They agreed on one beer. Until Vyn challenged them with tequila shots. ("The loser has to bottom for Percy!") Sloshed, they were singing as they went over to Ryan's.

As it turned out, Ryan was too sick to go. However, he entrusted Eyes, the least drunk of the trio, with his car. Long called shotgun. The better part of Vyn hesitated before getting in the back. The whole thing was wrong. But the voice! The voice who now suggested to pass around a flask of rum.

Car rides made Vyn drowsy. Yes, he could drink pitchers of beer before getting unconscious but long rides? Eyes was telling Long about a boy he was dating when Vyn fell asleep.

Long and Eyes's yells woke him up. The car swerved off the road. All they could see were branches. Vyn was rubbing the sleep off his eyes when a crash forced his body forward. He flew and crashed through the windshield.

Pain. Lots of pain. And the sound of the voice laughing.

He woke up at the hospital. Sugar was arranging the flowers inside the room. Seeing he was awake, Sugar told him his family had dropped by when he was out cold, but they promised to return tonight. Vyn stirred, his body aching.

"How's Long? Eyes?" Even talking hurt.

Where do you think?

Sugar combed his hair. "Long's recovering. You're fine too, sweetie."

"Eyes?"

Sugar's silence was indicative. Vyn's body shivered.

Eyes is where you'll be soon, Vinnie.

The pool air must've done Long some good as he stirred. Looking up at Vyn, he nestled on his chest. Intuitively, Vyn wrapped his arms around him.

"I'm sorry, Vyn." Long's breath reeked of alcohol. "I really am, Vyn. I'm really sorry, Vyn. I'm sorry."

Wishing Long would stop, Vyn hugged him tighter.

Spit was coming out of Long. "I'm sorry, Vyn. You'll be okay, soon, I promise, okay. We'll be okay."

"I'm sorry too," Vyn replied.

No, you're not. You hate Long. You hate him. Hate him. It was his fault!

Vyn held Long's face. "It wasn't your fault."

"It wasn't yours either."

The guilty comforting the damned. What would Eyes say?

⏪

Eyes had once said Vyn's head was a funhouse. He must've meant an asylum where his thoughts danced around the halls. What was once a happy place now reduced to ash.

Percy was in med school. Vyn called him out of desperation. After talking about the voice, Percy told him he needed to be committed before hanging up.

Ironically, at work Vyn was functional. He was a policy researcher who worked with the urban poor in the slums. Vyn's mind was sharp when he walked through the cardboard houses under the bridge. The people he interviewed paralleled his own abandonment. They were all a statistic.

Years ago, he had been the boy who spread his ass cheeks in front of a police officer yelling, "Fuck me in the shit-pussy you cunt-sniffing twat!" Now he was silent in the center of the city's poorest area, helping a homeless woman who had just given birth in front of the Apple store. Vyn was trapped between the most horrific reality and the most evil façade of it. The voice mocked. It condemned. It taunted. There was no escape.

⏩

Vyn cradled the now-asleep Long.

Pathetic. This boy is why you can't sleep.

"Shut up!"

"What ya say, Vyn?" Long said, in between snores.

Concerned he was talking out loud, Vyn nudged Long back to sleep.

Look at that fucker. Why does he get to rest and you don't?

Vyn chose not to answer. Yet his silence taunted the voice further.

Why don't you choke him? Right here, right now? What's the worst that could happen? They already think you're cray-cray. When was the last time they called you?

The voice was right on that note. This was the first he's been with friends since the accident. *We're coping! We're only human!*

But they're your friends! If they cared, they'd have found a way.

The voice shifted around and took form in front of him. Occasionally, it manifested in various shapes. Sometimes it'd be the old man that yelled at kids to get out of their lawn. Sometimes it'd be the smug little girl with a balloon. All random until now. This time though, the voice turned into a mirror image of Vyn, wearing his Halloween costume. The only differences were the clown makeup and the word "TOP" on the box was replaced with "POT".

Choke him.

Vyn's hands wrapped around Long's neck. Vyn resisted but the voice pressed down.

Long coughed. In tears, Vyn clamped down harder. He was so focused, the sleepy mumbles of Long almost missed him. "I'm really sorry, Vyn. I'll take care of you, I promise, okay? I'm sorry, Vyn. I love you."

Long's words worked like a spell. Regaining control of his hands, Vyn released Long's neck. His whole body vibrated, as if waking up from a century-long slumber.

The voice flickered in front of him. Lowering Long into a chair, Vyn stood to confront it. *Run.*

Whatcha gonna do, psycho?

Nine. Vyn marched toward the voice. *Eight, seven.*

Get away from me!

Six, five, four. Come on. Make my day.

You think this will free you? He will leave you! They all will!

Three. Get ready. Vyn was cornering the voice to the edge of the pool. *Two.*

Do it. Kill me.

One.

Vyn put his hands around the voice's neck and stepped forward. What he didn't notice was how they were no longer on solid ground. Both the voice and Vyn fell into the pool.

Submerged, Vyn adjusted his eyes. The fleeing voice was swimming away. Kicking his legs as fast as he could when fully dressed, he followed. The voice was not going to escape.

He struggled to breathe. His clothes were bogging him down. The mess of bodies made it hard to navigate. *Almost there!* He reached out and pinned the voice down.

He got in a solid three punches before hands dragged him up.

Just Like Fire

FIRST, THE SLAP REYES GAVE TIMMY. Then Percy's two boys (almost) had a fistfight. *Missed moments.* A stripper fainted with his dick hanging limp. To top it off, they had to fish out the whacko who jumped into the pool fully clothed.

King grinned. If this wasn't like the good ol' days, then he had no interest in going back to those dull times.

At the edge of the pool, his legs splashed around, as he watched El, Ryan, and Chase drag Vyn to dry land. Poor kid was spluttering water all over. *Three, two…there we go.* Right on cue, good ol' Doctor Naveen was kneeling at his side to check his pulse.

What a waste. He could've just told Naveen. Vyn was fine. Vyn was always fine. Kooky, yes, but still fine.

This is how you throw a party! Thank you, King. He had to thank himself for no one else would. If the party were successful, Percy would claim all credit. Good ol' Percy. Who brought the twins? Who pressured Ryan for a stripper? Who told Sugar to bring all his drugs? All in a day's work for the King.

He was deciding what they should do next while Timmy was kicking waves at Wallace. *Where was the other (and arguably better) twin? There!* At the other edge, Joule was teasing Angelo's ear. *Good for them. Well, good for Joule. Angelo could do so much better.*

Needing a drink, he surveyed those who weren't swimming. There was Long, but he was passed out at the other end. A few feet from King sat a grumpy-looking CC. Had Ryan asked him, he wouldn't have recommended inviting their exes. Might as well put them to good use.

"Hey-yo," King called out. "Grab us a beer, wilya?"

CC looked annoyed, yet he was on his feet. Sugar, who was rushing over to Vyn, saved him by scolding King with a "Sweetie, he's off the clock. Don't be a dick."

Disgruntled, King turned to Timmy. "Strip poker?"

Timmy splashed water in his direction. "We're all in our underwear."

"Well, we could put our clothes back." Wallace swam away from Timmy's hyperactive arms. "Some folks're getting dressed anyway. Oh, no one better step on my shirt. It's brand new, Peruvian silk. Can't get wet or it'll wrinkle—"

"Shit like that, Wallace," King said, "is why you don't get laid."

That quieted Wallace, who turned to climb out the pool. Triumphant, King kicked waves back toward Timmy. "You're welcome."

As he roughhoused with Timmy, two boys swam their way. Badger tapped the edge first, Si flapping behind him. "King, what's the plan?"

"Dunno." Feigning innocence, King turned to Si. "Why don't you ask your boyfriend?"

"Go talk to Precious Percy, Si," Timmy yelled.

Si was pissed off, but god bless good ol' Si, always able to take a joke. "He'll probably say it's time to go home." *He probably would.*

"Alright, how 'bout a game?" The three boys leaned in. Whenever King proposed something, there was guaranteed fun. It was always naughty, for sure, but still good fun.

King yelled at CC and Wallace to join. CC gave a stern "I don't swim." Wallace was straightening his shirt and ignoring King. Their loss. But Reyes, good ol' Reyes, back from the washroom wanted to join. Though King was taken aback, he gladly roped the new guy in.

With everyone set, King started. "Y'all know Never Have I Ever, right?"

"Boring." Timmy splashed waves toward Badger and Si.

"Well, let's make it fun." King kicked the relentless Timmy. "First person to get to ten has to swim one lap and back naked." That shut Timmy up. Even Badger and Si mumbled reluctantly. But with alcohol having hold of their better judgment, they all agreed.

The first few questions were relatively harmless. For instance, Si said he had never rimmed before, while Badger had never experienced a gloryhole. ("What're y'all doing with your life!" King said.)

Things got ugly during the third round. Badger said he had never been in love, a ploy against Si, who punched his shoulder. Reyes was getting into the game. He targeted Timmy with an "I've never kissed my twin brother." Amid mockery, Timmy drew a finger.

King laughed. "I'll do you one better. I've never been tied up with my twin brother."

Timmy gave him a dirty look as he drew another finger.

Badger slapped Timmy's behind. "We'll see your pale ass soon."

"Don't be so cocky. At least I get laid." Timmy glared at King. "My turn. I've never thrown a birthday party no one attended."

Damn Timmy. Guess the gloves are off. King put up a finger. The middle one.

◄◄

Ever since their group splintered, King relied on the twins for a social life. Unlike everyone in their school, he didn't mind the twins. They were the two people more misunderstood than him. Hanging around them made King feel normal.

Yet given the twins' inside jokes and mischief, King would choose his old crew any day of the year. In an ideal world, he'd hang with the gang for three weekends in a row and then spend the final weekend plastered with the twins. *That'd be grand.*

The birthday party Timmy alluded to happened a long time ago. While his friends were buried in college textbooks, he landed a new job. Tired of his father's garage, he charmed his way into a travel agency where he hosted daily trips for the tourists. Decent pay and King loved the attention old folks gave him on their bus rides.

Proud of himself, he invited his friends to dinner on his birthday. His treat. His friends always joked around that he wouldn't amount to anything. While the birthday party was a celebration of the many years the King had graced this planet, he also wanted to slap them in their faces. *Hey, bitches. Impossible? Please.* He did it all with ease.

Knowing that Percy or El wouldn't set foot in the diners he frequented, he booked a table at a high-end Japanese restaurant. He contacted all seven of his friends to confirm their attendance. Though some had prior arrangements, King squeezed out a "yes" from all of them.

On the day of the party, the "yeses" became silence. Ryan was first to cancel from the flu. Long had urgent classwork; so did Vyn. There was an emergency at El's condo. Percy didn't give an excuse. He just didn't show up. And Sugar, good ol' reliable Sugar, regretfully said the person he was switching shifts with canceled on him. Of them all, King believed Sugar's sincerity the most. It was impossible to dislike Sugar.

The waiters dropped by periodically to ask him to relinquish the table. *How fucking depressing.* When he told the story to the twins, they laughed so hard. If King thought Percy and Eyes were insensitive, he was yet to meet the twins.

But what he left out of the story was that he wasn't alone by the end. For one person did arrive, albeit incredibly late.

"My dear, such a large table for just two of us." Taking off his sunglasses, Eyes threw his bag down on an empty chair. "I might get spoiled."

While King was grateful at least one person showed up, his appetite was gone. He asked Eyes if they could go elsewhere. Already perusing the menu, Eyes turned the proposal down. "Oh, don't be ridiculous, my dear, let's eat for eight."

And eat for eight they did. Course after course, they indulged in the duck, the poached eggs, even the salmon (which Eyes normally hated). They washed it down with a pineapple shake and red iced tea. Burping, King unbuckled his belt. Had the other lads been around, they would've been grossed out, but Eyes only rolled his eyes.

"Thanks for being here," King said later as they were walking to the bus stop. Even between two hungry boys, there were loads of food left for King to take home.

"My dear, I almost forgot." Opening his bag, Eyes handed King a badly-wrapped package. "Happy birthday, my dear, and all the best."

King unwrapped it to find a golden candelabra. "Wow." He wasn't sure what to do with this. He thought it was a rejected present Eyes was going to give their more affluent friends.

"Saw it at the thrift shop and it reminded me of you," Eyes said. Arriving at the bus stop, Eyes leaned against the pole. "It's you. You're just like fire."

King was dejected. "Destructive?"

"More like wonderful. You are just like fire, my dear, you burn with every step you make. Oh, my dear, I wish I had your fire. You know what I'd do with it? I'd light up the whole wide world for a single day."

All that for a candelabra. It was shiny, the way it played with his fingers. Moreover, King was happy someone gave him a gift.

Eyes kissed him on the cheek. "You are fire, beauty, madness, charade."

Instead of going home, King spent the night with Eyes, showing his friend just how much like fire he really was.

Folks were swimming over to watch the rest of the game. As King had predicted, the game was lit. No one was pulling their punches. Funny thing about this game—the real objective was dropping your friends' secrets in the open.

"I've never been slapped at a party."

"I've never provoked a doctor to a fistfight."

"I've never had a glass of water thrown at my face."

King loved the intensity. This is what he lived for. That colorful charade. Yet with nine fingers up, King was losing. Si tied with him at last place. Timmy wasn't far with eight fingers, and Badger had seven. Way too nice for this game, Reyes had a mere two.

Timmy's turn. King pleaded. "Get Si! Si, not me!"

The glimmer in Timmy's eyes spelled doom for King. He wished he didn't provoke the Trouble Twin by revealing the time he left them tied up together for a few hours as a dare.

Timmy gathered them closer. In a whisper only the players could hear, he said, "Never have I ever, directly or indirectly, caused a car accident."

That faithful party at El's cabin was supposed to be just another party.

As schedules were tight, the gang couldn't drive together to El's cabin. King was supposed to ride with Ryan. At the last minute, he apologized but he was at capacity as Eyes was bringing a date. *No worries.* King went to Percy who laughed at his face. There was no way he'd let King into his new car.

That left El. King didn't want to go with Golden Boy as El planned to leave early to set up and King had tours scheduled. But the prospect of sitting out the party made him call in sick and hop in El's van.

The drive'd been uneventful. El sucked at driving games so they were passing stories around. Yet El's tales went way above King's head. He'd been talking about the summer he spent in a village in France and how he mixed the French words for "chair" and "bitch", which almost got him kicked out of the bus when he was offering his chair to an old woman.

King would rather French kiss an old lady than continue listening to El. Thankfully, they passed a large windmill which marked a town famous for its microbrewery. King pleaded for a detour for booze. As they were on schedule, El was hesitant. But whenever King made a party suggestion, everybody listened.

El drove toward the microbrewery. More drinks wouldn't hurt their supply. They bought a few boxes and they were loading them into the van when King ran into an old acquaintance, a dealer he met through Sugar. Afraid of more stories of France, King bought shrooms.

Back in the van, King offered El some. Once again, El hesitated, but King convinced him one wouldn't hurt. They'd stay in the car until the effects run off. Besides, they'd make it to the cabin before Percy. Loads of time. So, they took shrooms. It was the first time King had done mushrooms. The car expanded into infinity. El blabbered in French but all King heard were ooh-la-la's. The town buildings were collapsing on themselves. He was walking on a wire, bouncing higher and higher and—

El's phone rang. Percy had arrived at the cabin. *Damn.* Drugs from town are more potent. Lesson learned. El apologized for the delay and told them where to find a spare key.

The drug waning, El revved up the engine. *But wait!* King knew a shortcut through the forest path that'll save them a good half-hour. For the third time that day, El took King's poor advice.

They drove down the main road and turned toward the forest path. It was muddy and rocky. After a few minutes, the car stopped. "I got this, I got this!" King jumped out. He did spend years at his father's garage.

"I'm calling Ryan," El said. "Maybe we can squeeze in his car." As King tinkered with the engine, he did just that. "They're on their way."

"Ye of little faith." King shut the hood. "Carburetor needed a good kick. Should be good now."

El started the engine and, lo, the van fired up. The boys got back in. "Should I tell 'em to just head on there?" King asked.

"Nah." El's voice carried a trace of annoyance. "Let's convoy in case the engine breaks again."

The engine will not break again but King held his tongue. He'd gotten El into a spot of trouble today. They headed back to the edge of the forest path, right where it intersected with the main road, and waited. A slight fog rose.

Bored, King took more shrooms. He even offered some to El but good ol' El was too irritated by the delays. While waiting, King once again hallucinated. He was magic, flying free, disappearing from the car, and watching from above.

As King hovered in the sky, he saw Ryan's car rolling down the main street. King waved at them, but something was wrong. The car was swerving dangerously left and right. Instead of turning at the forest path, it kept going forward. "Watch out, you fools!" but too late. The car skidded off the path and kept going until it crashed into a tree.

It was the loudest sound King had heard in his life. Metal hitting wood, birds fleeing, yelling. His inner drum was shaking so much, and yet in all the din, he could hear the voices crying.

"Watch out! Watch out!"

"Shut up!" El slapped him. He was back in the car. His breath was rushed and his mouth uncontrollable. Everything around him moved as El drove off.

He couldn't sit still. "Call someone! Call the police! Call the ambulance! Call the priest!"

"Shut up!" El banged on the car horn. King never saw El like this. This was Golden Boy, mister perfection himself, scion of the richest house, reduced to a mess of a man, gurgling and sweating like any guy from the street.

King himself was frazzled the entire trip, alternating between yelling at El and attempting to jump out the window. After more shouting, El drove them to a motel. After checking in, they sat at the edge of the bed. The adrenaline must've overridden the drugs for King was perfectly sober.

El called 911 anonymously. King stopped himself from hitting El. *Why did we flee?* Maybe they could've helped. But King didn't need to blame El. The guilt was all over his face. It was his reputation. His inaction. Golden Boy seeking self-preservation.

They lay down, ignoring their ringing phones. Neither boy could take the call. They were hugging each other for consolation. King prayed no one was hurt.

Eventually King had to answer Sugar's call.

"Strip! Strip! Strip! Strip!"

The chanting was wild. King stood at the edge of the pool. Everyone wanted to see King naked and humiliated. "We're seeing dick after all!" someone yelled. *Good one.* He would've yelled the same thing.

They'll get what they want. They'll get a naked King but not a humiliated one. He put his thumbs inside his boxers and, in one swoop, pulled them down.

"You will not jump into my pool butt-naked!" Percy stormed toward him.

"Eat my shorts." King flung his underwear right at Percy's face. He faced the pool and jumped.

As he swam to the other end, a gripping fear took over, a sensation lost since that night of the crash. A fear that he's running out of time and no one could stop him. His stomach tightened but he kicked through. The claps propelled him faster, fast enough to escape the fear.

He made it! After touching the opposite edge, he tumble-turned back. A fancy move that the audience appreciated with their cheers. The return lap was longer. With every stroke of his hand and kick of his foot, he was escaping, rushing toward the inexplicable. He rushed like he didn't that night Eyes died. If only he were faster. He needed to go, he couldn't be stopped, he was the King.

Victory! He climbed up, raised his fist, and drowned in the applause. He was the King. He was just like fire. No. He was fire. This was his party. No one, no one can ever be just like him.

He looked around at Percy's disapproval, Sugar's concern, El's glee, Long's disbelief, and Vyn's absent-minded stare.

No one indeed could ever be like him in any way. *And thank god for that.*

⏸

Just Give Me A Reason

LIKE A WET DOG, Lee shook himself dry. Clambering out of the pool, he put on his pants.

Other guys who'd just been broken up with would've gone home weeping. Not Lee. He knew Ueliton hadn't really broken up with him. It was just the mix of emotions and nostalgia. *Yeah.* That was what caused the momentary lapse in judgment. Ueliton would be back in a day or so. *Surely.* Lee wasn't worried.

Bored with swimming or cold from the night air, everyone started getting dressed. Lee didn't know half the people here. He and Ueliton were two years older than Eyes's class. He did have a passing acquaintance with some. Ryan, Sugar, Percy, etc. They used to play video games when he and Ueliton would visit Eyes.

Fully clothed, he walked down the path to the house. *Where's Ueliton? Is that—no, that's not him.* Behind him, Mickey and Zeke were holding hands. *Guess everyone's coupling up.* They caught up with Lee, flanking him on either side.

"Heya, you." Zeke rubbed against his shoulder. "'Sup with you and Ueliton?"

Before Lee could reply, Mickey cut in. "We should have dinner, the four of us. A double date! Dying for some Korean. You been to the one at the plaza? Been hearing wonderful things."

"They're booked to the holidays," said Zeke. "Our company tried to get a table the other week."

"I always have an in," Mickey said. "The maître d' owes me a favor and I'm dying for some chicken."

"You and your connections," Zeke replied. "How'd he owe you a favor?"

"Well, I…"

Lee droned out the rest. He had his own relationship issues. Mickey and Zeke didn't seem to mind as they argued about Mickey's relationship with the maître d'.

He and Ueliton didn't go to restaurants that much. Lee was a superb chef. He loved experimenting in the kitchen and Ueliton's transparent reactions made him the perfect taster.

Stop thinking about Ueliton. He'd come back when he was ready. As he entered the house, his resolve was tested by seeing his partner and Ryan disappear into the hall.

Lee's face flushed. *Where is Ueliton going?* He had half a mind to kick down every door and drag Ueliton home. *Ryan must be poisoning him against me.*

"Shall we pencil something for Friday?" Mickey interrupted Lee's dark thoughts.

"That sounds like a—well, actually, I don't know. Ueliton keeps our schedule. Lemme check and circle back, okay?" That was the excuse Lee needed to walk away. The sickeningly happy couple made him vomit. After all, he and Ueliton were supposed to be the sickeningly happy couple. That was their thing.

Life was hard for Lee. As a transman, growing up was hell. Especially school. Lee struggled to understand his position in a world that was biased against him.

He and Ueliton were partnered for a lab experiment. Right from the start, Lee was smitten. Maybe it was how he sat, how he wrote down formulae, or how their hands brushed as they grabbed a flask.

After gaining the courage, he asked Ueliton out on a casual hang-out. Not a date. Ueliton might reject him if he were too forward.

Spring season meant carnivals. He brought Ueliton to one of the popular ones. They clapped at the fire-eaters, chased each other at the mirror house, and got splashed at the mermaid exhibit. Ueliton was chill. He grazed his fingers at Lee's arm. He squeezed his shoulders at the trapeze act. Lee was finding it harder and harder to hide his feelings.

Later, they passed by the ring toss booth. Ueliton pointed out one of the prizes, a cute bear sitting on a heart. Lee—who was always good at sports yet wasn't allowed to play—took a hoop and, in one try, won the stuffed toy Ueliton wanted.

What he didn't know was that the bear had a card attached. "Thief, you stole my heart," Ueliton read. Lee blushed. He wanted to hide inside the creepy clown house.

Ueliton didn't say much but soon Lee's hand was sweaty as it gripped Ueliton's. Terrified by the more hair-raising rides, Ueliton proposed a go on the Ferris wheel.

As the wheel spun around, Lee's heart rate steadied. At the highest point, overlooking the city, the silence was their music as he shared his first kiss with Ueliton. If Ueliton did steal his heart, he was a willing victim.

Having a partner made high school a bit more tolerable. Someone to share glances with. Someone to hold hands with under the table. Someone to walk the treacherous corridors, someone to cry to when children were mean, and someone to kiss when nothing else mattered.

Their favorite pastime was playing videogames. Though they played all genres, from battle royales to city-building simulations, their favorite games were fantasy RPGs. Those epic adventures with a protagonist Lee had spent hours in character creator. Lounging on a sofa, their legs entangled, they found escapism in videogames.

It took them a while before they had sex. Lee was uncomfortable disrobing in front of others, even someone he was crazy for. To Ueliton's credit, he never pressured Lee. But Lee still felt Ueliton's erections rubbing against him. He wanted it too. They agreed to have sex after prom.

Lee would never forget prom night, although for different reasons. All he and Ueliton wanted was a night of dancing, holding hands, and sweet nothings. Though nervous, Lee was looking forward to losing his virginity. Ueliton'd been whispering all the nasty things he was going to do.

As the clock chimed eleven, the host got onstage to award the prom king and queen. The king was a basketball jock. Expected. Modest applause. The host cleared her throat to announce the queen. The room was silent. Queen was the highest and most controversial category. Traditionally, the crown goes to the girl with the curliest locks and the loosest legs.

"Our prom queen is…Lee."

Ueliton's hand released as a spotlight scoured the crowd. Lee hid, but too late. In front of him, his classmates parted. There he was. The queen of the prom. The most coveted position was his.

Lee wanted to die.

Lee shook the memory off. This wasn't the time to think about Ueliton, let alone the most traumatic memories of childhood. He needed a drink. *Fast.* As they had arrived late, everyone was already in various states of inebriation. He needed to catch up.

He went to the bar, expecting to see King in his usual position serving drinks, yet the only person there was the stripper. As Lee got himself a beer, Chase leaned forward to ask him where Ryan was.

Not wanting to get involved, he told Chase that Ryan was talking to someone privately, but he'd be out soon. He offered Chase a beer. They brought good stuff from a microbrewery outside the city. *Ueliton had fine taste. Dammit!*

"I'm just gonna get my pay," Chase told him. "Then I'm gonna bounce."

"Already?" Lee took a long swig. Dark and fruity. *Well worth it.* "Thought you were gonna have a do-over."

Chase chuckled. "You boys can keep on dreaming. I'm done. Besides folks're too excited."

He wasn't wrong. The dip in the pool was the jolt that gave life back to the party. While everyone was too tired to dance, the volume in the room was at its max.

"Some party," Lee agreed.

Chase stared at him. Lee got uncomfortable when people look at him for far too long. "What's your deal?" Chase asked. "Are you a guy? A chick who wants to be a guy? Sorry, just curious."

Just curious. Lee gnashed his teeth. *Just curious* was an excuse he heard millions of times. It was the excuse coworkers made when they asked what was between his legs. Or the one his barber made when he asked for a close shave. Or the one call center agents made when he asked them to stop calling him 'ma'am'.

He was about to snap but Chase cut him off, "Know what? Never mind. Doesn't matter. All the same to me. You're hot, that's what counts."

Would Chase have asked that if I looked different? The compliment went past him. He was pissed. How he presented himself was a major cause of anxiety, to the point he meticulously planned his outfit. He was in a crisp powder blue shirt, blazer, and slacks. Ueliton, who looked like he stumbled out of bed with his baggy shorts and t-shirt, would never've been asked that.

Lee chose silence as he stared at his beer. History taught him to choose his battles. Chase adopted a more apologetic tone. "Hey, y'alright? Sorry if I offended, y'know?"

Lee didn't want to drag it further. Anger could do so much. Besides anything to get Ueliton off his mind. He gulped down the rest of his beer. "I'm fine, thanks."

"Where's your boy?" Chased asked. "Blondie in shorts."

"Wish I knew," Lee said, more to himself. "He's with Ryan."

Chase looked thoughtful. "Are they banging?"

"Hope not." Lee chuckled at the thought. A decade of knowing Ueliton was enough to figure out his type. Ryan was pretty, but no.

"You two have a fight?" Chase asked.

Jesus damn Christ, are all strippers this damn invasive? Well, Lee wouldn't know. Chase was the first stripper he'd met. He and Ueliton were homebodies. A strip club is the last thing that'd cross their minds on a Saturday night.

Is there no one else I could talk to? Someone more in tune with relationships who could give me advice on how to win back Ueliton? Having spent half the evening running around with Ueliton and the other half doing laps in the pool, he had yet to meet anyone interesting. *Urgh. Might as well settle with the stripper.*

"Sorta, I guess." Lee opened another bottle of beer. "He might say we've broken up, actually."

He handed Chase another beer. Chase peeled off the label. "Who cheated?"

"No one." Lee leaned back on the counter.

"Well, if no one's boinked outside the bedroom, why're you fighting?"

Damn if Lee knew. That was the question racing through his mind while swimming. There was no reason, no reason for them to split up. *Dammit, Ueliton. What else can I give?*

When Lee and Ueliton were in university, they lived together in an apartment off-campus. At the start of one summer break, Lee had his top surgery, so he could recuperate before classes started.

He remembered going under. When he came to, his chest was aching. Dozing off on the sofa was Ueliton, who was there throughout the process. A blue stuffed bear sat on the side table. It held a card saying, "Congratulations, it's a boy."

Lee laughed, but the pain stopped him. Ueliton had to wheel him to the sidewalk. He fell asleep on Ueliton's shoulders on the cab ride home. (Ueliton said he drooled all over his shirt.)

It took a week for the scars to heal. Lee planned to remove the bandages by himself. A rite of passage. As he was about to peel them off, Ueliton arrived, asking if they could do it together.

The bandages went off and Lee admired his new self. Though he liked what he saw, the scars didn't look pretty. Through the mirror, he saw Ueliton's hands on his shoulders. Ueliton ran his fingers all around the scars and, with every touch, it felt as if Ueliton's fingers fixed them. They stood, two boys in love. Lee grabbed Ueliton and kissed him harder than he ever had in his life.

After graduation, they started working at a video game company, making the same fantasy RPGs they adored years earlier. They would spend days designing and talking about made-up worlds. Lee had everything now. His dream job. A partner. Three pets. Life was almost picture perfect. Until Eyes died.

Ueliton didn't grow distant, no. But loneliness hung around him. Lee offered his ear but when that wasn't enough, he suggested a grief counselor. Yet, Ueliton shrugged them off. *He's fine*, he claimed.

Ueliton lost a brother. This was a pain Lee didn't understand. But he wished to all the gods he believed in that Ueliton would share this pain with him. But no. *He's fine*, he claimed.

Lee wanted to pretend but there were moments. Moments when Ueliton would stare at their portrait. Moments when he stopped caring about how he dressed. Nights when their bed was drenched in sweat. Lee was out of options. No matter how much he reached out, Ueliton remained stubborn. *He's fine*, he claimed.

Some time ago, Lee was reading in bed when Ueliton mumbled in his sleep, "Eyes, Mommy, Daddy, Lee." Lee threw his book away and scurried to hug him. "Enough," Ueliton continued. "I'm so tired. I'm so lonely. I've had enough."

He's fine, he claimed.

This is good beer! Score another one for Ueliton. Dammit! Stop thinking about damn Ueliton.

Checking out his reflection on a bottle, Chase preened his hair. *Jeez.* Chase was the last person Lee'd confide in, but he was the only one listening. "Ever been with someone, like someone you love, right, and he's lying beside you, but all you feel are empty sheets?"

Chase took two gulps before responding, "I get paid for sex. What do you think?"

From the hallway, Ryan and Ueliton emerged distraught. Ueliton was wiping his eyes. Sadness came upon Lee. Every bit of him wanted to run over and comfort Ueliton. But he couldn't even comfort himself. *Fuck.* He signaled Chase about Ryan's arrival, but the latter shrugged and stayed put.

Across the room, a bald guy walked toward Ryan and Ueliton. Lee blinked and Ryan vanished. The bald guy must've been looking for him as he didn't stay long with Ueliton.

Ueliton was now talking to Sugar by the sofa. Lee left him alone. There was a gurgle in his stomach. There were so many things to say, so many questions. But he was so far away.

"The problem is, I think, the problem is maybe we got so used to each other that we took us for granted. But, maybe, if we try, we could know each other again."

"If you ask me, you're spitting out excuses. Hand me another beer, won't ya?"

Lee had been drinking a lot in a short span. At most, he and Ueliton would have two glasses of wine on a special evening. *Dammit! Stop thinking about*—He got a couple more beers for him and Chase.

He opened his beer, drinking half in one gulp. "How can I live knowing that we're broken?"

Drumming his fingers on the table, Chase leaned back. "Met a guy once. Special guy. He wasn't a client, no. He knew shit though. I remember he told me, no one's ever broken. We're all just a bit bent."

"Must be a damn sage." Lee chugged the other half. "I thought we had everything. It was in the stars, y'know. We were happy. Shit."

"Nothing is ever this bad," Chase replied, taking his time with this beer.

"Dammit!" Lee's voice was rising. "All I want, all I want right now is a reason. Just, just give me a reason. A reason it all ended. What I did wrong! What I could do to fix it! Just a damn reason! Just one!"

Lee had been slamming his bottle against the table with almost every line. Noting a few ears perking their way, he composed himself. "Even a little bit would be enough."

After a sip, Chase flexed his arms, covering a yawn. "Why? Why d'you need a reason? Why does anything? Life ain't got no reason. Sometimes, it's just life. You let it be. You learn. People do all kinds of shit, it don't mean nothing."

Lee steadied himself. That was too much to think of. He understood half perfectly, the rest he needed to digest. "How'd you get so smart?"

Chase smirked. "I get paid for sex."

A thought came upon Lee. "You're not soliciting me, are you?"

The idea must've been funny as Chase roared in laughter. "Last thing on my mind, but now that you've mentioned it…"

Lee stole a secret glance toward Ueliton. He swore Ueliton looked their way a few times. But maybe it was the drink playing games. It was over now. Lee and Ueliton was no more. It was just Lee.

However, the trail of Chase's proposition hung over them. "I'm just a pity lay—" Lee began.

"Half-price."

"Well, it's very tempting—"

"There's a room over there—"

"Yeah, but Percy—"

"Okay, free."

"But right now—"

"You're saying no," Chase ended abruptly. "Don't have to say no more. It's all over you. Ah! The ones who're interesting are the ones not interested!"

Chase was joking, of course. The smile he gave calmed Lee. He had to deal with Ueliton at some point but maybe not tonight. There would be tears, there would be grief, and maybe, there would be acceptance. But tonight wasn't that night. He opened the refrigerator and got out a couple more beers.

"Thank you for listening, Chase," he said while handing him a beer.

Chase took the beer and then offered his hand. "Chester."

●

Don't Let Me Get Me

"BUT, HEY, IF YOU ASKED Me years ago if I'd see myself in this line of work, I'd laugh. Now, look at me. We were so silly. If I could, I'd slap my younger self and tell him to start investing! Might've gotten that car a few months earlier. Oh, well. *C'est la vie.*"

Wallace was in the middle of his favorite topic. He wasn't sure how the conversation started. After getting back inside, he spotted Reyes, Angelo, and Joule. *Ah!* They had been talking about high school or dreams or whatever people talk about when they get together. Wallace wasn't sure. He wasn't invited often.

Pat on the back. He managed to stir the conversation to its right track: investments. He was close to convincing Reyes to invest money into his account. Wallace didn't know why Angelo didn't get Reyes to invest. *More for me.*

"It starts with a yes," Wallace said. "Just a bit. Put in a little bit at a time. Will you notice one percent of your paycheck?

Won't be enough for coffee. It won't hurt, I promise, but you'll be glad you put it in."

Joule scoffed, "Phrasing."

Wallace ignored Joule. He had no interest in the Trouble Twins.

"I dunno," said Reyes. "Sounds like a scam."

"It kinda is," Angelo murmured.

"No, no, no." *Why is Angelo undermining me?* That's not how coworkers act. Had Angelo been making the pitch, he'd back him up a hundred percent. *Most definitely.* "You're not understanding. Okay, so the money goes—"

"You know I'm a student, right?" Reyes said.

This was news. Angelo's eyes glimmered. They had no need for students. Students were heavily in debt and wouldn't be solvent until they were forty. *Well, that was time wasted.*

"That's fine." Wallace resorted to his most gracious exit strategy. "Here's my card in case you win the lottery or something."

Wallace lost interest in the conversation. Joule was asking Reyes about his law studies, stating he and Timmy needed a copyright lawyer, a remark which caused Angelo and Reyes to pressure him for stories about being a YouTuber.

Law. Showbiz. Rolling his eyes, Wallace walked away. *Such mundane careers.* Lawyers are glorified liars. And making a living from bouncing around in front of a camera—that couldn't be very lucrative, *could it?*

On his way, he passed by El. Instinctively, Wallace's eyes dropped to the floor. Earlier, he had talked to El about investing, only to be told that his family owned a controlling share in Wallace's company. A definite low for the evening made worse when El got him to join a petition, something the defeated Wallace had no choice but to sign.

Badger and Sugar were laughing on the sofas, the latter soothing a sleeping Long. Wallace avoided them and headed toward the hall. He knew better than to ask Sugar for money and he had already approached Badger, only to be walked out of in the middle of his spiel.

"Looking for someone?" Wallace turned to see Ryan, coming out of a room, Percy behind him.

"Ryan!" Wallace patted his shoulder. "Happy birthday!"

"It's not my birthday."

Off to a rough start, yet this was great for Wallace. Percy's family was a few rungs lower on the social ladder than El's, yet it was far above everyone else, while Ryan was making a name in the arts. Wallace hated hipsters but Ryan's name'd been in the paper enough that he must be making bank.

"Sorry, chap. Figured that's why we're all here." Wallace turned on his salesman mode. "Got a minute? Do you play the market? If you're open-minded, I got an opportunity—"

"Dear god, not this again." Percy rubbed his forehead.

"We're actually on the way to—" Ryan fumbled but Percy was blunter.

"We're not interested in your pyramid scheme."

Percy dragged Ryan away. Ryan chuckled and shrugged but he followed Percy anyway.

Still fine. Wallace wouldn't be as successful if he got upset over every rejection. In sales, people used to tell him he had to be prepared for rejection every day.

What they didn't know was Wallace had a lifetime to prepare.

Wallace wasn't a nobody in high school. Nobody meant zero, that which didn't exist, the people who walked in shadows, and the faces no one remembered. *Oh, no.* Wallace wasn't a nobody. He was less than nobody.

He was the guy who genuinely wanted to succeed but faced failure at every corner. When he tried out for the basketball team, he found himself tied to the hoop, with his shorts pulled down as Si and Badger high-fived. In debate, he was outclassed in every round by Ryan and El. Even in the inclusive drama club, he ended up being chased throughout the gym by a surprisingly angry Eyes after Wallace accidentally switched off his lapel during a show.

No matter where, Wallace couldn't do anything right. Even his class performance was laughable. He passed his subjects by a hair. His subpar command of English led to habitual grammar mistakes that caused everyone to burst into hysterics.

One time, his English teacher offered to tutor him. Tired of being the class dolt, Wallace agreed. They met after class. His teacher was beside him as they went over his latest F. The personal attention was a marked difference. The teacher went at a pace Wallace was comfortable with. Everything was good. Until it wasn't.

The teacher was explaining the difference among 'there', 'their', and 'they're', when a hand crept behind Wallace's back. Initially, he disregarded it. *What was a friendly shoulder hug?* But then the hand crawled down his spine. "There with no apostrophe as in there running back to the hall?" Knees shaking, it was hard to concentrate.

"They're. Apostrophe r-e." His teacher was only a few millimeters away now. His other hand was rubbing Wallace's thighs. There, their, and they're. Wallace was blanking on the next question. There was a hand on his thighs. Or was it their? It was creeping up on his crotch. There skin was touching. Their! They're!

The clock chimes saved him. After telling his teacher his mom was picking him up, he ran as fast as he could toward the parking lot. He'd been so focused on getting away, he left his homework in the classroom.

The next day, Wallace gathered the nerve to tell the principal what happened. But this was Wallace. Everyone, including the principal, had more than a passing knowledge of his reputation. Tough break. She didn't believe him. Worse, he was accused of inventing stories to improve his rep.

Wallace fought. *Why would I make this up?* The principal snarled at him. Reduced to a whimper, Wallace was warned that if he repeated what he said to anyone, he would be expelled. As punishment for wasting the principal's time, he was sentenced to a week's worth of detention.

English class, he couldn't look at his teacher. They were reading *Crime and Punishment*, and Wallace was so behind he hadn't even gotten to the crime part. Later, he shuffled into detention hall. At the corner, Eyes and the Trouble Twins were stifling a laugh. He ignored the trio and sat in front.

After getting out his things, he took a shoe off. His foot was itching all day. As he scratched it, his fingers snagged on a couple of holes.

Behind him, the twins groaned.

"My dear," Eyes said. "Did you run a marathon?"

Without responding, Wallace put his foot back in and stared forward. No need to dignify the bullies. *What did they know?*

At home, he sniffed his socks. Okay, they were rank. *Phew!* After tossing it to the laundry, he stared at the mirror. He imagined he was Eyes, grand, dramatic, and glorious, flanked by the Trouble Twins. He tried saying 'my dear' in Eyes's famous accent, but it fell flat. He let the reflection go. He'd never be as mean as Eyes.

The next few detentions went by without a hitch. Afraid of the principal's warnings, he didn't tell anyone about the incident with his teacher. He didn't have anyone to tell, regardless.

The other boys in detention giggled every time he moved. He wasn't sure what he was doing. Sometimes, he'd lean over to open his bag, and they'd start laughing. *What was weird?* He glared at them once, intimidating and pleading to stop, yet that glare caused the loudest round of laughter.

As he did his homework, Wallace wished he were Eyes. *What would it feel to not be a loser, to not look like a loser, not smell like one?* He would've given anything to walk down the halls and not be laughed at. Eyes was so popular, so beautiful, so talented.

He was the most intelligent guy at school, though he barely applied any effort.

Not only did Eyes have impeccable grammar, he also had a finesse with words. Eyes could challenge a teacher if he felt the lesson was taught incorrectly. And perhaps the best thing about him was that Eyes would never be groped and left unheard.

When the bell signaled the end of detention, Wallace watched the trio leave. He studied Eyes's signature strut. He came to a decision. He would become Eyes.

First, he copied how Eyes puffed his hair. Mousse and hairspray. *Easy.* Then he went to thrift shops for vintage attire. A cape and zebra leggings will do. He borrowed his sister's boots. Personality was harder to mimic. The eye roll. The dismissive wave. The speech pattern. The damn speech pattern.

After weeks, he was ready. Hair, fashion, personality. Outside the school's looming doorway, he braced himself. *My dear, go for it.* He pushed the door open.

In the manner carefully studied, he strutted all the way to the lockers. He smiled, he waved. Everything. *This charade might actually work!* No jeers, no snickers, no side comments, only a steely silence. This was it. This was power. This was his moment.

When he got to his locker, he turned around. *Wow.* There was a sea of students staring at him. He blew them a kiss. The whole hallway erupted into laughter. People were pointing at him, Vyn was banging his locker, unable to contain himself. Even Angelo and Reyes were hiding their mouths behind their books.

He wanted to die.

"What the hell are you doing?" Ryan was in the middle of taking a sketchbook out of his locker. He was only a couple of lockers away from Wallace, but this was the first time Ryan had spoken to him.

"My dear, whatsoever do you mean?" *Dammit!* Wallace had been speaking like Eyes all weekend it was hard to turn off.

The noise was hard to drone out. Leaning by a classroom, his English teacher was part of the mocking crowd.

Fighting tears, Wallace dropped his wicker bag. He would not give these assholes, especially his English teacher, the satisfaction of seeing him in tears.

Blanking, a pair of arms were leading him somewhere. The next thing he remembered was Ryan closing a door behind them. They were in a classroom. The walls did little to stop the noise but eventually, it simmered down. Ryan gave him a hard look. "Explain."

Wallace cried. Not a simple cry. He was wailing, unable to control himself any longer. Nothing worked. No matter what he did. No matter if he became the most popular person. He sucked.

Ryan's reaction was hard to gage. He remained unmoved and quiet, staring out the door occasionally.

Wallace told Ryan everything. How he was bullied daily. How Eyes treated him at detention. How he hated himself. Even how he was groped. He took his time. They were already late for their class, but Ryan showed no intention to leave.

"Why do you wanna be someone else?" Ryan asked after Wallace had finished his rant.

Wallace turned away. "I have to change everything. Look at me. Look at Eyes. He's so pretty."

Ryan scoffed, "But that's not you. Trust me, I know Eyes. Jesus, lord, sodomites, and bedwetters. God knows we can't handle two of him."

"I'm a danger to myself."

Ryan stayed silent staring at Wallace. Drying the tears, Wallace composed himself. "You know, like Eyes is the type of guy I want to be friends with. I don't wanna be friends with myself."

Ryan stood, offering his hand. He didn't say anything, and Wallace didn't need him to. His presence was enough. He took Ryan's hand.

As they made their way out, Ryan gave parting advice, "Don't be your own worst enemy. Don't let you get you." Wallace nodded.

Within two weeks, their English teacher was fired. All thanks to Ryan's editorial cartoon in the school paper, showing a teacher molesting a student. It was captioned "They're Gone: There Is No Place for Their Kind". Wallace now knew the difference between 'their', 'they're', and 'there'.

Look where I am now, bitches. Look at my new car, my fancy job. Who's laughing now?

No one would've thought Wallace would make it, but he did. He took to heart Ryan's advice. He would no longer let himself get in the way of what he wanted.

He wasn't the guy that would stop time, nor the guy everyone would look to for answers, no. He was the guy that could take a punch, that would stand up once pushed, that had been called every name in the book and survived. There was only one job for him: Finance.

Dammit, he worked hard to be where he was. Where he struggled, he took lessons. He enrolled in seminars, lectures, pep talks. He would sit front row with a fresh notebook every time. Even though people at work found him odd, he proved them all wrong.

Now, if only he could show these people from high school how far he'd gone.

At the hall, two unfamiliar boys were taking off their jackets. *Opportunity!* Unfamiliar with his past, they might be more receptive to a sales pitch.

They introduced themselves as Drew and CC. "Having a good time?" Drew asked.

"Lovely," Wallace replied. "This is an excellent birthday party."

CC and Drew stopped in the middle of hanging their jackets. "It's someone's birthday?" CC asked.

Was it someone's birthday? He could've sworn it was, but he didn't listen that much when Angelo told him to come. He heard 'high school gathering' and he was in.

He shrugged, saying maybe he was wrong. The other boys sighed in relief as they discussed the labor laws in the city. Wallace cleared his throat. This was his moment. They may not be his old classmates but *by damn* he will sell them his soul.

"So, gentlemen," he began. "If you would give me a minute of your valuable time, be open-minded enough for I have an opportunity—"

Unfortunately, Wallace wasn't able to finish as Drew pointed to him excitedly. "Oh, you! I know you! Sugar told me about you. You're the big-shot investment guy, right?"

What? Someone was talking about me? Granted it was Sugar, and it was impossible to dislike Sugar, *but still.* His revelry was added on by CC who said people were talking about his car.

"Take us for a spin later, yeah?" CC laughed.

Wallace got light-headed. He's been here for god knows how long (arguably too long), and all this while he thought people were ignoring him. But someone said he was a big-shot? And people talking about his car?

Turning away, he faced the oak doors. There he goes tearing up again. It was shallow, it was meaningless, and it was all cheap talk no one'd remember in the morning. But this was the moment Wallace was waiting for. After all these years, he was recognized.

It had to come, of course, from the two people who never went to their school, but it didn't matter. He made it. He flashed to the day he was crying in the classroom with Ryan. *I didn't, Ryan!* He wanted to yell. *I didn't let me get me.*

"So?" Drew asked. "We gonna hear your pitch or what?"

Wallace wiped his eyes. He turned back with a charming smile. "Nah. It's a party! Have fun. Never mind. Let's go back?"

He'd never felt as accomplished as he did when he followed Drew and CC back to the living room. Yes, no one else would compliment him to his face, whether from the embarrassment that someone like him made it or from the envy that follows crowds like this. But it felt good! He felt good. A moment ago, he was ready to declare the party a bust. *But now?* Now he felt good.

He was Wallace. Annoying. Irritating. Un-pretty. And he reveled in it.

Are We All We Are

DREW'D BEEN ENJOYING discussing politics and sharing a joint with CC. It was a shame he and Wallace had both left to talk to other friends. *Oh, well.* He'll catch up with them later.

Walking back, he tried catching Dr. Naveen's attention, but either the doctor didn't recognize him, or maybe Naveen also needed to forget he was a doctor for a night. Resolving to speak to him before leaving, Drew retreated to the corner where Sugar was taking care of his passed-out friends.

"Florence Nightingale," Drew joked.

Sugar gave him a tired smile. "Oh, sweetie, I can't leave these two alone." Long and Vyn were sleeping on the sofa. "Poor Vyn, still a bit wet and, oh, poor Long, he'll regret this in the morning."

Both looked like they had the plague. Sugar's caring touch was called for. As the two guys snored, Drew asked if he should call them a cab. Sugar shook his head, arguing it'd be best to let them crash here for the night.

As Sugar knew these boys longer, he deferred to Sugar's expert opinion. After all, they were in good hands. Sugar painstakingly took care of Drew when he was sick, making him soup and applying vapor rub on his throat and back. It was impossible to dislike Sugar.

Drew'd never met a guy like Sugar before. They clicked ever since Sugar interviewed him as a potential roommate. But one friend wasn't enough. The biggest challenge to a newcomer was making friends. He was aching to join a circle of his own. City folk weren't as prone to talk to a stranger, let alone allow him into their lives.

He told Sugar he missed an active social life. Without hesitating, Sugar invited him to this party. "It's mostly old friends," Sugar had said, "but I'm sure they'll adore you." Drew hesitated. Friendships that lasted years were embedded into one's being. Weaving through these tangled lines was a chore. Yet Sugar's insistence whittled Drew to come here.

And he was having a good time! Another point for Sugar. Yes, the relationships were far too complicated to understand in a few hours, yet that worked in his favor. Sometimes *complicated* wasn't what people needed. Often, people needed a stranger.

So far, no complaints. Everyone had a story and Drew had a blast listening to them. Back home, the daily chatter was the blabber of shopgirls and grocers. In contrast, the issues of city kids seemed quaint. He held his tongue in fear of offending, yet some of these boys needed a good shaking.

Take CC, for example. *Wonderful guy, sharp as sharp can go,* and yet when talking to him Drew got confused. *Sometimes, the best route is the direct one. Forgetting doesn't mean it's gone.* But the way CC compounded his issues in his head puzzled Drew.

Or Percy, even. Drew was afraid of Percy, but anyone with a passing knowledge of human nature would see that the hardened exterior was begging to be broken. Perhaps then, the pain wouldn't be as bad. He didn't know how to say this. It would be awkward to tell a stranger his pain was guarded. And if his perception of Percy were correct, he was afraid he'd chase him out the house.

And, of course, El. Golden Boy himself wandering around asking people to sign his campaign. Drew did sign it earlier, but El got distracted and left him without further discussion. *Leaders of the future.*

Very interesting boys indeed. What if these boys looked further than they could see? They would've conquered the world by now. God is fair. But that was the problem with people. They refused to see through their own illusions.

There was a reason Drew found these concerns trite.

Before moving to the city a few months ago, he had lived in a nearby town, unremarkable save for the microbrewery where almost everyone worked. The type of place everyone came from but was ashamed to return to.

He had no interest in moving to the city. He was happy where he was, and contentment was hard to come by these days. There were times he'd mock the country mice who proudly rode the train to the city only to flee home, their tails between their legs.

He was one of them now. But it was difficult to assuage the cravings of a man sentenced to death. For Drew had Stage I Leukemia.

After the local family doctor (whose patient list covered half the town) had given him the diagnosis, Drew shrugged it off and went to the baker for a loaf. Drew had originally gone to the plaza to refill their cupboard, but it was the persistent pain and the fact that the doctor's office was right above the baker's that made him climb to the waiting room.

It wasn't a surprise. One of his uncles died from tongue cancer while his grandmother quietly went to sleep from an undiagnosed ovarian cyst. As sad as these stories were, they weren't uncommon. No one could afford chemo, and even those that sold their house to raise funds would struggle to find a specialist.

Nay. In their town, cancer was a death sentence. It was the reverent nod on the way to church. It was the smile that comforted a marked man. It was the silence after your name. There was no shame in death, only honor and honor of the highest order. For those who passed reminded people about the fragility of living.

His numbered days did little to change his disposition. The next day he was shoveling coal at the quarry. Friday, he sang shanties at the pub with his mates (The microbrewery was mostly for tourists). He listened to the priest on Sunday. There was a concept exclusive to small towns that folks end at the beginning. Drew was born here; he was fated to die here. And Drew respected tradition. In fact, he shared them.

But the bad days got worse. He was confined in bed, counting the ceiling cracks he'd promised to fix, as his body betrayed him more each day. He didn't want to die staring at the same cracks his father saw, and his father before him.

Maybe it's time to see the world before it ended. One day at sunrise, Drew packed his bags and boarded the train.

There went Drew. Dead man walking. But the dead were gifted that way. The dead could see what the living refused to.

Here was a fresh start. He didn't tell people about the cancer. Not even Sugar as they sipped tea after work. The apartment they lived in was cheap but homey. Though they were at the heart of downtown, the neighboring condemned properties caused tenements to roll back on rent. The low rent meant Drew didn't need a full-time job. He was hired on a casual basis at a data entry firm. Yet even with reduced hours, his body was stretched to its limit.

But if Drew refused to die with a whimper back home, he wouldn't be content to live his final months in bed. His newfound perspective led him to an activist organization. Challenging the lenses people view society, Drew pushed himself to a leadership role. Though the stress of mobilization, mass demonstration, and education hurt his body, his spirit had never been more alive.

One day as he was coming home from a rally, he collapsed at the front door. God must've blessed Sugar with divine hearing as he heard it all the way from the kitchen. Sugar rushed and brought him in. He owed his roommate the truth. He told him about the cancer.

Sugar scolded him. *Why didn't he go to a doctor?* Through the heavy sweats, he admitted he didn't have money nor insurance nor caretaker. Drew grossly underestimated Sugar. Right away, he had Percy on the phone.

Drew wanted to stop Sugar. He didn't want to burden Sugar with his problems. God would solve them in his time. He had faith. People from home had been calling him to say they've been offering novenas for his recovery.

But Sugar wouldn't have any of it. He pulled a favor to get him a free appointment at the hospital. Though apprehensive, Drew agreed to go. He had come to the city to die but now he wanted to live.

The next day, he was sitting at the hospital exam room opposite a kind-faced doctor. Naveen perused the charts sent by the town doctor. After a round of questioning, he recommended a nearby cancer clinic that produced positive results with stem cell treatment.

That sounded fancy. And expensive. Drew smiled and said thank you. *Coming here was worth a try*. But Naveen wasn't finished.

Laying out brochures, Naveen discussed bursaries and emergency aid he was eligible for. Naveen stayed with him for an hour, helping him fill out medical forms. Drew'd been ready to bolt but Naveen had a solid response to every excuse Drew gave.

By the end, Drew had one hand at the door, when Naveen gave his final plea, "I know that look. I see it every day in the ICU. You're ready to die. I'm a doctor. I don't judge and I don't force. When you leave, you can choose to never return. I won't hunt you. But bear with me.

"You're a religious man. You believe in God and you believe in salvation. Why not give God another chance?"

He never said it, but the good doctor's words struck him. *If only doctors could be tipped!* He smiled in gratitude before leaving. And the rest came naturally. He prayed and, as Naveen predicted, he got government and private donations. He went to the cancer clinic and they scheduled him for chemo next week.

Tonight was the last night he could drown in the party atmosphere, and he planned to enjoy every minute. Chemo terrified him, but Sugar promised he'd be beside him every step.

Long and Vyn settled into a comfortable slumber, Sugar still humming beside them. *Soon enough, Sugar'd need to get a caregiving license.*

The past few tracks were EDM and that wasn't Drew's sound. He asked Sugar to play something on the piano. Sugar waved him off. "Everyone's enjoying Mickey's music." Insistent, Drew dragged him to the piano.

With a resigned "fine, fine," Sugar drew his fingers across the keys. *Oh, sweet melodies.* Sugar'd mentioned he dabbled on the piano, but Drew never had the privilege of hearing him until tonight. And he loved it.

The tune brought Drew back to simpler days, when he and his pals would race from the town square all the way to the treacherous forest path. Some songs made him cry, some songs made him fall in love, but the best songs were those that asked the hardest questions. Sugar's haunting melody kept asking him, *Are we all we are? Are we all we are? Are we? All we are? Are we all? We are? We all? Are we all we are? We all are? Are all we? Are we all we are?*

He bathed in the glorious tunes. Ryan turned off the sound system as people gathered around the piano. Sugar ended on a crescendo that caused everyone to applaud. Sugar was blushing. *Good for him. Really though. He never gets enough credit.*

"Encore!" Drew yelled out. "Encore!"

The word was on everyone's mouth. Drew bet Sugar'd never been the center of attention like this. Standing, Sugar invited El to come up with him, and soon both were doing a duet.

This time, the song took a sadder twist. Even the crowd's breath chilled, couples snuggling closer, as every keystroke called out to him. Though two people were playing, Drew could differentiate between Sugar and El. El's strokes were masterful, rich, and vibrant, the product of rigorous training. Yet his music had a formality, a detachment. Sugar played solely by ear, schooled by the grandmasters of life and poverty. He commanded the choir angelic. His occasional slips betrayed a lack of musicology, but his song came from the heart.

Not to diss El who was highly capable of anything. But boys like Sugar and Drew were the kids that refused to be silenced. The souls that were forgotten. The people no one'd ever get the best of.

Mesmerized, his eyes caught Dr. Naveen's. With his arm around Percy, he too was transfixed by the music. Yet Naveen's eyes remembered him. For seven seconds they stared. Not a doctor talking to a patient, nor two people about to hook up, but a mutual gratitude. *Are we all we are, indeed.*

The worst part about music is that it ends. People clapped, as Sugar and El bowed. Badger rushed forward to escort Sugar back to the sofa. And, as if nothing had happened, the sound system was on and people went back to what they were doing.

Drew didn't return to Sugar. Instead, he walked toward the piano where El relaxed his drink. Seeing him draw closer, El motioned for Drew to sit beside him on the bench.

"You play?" El asked.

Drew stared at the keyboard. "No." He never had the opportunity, though as a child, he saw a touring orchestra and fantasized about being a maestro.

"Funny thing, the piano." El covered the keys. "It's the most fucked-up instrument. It's an entire band in one. A Filipino composer once said that."

El was like that. He quoted stuff from important people Drew'd never heard of. *Too smart for his own good.* With El at a happy state of music and alcohol, Drew figured this was his chance.

"I never saw you again, El."

El's incredulous stare made Drew laugh. There was no way El would've known it was him. He dropped another clue. "I missed you at our meetings."

Seeing the truth dawn in El's eyes was golden. "Please, please don't tell me you're the guy from Grindr."

"Eat a bagful of dicks, you bourgeois trust fund oligarch."

Drew watched in amusement as El spilled the drink sitting on top of the piano. "Damn."

"For what it's worth," Drew said, "seeing you on the streets made me imagine how you'd be under the sheets."

"Shit." El couldn't stop laughing. "Nah, man, I'm just a coward."

Drew let El simmer down. In one gulp, El swallowed his drink. "A wise man—no, a friend—once told me my problem was that I'm a bored rich kid. And bored rich kids are too perfect for this world. At best, we do nothing. At worst, we are nothing."

"Maybe it's not boredom," Drew replied. "Guilt?"

El scoffed, "The proletariat again."

"That's something else, but no." Drew was careful. Rich kids do fuck everything up. "What you told me on Grindr? Your friend's accident? Man, you didn't join a political party, or rally at the plaza, or immerse in the slums because you're bored. It's because you're guilty. Bored people buy yachts. Guilty people seek atonement.

"That's why you left us, wasn't it? Because we were doing the right thing and you couldn't forgive yourself."

El was silent. He stood up and leaned against the patio door, staring outside. Worried he'd overstepped boundaries, Drew observed El's posture weaken. "It's my pattern," El said. "You remember the story. I ran away. Bolted across town like a fucking coward. He was my friend, but at the moment I needed to make a split-second decision, I chose to save my reputation. If only I stopped, if only I checked, if only…"

"But even if you did, it might already have been too late. You were young. You couldn't have known—"

"What would you know?" El turned harshly. "Do you live my guilt?"

It was Drew's turn to be silent. Perhaps, he had judged prematurely. In front of him was a tough kid from the upper echelons of the city. The Golden Boy owned the city, but his past owned him. Drew didn't know everything. He wasn't a savior. He too needed salvation.

"It's nice what you're doing with the signatures. We'd really love to have you back," Drew said. "You know, El. We are not all we are. We are often more. The sum of our parts and more. Our experiences, our friends and family, and more."

Walking toward the patio door, Drew stood beside El as he continued, "A very, very selfish part of me is grateful. I thought you left us because you didn't like me."

"Don't be silly. I left because I didn't like me."

Drew gave El a hug. Thank God he came to this party. *Sometimes you put your faith in a Divine and They deliver.* Drew was not the walking dead. He was alive. He had never been more alive!

Revenge

THE OWNERS OF THIS HOUSE really need to up their security. Ambrosius scaled the back fence of the mansion. Okay, he'd been trying to scale the fence for an hour, nonetheless he expected a security system more advanced than tall walls.

Upon arriving at the gates a few hours ago, he had spent an inordinate amount of time surveying the area. Ambrosius lived for this. He followed a detective podcast and binged on crime shows. They taught him to expect laser-activated fields, nanotech drones, and attack dogs. During his patrol, he thought he had stepped on a mine. He stood frozen for ten minutes before realizing it was an oddly shaped rock.

The best place to enter was from behind. *That's what she said—Phrasing* (Ambrosius was learning gender-inclusiveness). He had to wait around half an hour before he could climb the walls, as he could hear loud laughter and splashes nearby. They must be having a water aerobics class. Or training Navy SEALS. Or just seals.

While waiting for people to go back in, he ate a baked potato, topped with mushrooms, anchovies, and kale (He hated kale, but it matched his emerald hair). *Are these folks Canadians?* How could they go swimming while he was shivering in his bomber jacket?

Inside his bag were a long piece of rope, binoculars, a lockpick from Amazon (he was yet to test it), and a *Teen Vogue* for when he got bored. If the mission got dicey, he brought weapons. He voted against guns and didn't want to betray his district representative. A knife might cause issues if he ran into the police. He settled for a ping pong paddle, a pair of handcuffs, and a paintbrush. Don't laugh at the paintbrush. He once poked himself in the eye with it. It could hurt someone. *Hopefully.*

The wall wasn't even that tall. When he measured it, he scoffed. Heroes in action films climbed taller walls. *What a joke.* He forgot to factor in how he'd never set foot in a gym and, back in school, the climbing wall made him hyperventilate.

But, see here, revenge was a powerful motivator. And vengeance was deep in Ambrosius's heart. Though, perhaps not that deep. It was there, but was it deep? While he pondered, he forgot to hold on to the rope. He fell down.

This was the third time he'd fallen. And he was so excited. *Third climb is the charm bullshit.* His knee was skinned, his elbow bruised, and his stomach wanted to hurl out the baked potato, but *to hell with them!* Ambrosius was on a mission, and a mission he would accomplish. If the rope held.

Maybe fourth time's the charm! Ambrosius threw the rope up. This time it latched on to the base of a wall lamp. Palms sweaty, he clambered up the wall. He put his right foot in, then he put it out, but he didn't do the Hokey Pokey. *Revenge!* With a grunt, he lifted himself to the top. If only his gym teacher could see him now.

Now that he was on the wall, he had no clue how to get down. Must be sorcery, but the ground looked much further from above. In fact, everything looked further up from here.

Did I develop a fear of heights? He should talk to one of his therapists soon. But not the Freudian one.

From here, the living room was lit AF. Whoever designed the place took the placement of lamps seriously. The noise carried to where he was. *Ah-ha!* In the middle of the room stood the silhouette of the guy he was searching for. Even from afar, Ambrosius recognized the figure. He gnashed his teeth. This guy was responsible for all his misfortune, the death of his career, and the decline of his genius. He was being melodramatic again. As his therapist said, *remove blame from the equation.*

The things I'll do to him! Actually, he didn't know. Just like everything tonight, he hadn't thought it through. Murder was obviously out of the equation. He considered torture, but he didn't want to violate the Geneva Convention.

I will take it! I will take everything from him just like he did. Though what 'everything' was, he wasn't sure. He'll play it by ear. *Small concern.*

He lowered the rope down the opposite side. Why did spy shows only show people climbing? Wasn't getting down just as valuable a skill? He lowered his feet, making sure his hands were grasping the thread-bare rope. Slow and steady. Yet, he hadn't budged an inch when gravity decided to be a bitch. *PLOP!*

People started peering outside. *No matter! I am Ambrosius!* Ignoring the pain on his leg, he jumped up. *These pedestrians will not see me on my ass.* (Though he did make a series of self-portraits of his ass.)

Clutching his leg, he shuffled to the house. Before he got near, the patio door swung and out stormed a haughty guy. His commanding air meant he was the owner of the place.

"Get out," the guy said in definite terms.

Ambrosius pushed him aside. He barely stepped in when a group of muscular goons blocked his path. *Wait, are all these guys?* Ambrosius searched for a female. That was quite odd.

"Get out!" The haughty guy made his words hit the spot perfectly.

"I am here for Ryan!"

"Uhm, hi?" Ambrosius recognized that voice. Over by the back, his head was peeping out. It was him! The guy who destroyed his life.

"Revenge!" Ambrosius stormed toward Ryan. In retrospect, he shouldn't have done this. He'd never been in a fight. He didn't even know how to throw a punch. The worst they could do was flap their hands hoping a slap would connect.

That hypothesis would never be tested as two pairs of arms restrained him.

Well, this ended terribly. Two guys were grabbing his arms, as people discussed what to do.

"I'm calling 911," said the haughty guy. "He can rot in jail tonight."

A blonde curly-haired guy scurried over to him. Ambrosius strained his ear to catch what blondie was whispering. He caught fragments of "drugs", "raids", and "press."

Everyone was giving him dirty looks. Even the boys restraining him weren't gentle. *Wait. Blondie said drugs. Did I inhale drugs?* One of the guys holding him looked exactly like the guy sitting on the fat guy's lap. *These boys have mastered cloning.*

Another guy came over, announcing he'd take care of the intruder. Ambrosius's gut sank. *Are they going to waterboard me?* He liked all his fingernails, *thank you for asking,* and didn't want them ripped off.

With no dissent, the newcomer proclaimed victory. He told Ambrosius's captors to follow him. The two dragged his struggling body toward the hall. *Do rich people have dungeons? Maybe they're cannibals!*

It was neither. They entered a small room off the hallway. The boys pushed him down on the couch. The guy in charge took a chair, spun it around so the back faced Ambrosius, and sat down. "Who the bloody hell are you?"

What would a spy do? "James," he said.

"Yeah, James what?"

Quick! The only thing that came to mind was blondie. "Blonde. James Blonde."

The guy laughed, before telling the boys to check Ambrosius's pockets. They managed to find his wallet. *Next break-in, leave the wallet at home.*

"It's Ambrosius." One of the guys passed him the wallet.

"Ambrosius." The guy in charge enjoyed how the letters sounded. "Odd name, innit?" He tossed the wallet back. "They call me King. And my two henchmen here are Badger and Timmy."

"I am not your henchman," both guys said simultaneously. Timmy added a 'fuck you'.

"Why're you here?" King asked. "Clearly, you weren't invited."

"Have you seen everyone here?" Timmy rested on the couch beside Ambrosius. "Clearly not everyone was invited or Precious Percy's lowering his standard."

The two bantered and it was left to Badger to gently remind them to get back on topic. And by gently, Badger called them dimwit fuckers who need to get their shit straight.

"What's your deal with good ol' Ryan?" King asked.

Ambrosius looked at his feet. "I hate him."

"Hate seems to be the ongoing theme here," said Timmy.

Before King could respond (and he looked like he had much to say) Badger jumped in, "What'd he do, paint you wrong?"

Ambrosius had a ready answer. A long one too. He came here to shame Ryan, so his response surprised him. "It's too personal."

The guys weren't happy to be denied the information. Just like Ambrosius, they were obviously winging it.

"Yo, King, check his bag," said Timmy after they exchanged 'what-do-we-do-now' looks. Though annoyed his 'henchman' was ordering him, King opened the bag.

"That's private." Ambrosius jumped up, only to be restrained. "I plead the fifth!" (He wasn't sure what the fifth was, but victims claimed it all the time on TV.)

His plea was ignored as King went through his bag. First was the remainder of the rope.

"Should we tie him?" asked King.

"This isn't porn." Badger took the rope from King.

Timmy turned toward Badger. "Give that here. I'll find a use for it."

King rolled his eyes and took out more items. Next were the binoculars. After trying them, King laughed saying it was a toy. He didn't give the lock-pick a second glance, probably thinking it was just a hairpin. (*It kind of was.*)

Then the *Teen Vogue*. King rifled through it, before throwing it to the floor. "No! Jeggings were never in!"

When King fished out the handcuffs and the paddle, the trio laughed. "It might be porn after all," Timmy said in glee.

It got worse when the long hard 9-inch paintbrush was revealed. "It is porn," King agreed. "Definitely."

After the boys had their fill, King told Ambrosius he seemed harmless enough, *the fuck's he doing here?*

Damn it! Ambrosius hated flashbacks.

So, why did Ambrosius hate Ryan? To answer that question, one had to understand the mind of an artist. Artists lived in their heads, but the head wasn't a good place to dwell in. It was full of misdirection, imaginary friends, and demons. Of all artists, painters were the worst. Maybe the visual nature of composition debilitated one's brain into madness. Or maybe paint fumes were toxic. Who knew?

Painters were like wolves, they lived independently. (Some wolves did form packs, but those were the wrong wolf.) Painters lived in caves and a one-bedroom apartment was kind of like a cave. They didn't socialize out of human necessity but to market one's work in the most notorious way, not unlike how wolves swung their dicks to compare. (Ambrosius was pleased he used his metaphor until the end of the paragraph.)

Anyway, Ryan. He met him at a gallery, as they hobnobbed with curators and agents. *Oh, he knew of Ryan.* The world of the arts was so small that everyone knew everyone. Depending on skills, one was either a colleague or a rival.

Ryan trod the line between the two. They came from the next generation of painters, went to the same shows, and got equal features on the arts section of the paper. (No one read the newspaper anymore though.) Yet in terms of aesthetics, canvas, subject-object relationship, perspective, the shit that mattered, the two were different. Ryan painted for the unwashed masses. Ambrosius was a genius, or so one reviewer claimed.

Digress, Ambrosius! Artists are so flighty. *So, Ryan!* They got to talking. Ryan was telling him about his difficulties with his upcoming exhibit, the *Dama de Noche.* Namely, he needed a venue and representation. Ambrosius had heard about the *Dama. Pedestrian.*

Instead, Ambrosius regaled Ryan by telling him he too was having an exhibit, but his was booked. It would be at the new art gallery, curated by the Marquis. (He was proud he could pronounce 'marquis'. He googled it.) Oh, and agents were dying to represent him.

This really wasn't the case. Ambrosius hadn't booked the gallery, nor had an agency made an offer. He'd been bugging people on the phone daily (once he called the curator Marky five times in an hour) that they gave him a meeting to let him down face-to-face. Ambrosius thought 'meeting' meant an advance for the millions he'll earn in commission. Over the next two days, the bad news was broken to Ambrosius. That was okay though. They were snobs and beatniks who couldn't tell the difference between a toilet and true art.

That comparison would be more striking after he read in the arts section of the paper (which no one read) that Ryan was now showing at that gallery. The exhibit was to be curated by the marquis Marky and the agent who had promised him representation was representing that hack.

Ambrosius's thoughts were invaded by Ryan. He couldn't paint, every new work he created reminded him of the drivel Ryan produced. He was late on rent, his 'partner' left him, stocks were at their highest, Serena Williams lost, his cat ran away, and the price of pork doubled! Granted some of those may not necessarily be Ryan's fault, but that didn't stop Ambrosius from blaming him.

This was supposed to be Ambrosius's life. This was his time. While stalking Ryan on Facebook, he found out about this party.

Ryan's not getting away with it.

⏩

"You okay?"

Ambrosius was jolted back into the present, as the other boys shook him.

"You were in a trance, murmuring about the price of pork," King said. This was news to Ambrosius.

The door opened and blondie entered with two other boys. One of them, a frail-looking wispy lad, went to King and whispered they should let Ambrosius go. *This was technically kidnapping and in violation of at least six laws.* Ambrosius disagreed. He was not a kid.

The other guy was older than the rest and he looked at the gash on Ambrosius's leg. After prodding, he wrapped bandages around it. With Ambrosius's leg fully bandaged, the guy shined a flashlight into Ambrosius's eyes. He turned to declare that Ambrosius was fine.

Everyone huddled close to King. It was all hushed, but Ambrosius could hear snippets like "taking advantage" and "not in the right mind" and "it's stupid, just damn stupid."

Blondie separated. He came to Ambrosius and ushered him outside. Ambrosius didn't know who blondie was but he liked him. He seemed nice. And it was impossible to dislike blondes.

As everyone left, Timmy and Badger remained. *What were they planning?* Timmy said he found good use for the rope. Maybe he was a boy scout and wanted to show Badger some fancy knots.

At the hall, Ryan and the haughty guy were waiting. The latter, in particular, didn't look happy, with his arms folded and his feet tapping. Ryan looked confused.

"Get out," the haughty guy said.

Blondie got in between them. "Oh, sweetie, let's bring him some water first."

"Wait." Ryan was staring at Ambrosius. "Leave us."

"You sure?" asked King. "I could stay in case he tries something."

The haughty guy was ready to burst, but his annoyance was now directed toward King. "There are twenty-three boys in this house right now. You are at the bottom of who I'd want with me in a fistfight. Actually, come to think of it, stay. I could use a laugh."

That shut King up as he, together with the rest, headed out of the hall. Ambrosius was now alone with Ryan.

"How's the exhibit?" Ambrosius mumbled.

"The *Dama*'s fine. I still need a centerpiece though."

"Yeah, great." Face-to-face with Ryan, all the harsh fantasies in his head were gone. He could throw a bucket of paint over his hair. If needed.

"Wanna come to the studio? I could use your input."

Ambrosius's eyes bulged. Ryan had just recognized him as the master, as the superior artist, the painter extraordinaire. *Why would Ryan get a nobody, why would their opinions matter?* Ryan wanted him because he was better. His eyes welled. No, Ryan wanted him because he was the best.

Plebs, fall on your knees. Ambrosius was back.

"Sure, I'm busy with my masterpiece but I might be able to drop by."

Ambrosius shook Ryan's hand. For the record, Ryan did get away with it.

Sober

LONG STIRRED. The music was pumping, the lights were flashing, and the people were laughing. So much stimuli made Long sick to the stomach. He needed to puke. Badly.

Stumbling from the sofa, he nearly knocked down poor Vyn. *Shh!* He took one step and everything, the lights, the music, the faces, swirled. His head pounding, he steadied himself by leaning on the sofa. All the while, he was forcing his stomach to not churn all over the floor.

"You okay, man?" Vyn was half-awake. Long managed a nod. The last thing he needed was to rely on Vyn to guide him to the bathroom. A fear well-founded as Vyn went back to sleep.

You can do this. You drank all the bloody booze, least you can do is puke in the toilet. In any other party, he'd settle for puking in a trash can, but this was Percy's. Experience taught him Percy'd make him clean it after.

All he needed was one step. That wasn't hard. Then another, then another. He'll make it. *Don't think about puking, drone out the lights and, why's the music so goddamn loud?*

Long'd been at Percy's more than enough times, he was on autopilot. He trusted his legs. After all, the walls looked the same. Any logical attempt would end in a mess. Thinking was hard.

One step. One step more. Light-headed, he contemplated passing out on the floor. At least, he wouldn't puke. *Cock, why'd I drink so much?* His left leg was giving up.

At the moment he was about to collapse, hands gripped him by the arms and steadied him. Two people were beside him, their arms around his shoulders.

"You can do it, sweetie." Sugar was on his left, Ryan on the other side. "We don't have to go too fast, okay? Deep breaths. Take your time."

Long did his best to follow Sugar. There was no need to rush. Inhale. Exhale. Be aware of the air moving in the body. "There's some steps, sweetie." Forewarned, he forced his legs up a couple of stairs.

"I'm sorry, guys." Long didn't want to be a bother. And tonight, of all nights. He just wanted to hang-out with his friends again. *Why did it always end like this?*

"Hush, sweetie." Sugar was reliable and it was impossible to dislike Sugar. Long felt he didn't deserve him. From the other side, Ryan joked about being like the old days. Sugar didn't care for the remark as no response came from him.

Just a few steps more! He was grateful his stomach was subsiding. *Positive thoughts.* He will get to the toilets without making a scene.

"Take it easy. Relax your mind, your body," Ryan said. Long appreciated it even if he didn't have the energy to respond. He feared opening his mouth would cause vomit to purge out.

Long wished he had a stronger tolerance for either alcohol or peer pressure. Both were his weaknesses and trips to the toilet weren't uncommon. In the past, he'd promise that if he survived the night, he wouldn't touch even a bottle of root beer. He knew better now.

As they arrived outside the bathroom, Long's stomach churned. Ryan banged on the door. *Emergency!* A hurried sound of water later and Mickey scurried out, apologizing. Of all the people in all the world, *not fucking Mickey.*

"Yikes. Take care of him." His ex's pity was aggravating. "I'll bring some tea."

Sugar helped him up to the toilet while Ryan stood guard outside. Long'd barely kneeled in front of the bowl when everything came out. *Disgusting.* It was a miracle Sugar could stay to hold his head and pat his back.

"I wanna die," he groaned, after the second round of puking.

"Oh, sweetie, it's just a little alcohol. Get it all out."

Long wanted to sleep right there. "What time is it?"

"Around 4."

"I don't wanna be the boy at 4 a.m. puki—" A third round of vomit was coming. As he continued, Sugar hummed, helping Long to stay awake.

After a couple more, he stayed kneeling in front of the toilet as if it were a deity in want of an offering. Getting the alcohol out soothed him but now his head longed for a pillow.

Sugar was fixing his curls in the mirror. Long forced his stomach one last time though only water came. Ordeal over, he stood and flushed the toilet.

Sugar helped him up. Long leaned on the sink. His reflection was a mess. His eyes were teary, his hair was all over, and there was a bit of vomit on his mouth. Sugar turned on the faucet, helping him wash his face.

Outside, Ryan was joined by Percy, sitting at the middle of the stairs. Long was expecting Percy to be upset. He'd been on edge the entire night; however, he didn't say a word. Sugar helped Long sit at the stairs right below Percy, who massaged his back, whispering medical terms.

"He alright?" King was coming toward them, with the tea Mickey had mentioned. Behind him was El, holding Vyn up. "Whacko here told us Long wasn't feeling well."

"He's good," Percy said. "Just had a bit too much."

Long was drifting off when he realized something. He and Percy were on the steps, Ryan was holding on to the banister, Sugar and King leaned on the wall opposite, and finally, El and Vyn squatted on the floor.

For the first time since the accident, all seven of them were together. Long was fully awake.

Funny thing, regret. If only Long knew when good things were happening, he'd frame the moment.

Take the last time the eight of them were together. It wasn't anything special. In fact, it was just coffee on a random Wednesday. Fresh out of college, their jobs consumed most of their time. Gone were the days they spent weeks together. Breaks were now a relief.

Call center agent, med school, artist, policy researcher, feature writer, tour guide, teacher, and whatever El did. *Wow.* Before they were the lords of school, now they were occupations.

They shared a lot, the eight of them. The golden moments that in a snap became nostalgia. The adventures and stories they'd tell their kids. The good ol' days.

If Long were to pick his favorite, it'd be that one afternoon a year after high school. El had come back from his year abroad, while the rest of them were finishing their freshman year finals. The perfect time for a reunion.

Of course, selecting the activity was cause for debate. "My dear, how about that one-woman show at the little theatre?" "Battle of the bands is free." "The twins' birthday?" "Just want a blowie." "No. Not here!" "I'm tired of the club."

In the end, Ryan's suggestion of a drive up a mountain won. The view was supposedly gorgeous, and it was only two hours away. They could have a picnic on the grass and watch the sunset. The gang'd never done this before. Long was so excited he bought a picnic basket.

They convoyed toward the mountain. Upon reaching the viewpoint, Ryan was smug. He didn't lie. It was beautiful. One side overlooked their metropolis. Though they were too far to pinpoint locations, the large landmarks stood testament to their city. But they didn't come here for the city view.

The opposite side overlooked a bunch of towns. This was the winner. Hilltops, valleys, lakes, even a snow-tipped mountain range. Ryan took out his sketchbook, as Sugar and Percy prepared the picnic. (Just Sugar really, Percy 'supervised'.)

Long's first picnic, he didn't have any expectations. They were city boys. They went to restaurants and bars. He sat on the blanket with sandwiches and salads while El flew a kite, Vyn and King raced, and Eyes lay on his stomach writing a poem. This was new. He chewed on a daffodil.

And then the sunset! The eight of them stood at the edge of the cliff watching the sun slumber into the West, her rays becoming gentler, her mouth releasing a last sigh. The clear sky turned orange. Their city never slept so seeing the sun sweetly say good night relaxed him.

For the first time, there was silence. No one was talking, bragging, kidding around, or being mean. It was quiet, but not the kind of quiet that followed an awkward pause. It was the quiet that lulled him to sleep, the quiet at the end of the storm, the quiet when everything was still. They were at peace; nothing could touch them up there.

Long wanted to say this but he didn't want to be the one who broke the silence. Besides, this time the stillness was celebratory instead of scary. He closed his eyes, basking in the setting sun.

He loved these boys deeply. Even though they were an exhausting bunch, they were worth it. Surrounded by boys he loved, he'd never been happier. *If only someone brought a camera!*

But no. The moment lived once and only once, not in photos, but in memory.

The memory of the time they were just eight boys at the edge of the cliff, watching the sun go down in perfect silence.

⏩

Long was relieved it wasn't just him. As the seven gathered, they reminisced about happier days. There were still the jokes, the one-upmanship (at this point the group had perfected it into an art form) but this was it. They started to feel like the group they used to be.

Sugar was regaling them about the time they went camping in a storm. Unable to leave due to slippery roads, they high-tailed it into an abandoned cottage. "And we were so hungry, remember?" El chimed in. "We left the food in the car!"

Long wished he could chime in to remind Golden Boy it was his brilliant idea to leave the food because 'did you know crickets poop on unwatched food.' But Long was content to listen. His stomach's protests had abated but talking strained him.

That trip though! Percy was so afraid of the cottage that Vyn pranked him by covering himself in toilet paper like a mummy. King told that part. Long wanted to remind King that he was also so terrified he almost peed.

No one talked about the essay Eyes wrote about the trip weeks after. Published in his magazine (and full of tiny embellishments), it won him his first literary award. Maybe they weren't ready to remember him yet.

There were thousands of things Long wished to say. He was the one who needed to be surrounded by friends. He was an easy-going guy, if somewhat simple. He didn't need gifts or dreams or recognition. Being with friends was enough. Being a friend was enough.

Eyes was the only person Long loved. It wasn't the love that was clingy or possessive or even necessary. Rather it was the release after being forlorn. Long couldn't pinpoint the moment he fell in love, but there were a few contenders. Like how they were the cuddliest in the group, snuggling as they slept beside each other. Or that time Eyes wrote him a poem about his loneliness. Maybe even when on his birthday, Eyes surprised him with a trip to the museum. It wasn't how he wanted to spend his sweet sixteen, but as they looked at a painting of the horizon, Eyes's head rested on his shoulder. *Best birthday ever.*

He never acted on it. Long preferred to love from afar. Friendship gave them that detachment. Besides love could be destroyed easily, friendship not so much.

Once, he confessed to Ryan about his feelings. The two met at the usual coffee shop. Ryan's attention was divided between Long and CC who kept coming over to talk to him. Long had forgotten if Ryan and CC were together at that time. They kept breaking up that it was hard to keep track.

"Honestly?" Ryan said. "Honestly, most of us know. Even Eyes. But what do you plan to do about it?"

"Nothing." Long was telling the truth.

CC passed by, winking at Ryan. Ryan rolled his eyes. "He's stringing you on. Come on, Long. Even you have to know that." The emphasis on the last sentence made Long squirm. The physical reaction wasn't lost on Ryan. "Okay, I'm sorry. But this is legit his playbook. Plus, he's in a relationship."

Long picked up his coffee and took a swig. He didn't taste anything, but he needed his arms to do something. Eyes had hinted on multiple occasions he had a boyfriend, though he refused to name him.

Perfect time for CC to come over again, with a muffin for Ryan. On the house. Ryan waved him away, but he did start eating the pastry. "Come on, Long. It's gonna be Mickey all over again."

Long knew all too well. He and Mickey had made a horrible couple. Though they broke-up on amicable terms, because they ran in the same crowd, drama happened. Long was grateful it wasn't him thrown out of the gang. But he knew perfectly well who would be kicked out if he and Eyes ever broke up.

"By the way, he's bringing his boyfriend to El's cabin," Ryan said, as CC picked up his plate. "Word of advice, my friend. Love makes you feel good. So does vodka. And vodka isn't high maintenance."

The conversation shifted to the present. As it'd been years, they needed to catch up on lost conversations and forgotten memories.

King had finished telling them about a tourist whose wig flew into traffic, and now Sugar was proudly announcing he got a promotion. Long sniffled. *Look where we are.*

Long had gone back to their high school, this time as a Phys-ed teacher. The walls had a fresh coat of paint. It was still crass, but it made the memories more poignant. Every room, every corner, every chair had a story to tell. The fat kid who struggled to run laps was their Angelo. The people he sent to detention were their Trouble Twins. The president of the drama club sat on the chair as Eyes did.

The job was overrated. His colleagues were detached, jaded from decades of walking down the same halls. The students alienated Long. They reminded him so much of days gone.

That was why Long turned more and more to drink. He wasn't drunk regularly. The occasional loneliness forced him to a bar, where he told the bartender to keep pouring until it dried up. He did it every year on the anniversary of Eyes's death, every year on his birthday, every year after graduation as his students tossed their caps in the air. As Ryan said, vodka wasn't high maintenance.

The topic of Eyes hadn't been breached. No one wanted to be the one to bring up their deceased friend. But inadvertently King asked Ryan about his exhibit.

"The *Dama de Noche*?" Ryan squirmed. "It's about, well, it's about us. And Eyes."

Commiseration took over the ecstasy of the moment. No one said much in response, save random things about missing Eyes and wishing he were here. No one truer than Long.

He drank the most on the anniversary of the accident. Once, the bartender let him pass out on the booth. They said alcohol helps to forget. It had no effect on Long.

Long was impatient. He just wanted them to get to El's cabin. They were the last group leaving and he didn't want to arrive at a party where everyone was already drunk.

Eyes was driving, Vyn snoring in the backseat. El had just called asking them to detour through a small town. With his car broken, he and King needed a lift.

Long looked around the boxy interior of Ryan's car. "Will we all fit?"

"But, of course, my dear," Eyes replied. "If we need to, the tops will sit on the bottoms so there's no hanky-panky."

Long stared out the window. The scenery was pretty as they passed by the windmill El had mentioned. "Ryan said you were bringing your boyfriend."

"Oh, but I am." Eyes smiled at him. "You're here, aren't you?"

"C'mon, tell me!" Long reached for Eyes's phone, only to have his hand slapped away.

"Jealous?"

Lost to the world, Long tickled Eyes in the ribs. He was incredibly ticklish and Long took every opportunity.

"Okay, fine!" In between laughs, Eyes tossed his phone toward Long. "It's Angelo, okay? It's fine, we're hap—"

Then it happened. Eyes lost control over the steering wheel. Ryan's car was old and had quirks only he could manage. The road leading to the forest path El and King were waiting on was full of potholes and bumps. The settling fog was tampering with their visibility, and at the last moment, Long spotted an animal right in front of them.

"There's a deer!" Long yelled. Eyes careened the opposite direction. "Hit the brakes!"

Too late. The car was swiveling madly. They drove off the road, shooting past the forest path into the actual forest. Long gripped his seatbelt as both boys screamed. Behind them, Vyn woke. It was short-lived for poor Vyn. Hitting a tree, the car violently stopped and Vyn's body flew through the car, crashing through the window.

Then only darkness. Darkness and sirens.

The next time Long's eyes opened, they were all in stretchers. Vyn was passed out but breathing. *Eyes? Eyes!* As they were wheeled into the hospital, Long kept yelling. "Never mind me! Take care of Eyes and Vyn! Take care of my friends!"

An injection sedated him for the next thing he remembered was waking up on a bed beside Vyn's. Vyn was unconscious, bandaged all over. *Where's Eyes?* Long sat up, but the nurse forced him to lie back down. *Where's Eyes?* They didn't understand. Long just needed to know. *Where's Eyes!*

The only place Long could find himself was at the bottom of an empty mug. He never felt as good when sober.

He was sober, surrounded by friends at a party, yet he still felt alone. He needed a drink. Being with friends was supposed to make him better. He needed to puke again. Steadying himself, he stood up.

Percy held on to his back as Sugar and King led him back to the bathroom. As he threw up the little left inside him, he cried. It wasn't just the tears when one vomited. He was falling, and he could only blame himself.

After cleaning up, he went outside to six pairs of concerned eyes. He gathered his energy to his throat. "I feel like the party's over."

Beautiful Trauma

RYAN WATCHED HIS FRIENDS head back to the living room. After their first real conversation in years, they had their arms around each other's shoulders. Ryan wished he could get swept back to days when things made sense, but he couldn't. Here they were, all seven of them. What used to be eight.

"Sugar," he called out. The rest left but Sugar hanged back. "Do you have anything on you? Happy pills?"

"Oh, sweetie, drugs don't make us happy."

"Save it, it's too late. Just something, whatever."

Sugar rifled through his pockets. "I handed a lot tonight. Only thing left is this here salvia." Ryan reached out, but Sugar held on to it. "Sweetie, this is…this is hardcore."

Ryan grunted. He'd be fine. Sugar laid it on his palm, complete with a list of side effects and warnings. He thanked Sugar and went into the bathroom. *Phew! What did Long eat?*

Tired, Ryan stared at the mirror. Percy's mirror was a bigger bitch than the one at home. His hair was flat, and his eyes were red. Worse were the circles under them.

He lay the herb on the sink. *Should I?* The night was over, the party was ending, and people'd be leaving soon. *What's the point?* He was exhausted. Tonight was supposed to be perfect. An evening of answers that ended up slipping through.

Enough. He swallowed the herb. Slapping himself awake, he stared at the mirror. *You're a real bitch.* His face was gaunt. *Wait, is that a pimple on my left cheek?* He stared intently. Either a pimple or a speck of dust or his imagination.

"I'd say all of the above." Eyes leaned against the towel rack. "My dear, people are dying from war, famine, and pestilence. You'll live."

"I have a show in a month," Ryan replied. "Less than a month. Fucking pimples."

Eyes sauntered over. They both stared at their reflections. "My dear, it's not your face they're paying for. Besides, you're pretty."

Ryan's head reclined on Eyes. "I missed you."

"Who wouldn't?" Eyes lit a cigarette. "I'd miss me and I hate me." The bathroom lights flickered. "Why are you by your bloody lonesome when there's a party outside? Your party, I might add."

Ryan was gonna say he needed a breather, that he was tired, but he knew better than to lie to his best friend. Eyes knew all his tells and would call him out before he could say two words. "Have you seen the party?"

Eyes rolled his eyes. "No, my dear. I'm dead, remember?"

"Come out then, maybe you'll get why I'd rather stay here."

Eyes stepped back in disdain. "Do you know what I've always found infuriating about you, my dear Ryan?"

Turning on the sink, Ryan washed his face. "No, but I'm sure you'll tell me."

"It was you, my dear. You were always the most infuriating thing about you."

Ryan grabbed a towel beside Eyes. "And can I tell you what I find most infuriating about you, *my dear*?"

"Enlighten me."

"Nothing." Ryan looked at him. "Nothing at all. Though perhaps I am furious that you're gone."

"Pish-posh, my dear, though I must say hell is a beautiful place. Four point five out of five."

Outside, a round of laughter was heard. "Wanna come see?" Ryan asked.

"Whatsoever for? It's a party, people're drunk. You've seen one, you've seen them all."

"You might be surprised."

Eyes put his ear on the door, but no other sound followed. "Well, I s'pose. Beats hanging out with Long's puke."

Ryan linked his arm around Eyes's as they headed out.

"Oh, but my dear, I am not dressed." As they rounded the hall, Eyes took stock of his outfit. Signature red cape, lounge shoes, but the pants? The purple shade clashed with everything.

Ryan gave Eyes a once-over. "Looks fine."

"Can you imagine what Percy'd say? My god, why did I buy these pants? Never ever trust a bargain." Eyes looked at Ryan's outfit. "Actually, stay close to me all evening. When we're together, I'll look like fucking Gucci."

Ryan laughed. "Shut up and walk."

Eyes surveyed the area. Conversations were wrapping up. The loud laughter was replaced by chuckles. Out was the din of ruckus in favor of quiet talk. *Goody goody!* Eyes hated loud noises.

No one had noticed them enter. Ryan took a deep breath. "Welcome to your party."

Eyes was ecstatic. "Everyone's so beautiful, I could fall asleep in their lovely, lovely arms."

"You know almost everyone," Ryan said. "Some a bit more than others."

"But, my dear, it doesn't matter if we know them. They're beautiful. Strangers are beautiful."

"Messed up, though," Ryan replied. They stood observing the guests. "Everyone here's kinda fucked up."

"Isn't that how we like our boys? Messed up, fucked up, lubed up, and all the rest of it."

Ryan's voice was irritated. "Sometimes, I wish you took things seriously."

"My dear, I am dead. I can do whatever the bloody hell I please."

That was the end of it. Ryan couldn't argue against the dead. Eyes was always flippant and nonchalant. Death made him more obnoxious, but this was Eyes in full glory.

Eyes smirked. He won. "Shall we meet the pretty boys?"

The first group Ryan went to was Sugar, Drew, and El. They were squeezing in on the piano bench. As Ryan drew closer, he could hear El inviting Sugar and Drew to the orchestra. Sugar's eyes brightened, but Drew's face was pained.

As Ryan gave Sugar a peck, Drew revealed the reason, "I'm starting chemo this week."

Ryan had seen that fired-up look on El's face before. "How about I bring my Yamaha to your hospital room?" El said. "Sugar and I can play for you."

Drew's mouth widened. "You sure?" he asked, looking at both of them. Nodding, El squeezed his arm. This was too personal for Ryan, so he asked if they needed anything.

Nope, they were all good. El suggested that the gang should get together for his exhibit. Sugar agreed, wishing him the best of luck. Ryan blushed. After thanking them, he walked away with Eyes.

"That hippie thing," Eyes asked. "El's new hobby, I presume?"

"That hippie thing is Drew," Ryan replied. "And, no, he's not El's new thing. You missed a lot. Say what you want, but El's trying to do the right thing."

"My dear, you can't see it, but the problem with rich kids, and Golden Boy in particular, is everything. They have everything, and they want everything, and everything's not enough. It's a hobby, my dear. No different from your silly paintings.

"Although that hippie thing'll be glad to get a sponsor. Chemo's so expensive these days. Even with donations, he'd be lucky to have a home at the end of the year."

"That won't happen," Ryan replied. "Sugar'd never kick him out."

"Oh, Sugar. It's true, no, that it's impossible to dislike Sugar. He's so sweet at his own expense. I need an insulin shot."

Ryan stopped. Something wasn't right. "That's not fair. You don't know his happiness. He's happy with life."

"He's content, my dear. Do not conflate one for the other though they are similar. A street dog is content with scraps for he doesn't know Fido across the yard has two bowls of dog food and a bagful of treats. We are not dogs. Though some of us like it doggy style. Do you think Sugar is happy? In his little call center? As he passes drugs on the street? That's his *raison d'être?* What a grand life! Nothing like playing the piano or something silly like that."

"Not all of us come from privilege. Of all people, I can't believe—"

"I am bored, my dear. Who else is here?"

"Isn't that brother dearest's boyfriend?" Eyes asked. Lee was preparing to strike the balls at the pool table while trash-talking Chase. *Why did Ryan invite the little boy?* Lee and Chase. Trash-talking. The world was mad.

Ryan whispered that Ueliton and Lee broke up earlier. Eyes would never tell his brother, but they were his #partnergoals.

"Hey, Ryan," Chase said, as they got to the pool table. "When I get fat and old, figure I'll make it as a pro pool player?"

"Ha!" Lee sunk two balls. The wrong ones. "Can't even beat me."

As Lee turned to survey the remaining balls, Ryan handed a small envelope to Chase. Eyes swore there was a moment's reluctance in Chase's eye, but it disappeared as did the envelope.

"You overpaid," Eyes scolded as they walked away.

Ryan smirked. "I don't make a habit of hiring strippers. Unlike someone."

"The power couple is over," Eyes said. "How unfortunate."

"You never know these days," Ryan replied.

"On the contrary, my dear, one always knows. One chooses not to think."

Ryan glanced back at the pool table. "You refused to tell me before, but I gotta ask. What happened between you and…him?"

Eyes expected this question, but he too needed secrets. "Him? Oh, nothing, my dear. He is a stripper. A harlot. A price tag. A gentleman caller. A knight of the night. The dark prince of the boudoir. He was nothing, my dear, but a prostitute. And whores with hearts of gold exist only in fairy tales and porn."

By the sound system, Mickey fiddled with the volume while Zeke struggled to stand. Sugar warned Ryan earlier that the two had broken up. With their sweet glances, they definitely didn't seem broken up now.

Zeke was too sleepy to talk, but Mickey could speak for more than two people. *How is Mickey so perky?* Ryan slapped his forehead. His job.

As he set up an easy-listening playlist, Mickey thanked Ryan for the invite, followed by an offer to have coffee with him and Zeke.

Ryan accepted. At his age, any invitation should be accepted. And he liked Mickey. Eyes was to blame for having him ghosted from the group. Time for amends. As Ryan turned to leave, Mickey tugged on his sleeve. "Really though, thanks for inviting us. Nice seeing all of you. And, I don't know how to put this, but I'm sorry about Eyes."

"Can you believe that bitch?" Eyes asked, when they got out of earshot.

Ignoring the insult, Ryan looked wistfully at Mickey and Zeke. Their hands were touching, and their lips hovered over each other. "We didn't have to choose, you know."

Eyes followed Ryan's stare. "What do you want me to say, my dear? That I'm sorry? That I regret everything? That I was drunk on power? My dear, Mickey annoyed me. Plain and simple. There was a chance to kick him out and I took it."

"I'm happy for him," Ryan replied. "He deserves love. We all do."

"What makes you think that's love, my dear? What makes you think things've changed? It's hormones, nostalgia, and alcohol. My dear, this is a party, not a life-changer. Don't delude yourself. Zeke would return to the routine he desperately craves, and Mickey would never stop planning the next big social event. It is their compulsion. What changed?"

Had Eyes always been this annoying? Yes. Yes, he had. His death freshened up the dark times, but he was an asshole. "Sometimes nothing's changed," said Ryan. "Except everything."

Laughing, Eyes patted him on the back. "You're learning, my dear. I'm so proud."

A few feet from the sound system, Joule, Angelo, and Reyes were dancing. Mickey's track was slow, and the three matched the tempo. Eyes was unhappy at how Joule and Angelo were touching each other. He scowled as Ryan joined them.

They bounced around, waving their arms in the air. The lateness was apparent as Reyes's eyes were half-closed. Still, they moved to the beat. Joule and Angelo's chemistry was sickening. Joule had his arms around Angelo's neck. Eyes wished Ryan would separate them.

Ryan leaned toward Reyes. "Doing fine?" Reyes responded with two thumbs up.

Eyes was at a loss for words when Ryan rejoined him. "Let it go," Ryan said. "You're dead. He has to move on."

"My dear, I am not affected."

"He deserves happiness. Your loss was a great blow to him." Ryan took a deep breath. "And not just him."

"I am ever so curious, my dear." Eyes ignored Ryan's reasoning. "That match is doomed. Put money on it. One week. Max. Both would resent each other like five tops at an orgy."

"Funny. I would've said the same when you were with him," Ryan replied.

Eyes laughed. "And you would've been right. Joule will cheat, or he'll ask for an open relationship, or, worse, a threesome with Timmy. It's just who Joule is. You're old enough, my dear. People are who they are. But Angelo will have none of that. He wants cuddles and the white picket fence and children. That's just who Angelo is. He should've hooked-up with Reyes. My dear, why don't you hook Angelo up with Reyes?"

Ryan's eyes rolled. "That's as gross as asking Percy to hookup Long and El. You're obsessed with hook-ups. We're not ruled by our dicks. Besides, Reyes needs a friend."

"That's your solution to everything. You're lonely? Have friends. You're depressed. Here, have some fucking friends. Friendship is not the answer to all your problems, my dear. Friendship is not marijuana."

By the sofas, Ueliton was questioning Long and Vyn. The two were responsive (or at least as responsive as they both could be), and Ueliton hadn't given up discovering what happened the night of the accident.

Watching Ueliton ask question after question in calculated fashion made Ryan guilty. In his mind, he and his friends had been the ones most affected by Eyes's death. He forgot people like Angelo, Chase and, of course, Eyes's damn brother would have a vested interest.

Given that Vyn was retelling the accident, Ryan didn't want to bother. He tiptoed in to ask if everyone was okay. Long and Vyn grunted, though their faces said otherwise. Ueliton merely nodded in irritation.

"He will never find peace, that one," Eyes said.

The sadness on Eyes's face moved Ryan. "If you were him, what would you do?"

"I would've thrown a goddamn parade."

And the sadness was gone. There was no winning with the dead, though Ryan was close to his limit. "Poor Long and Vyn though."

"What about those fuckers?"

"They were with you in the car. Imagine their trauma. It could've been them. Sometimes they wish it were them."

For once, Eyes remained silent.

After processing Ryan's revelation about Long and Vyn, Eyes shook it off. This was his night. There were too many boys to fuck to get stuck on two basket cases.

Who haven't we talked to? By the table sat the oddest pair of the evening: Wallace and a stranger with emerald hair. Wallace was pitching an investment opportunity. It sounded like a pyramid scheme, but both were absorbed in the presentation.

Ryan seemed hesitant to approach them. He skidded past them, giving them a nod, before returning to Eyes.

"Who the hell is this character?" Eyes demanded.

"Ambrosius." Ryan struggled with his response. "He's… uhm, he's a painter of sorts."

This is the company Ryan keeps nowadays? Eyes gave him a cold stare. "You should kick him out."

"He's alright. By keeping Wallace occupied, he's saving us from listening to more insurance scams. Fuck. If Ambrosius invests, I wonder who's more screwed."

"Kick him out."

"Nah. He's a bit…kooky."

With a shriek, Eyes applauded. "He can stay! We love our crazies! Can you kick Wallace out?"

Ryan was incredulous. "The party's almost over."

"Lesson number one, my dear. It's never too late to kick someone out."

The biggest group was convened by the bar. Here, King was playing a game with Timmy, Badger, and Si. Odd that none of them had a drink. Ryan chalked it up to being too late in the evening. Or too early in the morning.

The game was suck and blow. They had to pass a playing card around using only their lips. Ryan arrived in time as King roped him into joining. King had the card on his lips. As Ryan swooped in to suck it, King swiped it away and gave Ryan a smack.

"That's breaking the rules." Ryan wiped his lips. "You lose."

"I'm not sure anyone lost," King replied as the other boys laughed. Not wanting to kiss anyone else, Ryan left them to their game.

"My dear, if you're gonna sleep with one of our friends, please not King. Why not Sugar?"

Ryan was puzzled. "You do know Sugar's asexual, right?"

Eyes's eyebrows flew up. "Oh, that's probably why it's impossible to dislike him. And why everyone hates these boys, these lovely beautiful devils. These are the boys my momma warned me of. Or at least she would've if she weren't a bitch.

"These are the boys who love to fuck, though they're not very good at it. They are lost causes, devoid of a future and humanity. They are brash and uncouth and absolutely disgusting. And we love every bit of them, and we hate ourselves in the morning."

Fighting words. Ryan was fed up. *Why couldn't Eyes see?* He'd been showing him everyone, but the Eyes refused to see. "That's unfair. You don't know these boys—"

"What is there to know, my dear? People are people, they are horrible and mean and gross, and we love them because we're no better."

Where was Precious Percy? Nowhere in the living room. *Maybe he's busy putting more brooms up his ass.* The image made Eyes laugh.

Ryan pointed outside. There he was, sitting on the back porch with his boyfriend, Naveen. Ryan stepped out to the patio's cold air. "Alright, Percy?"

Percy turned, draping his head on Naveen's shoulder. "Peaches, Ryan."

Ryan shivered. "Thanks for the party. You've outdone yourself. I can't thank you enough. Eyes would've appreciated it."

Percy covered his blushing cheek. "You're always welcome, darling. Love you."

Eyes waited for Ryan inside. He hated the cold, and a cape was no match for dawn's chills. "You're speaking for me now?"

Ryan's face flushed in annoyance, yet he ignored the jab. "It's not my business, but sometimes Percy...I mean, obviously, Percy's still in love with Si. You remember. They made a good couple. I feel like he's settling for Naveen, and that sucks, and I want to tell him."

"You're right, my dear." Eyes turned toward the cuddling silhouettes of Percy and Naveen. "It is none of your business."

"I'm looking out for him."

"Why do you have this compulsive need to save people? Ryan, people are not dumb. Yes, he's a bottom, but Percy is still a person. What you said—they know that. Percy knows it. Si knows it. The damn doctor knows it. If it's a mistake, it's a decision they'll make. My god, my dear, just because you're an artist doesn't mean you have access to a higher plane of understanding. Life isn't a series of realities where people live in parallel planes of existence. We live together, the beautiful and the sordid, the genius and the crazy, the enlightened and the damned."

If Ryan's face hadn't betrayed anger earlier, now it did.

Ryan was boiling. This party was for Eyes and, now that he was here, Eyes was blindsided by his own philosophies.

"Almost all the boys came here for you. One last fucking memory. Say it. Say we're all fucked up, spending the night laughing, fucking, drinking, shooting, fighting, kissing, and for what? To hide trauma.

"You speak as if we were chaos. Guess what? You're wrong. Not everyone here, no, no one is as messed up as you make us out. We struggle, yes. We are sleep-deprived, broke, and lonely. But we're here. We made it here. And we make do.

"It was you. You're bloody Eyes, and you can't even see. There are boys here who wish they died instead of you. We're all coping. Vyn with his depression, Long with alcohol, Sugar with drugs, King with games, Percy with love, El ironically with politics, and then there's me.

"For me, it was you. Jesus, lord, sodomites, and bedwetters. You are my trauma. Why the bloody hell did you leave us, Eyes? We were on fire. We were gonna conquer the world.

"We loved you. You were our friend. You were one of us. Then you died. You know how long since I've seen some of these guys? Years, Eyes. Years! Years that you weren't here! So, go ahead. Judge. Laugh it off like another joke. If I'm fucked up, it's all thanks to you."

Ryan wiped his forehead. All the words he'd locked up burst out. He wiped his tears.

After a long silence, Eyes gave him a long embrace. Ryan sank into him. He missed this.

"My dear, I am so, so sorry."

They stayed for a good few minutes before Eyes paced pensively. "My dear, you're right. You're absolutely right. But just because you're right doesn't mean I'm wrong. We can both be right and also both dead wrong.

"Trauma. Funny. I wish I had more trauma. Might've made me a better writer. Trauma is sad. But, my dear, trauma is beautiful.

"I had to die, my dear. There are no mulligans. No checkpoints. No grand reasons. I died. I had to die. I am no longer your friend. I am your stronger. I am your will. I am your tears.

"My dear, 'high school never ends' is said by those who peak in high school and die in anonymity. We have to grow out of high school. You blame me for your falling apart. Perhaps. Perhaps, indeed. But, my dear, even if I were alive, the old days are done.

"You move on. You strive. You fight. You bleed. You strike back. There is no other option. But you are not alone. You have me, your trauma.

"Beautiful, beautiful trauma. Nothing will be fixed tonight. You wanted this shindig for closure. You were always so obsessed with closure. But this is a party. One night in 365. These boys, their stories do not end here. There is no happy ever after, that's all folks, curtain call. What about tomorrow, when they wake up hangover, pissed, and worse off? How about next week? How about next year?"

"What do you suggest?" Ryan asked.

"Take your beautiful trauma and live with it. Do not be afraid of it, don't run away as if you were being chased. Embrace your beautiful trauma; it is part of you, it will always be part of you. The days of wine and roses. The nights we stared at the sky. They will keep you smiling. But take the pain, the guilt, the heartbreak. Live with them, embrace them, they are your friends. They make you stronger, wiser, faster, and whatever else is in the Olympic slogan."

Ryan laughed. "Sometimes, you're full of shit, Eyes."

"We are the boys who wear pink. We eat trauma for breakfast, we puke it out to fit into our skinny jeans and leather jackets. We've been bullied, harassed, homeless, destroyed. But boys who wear pink laugh. Boys who wear pink never change. Boys who wear pink salute tomorrow with two middle fingers."

It was so simple Ryan wished he'd seen it that way earlier. But that was Eyes. Eyes could see everything. And he wasn't done.

"Speaking of closure," Eyes said, pointing toward a figure coming from the hall. Ryan followed his finger. CC.

Blow Me (One Last Kiss)

WHEN CC HAD ARRIVED, people hadn't even begun drinking. Now in the wee hours of the morn, the same people were packing up.

The evening had taken lots of twists. CC wasn't the best with names, yet he was entranced by the boys here. At times, he even had fun! Ryan wasn't lying when he had said they threw the best parties. What are the best parties if not regular parties with the best folks?

Yet, he still hadn't managed to talk to the one person he had come here for. It was laughable how CC couldn't catch Ryan alone. Either he was in a group or he was entertaining. On the rare occasion he'd spot Ryan by himself, he'd be gone the moment he reached him. *Magic!*

Not anymore. Coming back from the washroom, he was locked eye-to-eye with Ryan. No more disappearing acts. No more excuses. Maintaining eye contact, he walked toward him. "Can we talk?" Finally. And it only took eight hours.

They walked back toward the hall, mostly because the party was suffocating him as if he'd spent years here. Even the patios both front and back had lost their luster. Ryan agreed, "How's a walk down the block?"

The street was quiet. No dogs barking, no alarms ringing. A humid dawn took over the night's cold air. CC was thankful. There was a time he'd be huddled close to Ryan in want of heat and comfort. Not tonight.

"Nice neighborhood, eh?" Ryan said.

CC nodded. It was pointless to argue with small talk. Weather's crappy, trees are nice. He wanted to get things going. "How are you, Ryan?"

Ryan kicked some pebbles down the path. It took them a few steps before he replied, "People ask that question when all they want is someone to tell them they're fine."

CC touched Ryan's arm. "You don't give me enough credit."

"I'm fine, CC." Ryan moved away. "Really. I have an exhibit in a month. Aside from that, life is absolutely perfect."

"I read about the *Dama de Noche*. I'm surprised it's taken you this long to finish it. I might go."

They walked further. "What's new with you?" Ryan asked as they rounded a corner.

CC sneezed. It was getting cold again. "Well, we're serving a new strawberry danish. People seem to like it."

"Yeah, but are you okay?" Ryan sounded concerned.

CC bit his lip. "I've had a shitty day." He was wary of his words. They were pieces locked in a chess match. "On the whole? On the whole, taking it one day at a time. One shitty day, that is."

They must've been five blocks from Percy's. More than half the trip was spent in silence. CC didn't mind though. There needed to be a certain comfort between two people for silence to pass beautifully.

They passed through a park. "Look." Ryan pointed toward a big mango tree. "Do you remember?"

"Need you even ask?"

CC had met Ryan at the coffee shop he worked in. Ryan and his friends were so loud that the manager asked CC to shush them. He did the exact opposite. As he brought them their drinks, he flirted with Ryan.

After that, they kept returning. Keeping up the game, CC continued to flirt with Ryan. And it was working. Every time he'd pass by their table, they'd snicker while Ryan's face blushed. CC enjoyed it. There was little fun in making coffee.

It took a few suggestive lines before Ryan finally asked him out on a date. He had just put down a tray of drinks on their table. All Ryan's friends were staring at him, waiting for his reaction.

Flirting publicly was one thing: good fun. Dating was different. However, he felt awkward to decline the invitation in front of so many witnesses.

"One condition," he said. "No chaperones."

Their date was at a park. The city allowed people to drink alcohol in public if paired with food. Ryan said he'd bring the wine if CC would bring something to eat. He knew exactly what to bring—the coffee shop started stocking meat pies that'd been selling like mad. During CC's break, he tucked a few in his apron.

They strolled through the park, lunch in hand. The sun was out, but it wasn't too hot that umbrellas were needed. Right below a mango tree, they found the perfect shade.

As Ryan took the cups out, CC searched his bag. He forgot to bring a knife.

"I can bite at one end," he said, "and you can bite at the other. Then our lips can meet in the middle like *Lady and the Tramp.*"

Ryan poured wine. "Am I the Lady or am I the Tramp?"

"A little bit of both."

Unfortunately, what worked for pasta (and singing dogs) didn't translate to meat pies. Crumbs and meat scattered all around. A nearby couple pitied them they lent CC their knife.

CC cut the remaining pies while Ryan talked about art. After the pies were divided, he was wiping the knife, when a strong wind blew. Their arms flew to catch the flying napkins, cups, and wrappers. As Ryan's hands flailed, CC, who still held the knife, accidentally stabbed him on the palm.

"Jesus, lord, sodomites, and bedwetters," Ryan said, wrapping a handkerchief around the wound. It was a small cut, though it still bled. "It doesn't bode well for a first date when I have to do first aid."

CC winked. "We'll have a cool story for the grandkids."

Stabbing aside, that was CC's favorite first date. Favorite date, period. ("Meh, it's in my top five," Ryan said.) They enjoyed the same animated shows, they discussed classical philosophy, and they bantered for hours. And that was important. People would get ugly, but conversations would never stop.

The biggest surprise was when CC told Ryan that his mom, god bless her soul, used to be a painter and had enjoyed success in local galleries.

"Stop fucking with me," Ryan said. "You're her son?"

CC bowed. "The one and only."

"Dude, I studied her work. She was such an inspiration."

"Well, don't fall in love with me just because I'm her son!" CC threw grass toward Ryan. "I can't fall in love with you either. My therapist will say I have a mother complex."

Ryan blew the grass back toward CC. "Better find a new shrink then."

After four hours of lazing at the park, CC was in Ryan's bedroom. Maybe it was the wine or the shine in Ryan's eyes, but the moment the door closed, their lips were together.

"I don't usually sleep with guys on the first date," Ryan said. "Well, I mean, sometimes. Actually, I do it a lot."

CC undid his belt. "It's your turn to stab me."

Their first date was indeed glorious, and the ones that followed weren't less spectacular. On their second date, Ryan gave him a gift. A sketch of them in bed. It was a rough scribble, but CC appreciated a token of that special date.

Looking nervous, Ryan asked CC what he thought of it. CC stared at it, pretending to be deep in thought. When Ryan's head was turned, he kissed him on the cheek. "Thank you."

Unknown to Ryan, at that time, CC wasn't looking for a relationship, much less love. Yet, for a while, CC went along for the ride. Their schedules led to a lot of canceled dates. Ryan was always out with friends or working on a project. CC had rotating shifts at the coffee shop. The more they spoke, the less they could talk about.

All he had was that sketch of that first date. For CC, that was enough. A good memory of a good time. But just a memento. He had his fun.

They broke up.

"I thought it was a sign," Ryan said. They made it to the mango tree, Percy's mansion a good distance away. Ryan sat down. "I thought it was a sign. How was I to know you only blamed the wine?"

CC lay down beside him. He didn't have anything to say. He uprooted some grass and threw them Ryan's way, just like he did on their first date. A couple of cars drove by. CC wondered who'd be traveling at this hour. Only the most pious and the most depraved were awake so early.

"What's on your mind?" he asked.

"This was a shitty party," Ryan replied.

CC laughed. "It was alright. It was a good party. You should've brought me to more of these."

"I tried, CC."

◄

A year passed since that first breakup. Ryan had stopped going to the coffee shop. Occasionally, familiar faces from the group came, but CC didn't want to bother them. At his request, Ryan never introduced him to his friends. That was something couples did.

One day, CC got an invitation to an art launch. His mother's paintings were on display. She had faded from the consciousness of even those obsessed with art, so much so that an homage was apt.

He conveniently forgot Ryan moved in these circles. And there he was, staring at a painting and eating cheese. Comically, CC darted from panel to panel. He even hid in the toilet when speeches were made. Yet as he was swerving around a guy with emerald hair, he bumped into Ryan's shoulders.

"Are you stalking me?" Ryan asked.

CC laughed. He had been following Ryan's progress as an artist. He read articles about his work, even considered going to his shows. "Not stalking. What's the right word? Destiny, kismet, fate, serendipity?"

"Coffee," Ryan replied. "The right word is coffee. Let's go get coffee."

The thing with coffee was it would lead to a drink. Drinks would lead to dinner, then a walk through the park, and, of course, back in bed, square one.

Well, not quite. In their year apart, CC questioned if he had made the right choice. He missed Ryan. Seeing him in the paper led him to meditate. Maybe the human condition wasn't about the search for true love but the moments in between. People measured love in length. But maybe love couldn't be quantified in time. A love that lasted a minute could burn as strong as one that lived a century.

They did rekindle, although that wouldn't be the last time CC and Ryan broke up and got back together. They both had such strong personalities, and they clashed all the time. They broke up once over an argument involving hedgehogs and porcupines. When they got back together, CC joked, "We're like Ross and Rachel."

"Why are your references so heterosexual?" Ryan responded. "We're like Brian Kinney and Justin Taylor."

And then the day of Eyes's death. Ryan was supposed to drive his friends over, but he had forgotten he agreed to meet up with CC that day. "You always have time for your friends!" CC complained. "Always them and not me. Why don't you make Eyes your boyfriend then?"

He knew he was being unfair. He and Ryan were together a lot, and he knew Ryan needed time with his friends. But Ryan had just guilt-tripped him into taking a week off work to accompany him to an art tour.

CC would later regret convincing Ryan to tell his friends he had the flu. This date wasn't even spectacular. They kept arguing until Ryan got a call from the police about the accident. CC lost his mom years ago to a drunk driver. He understood grief. But grief hit people differently.

Ryan was an artist. His despair materialized in his work. His erotic paintings had become bleak. Gone were the mouths gasping in ecstasy. Here were various shades of black—CC hadn't imagined there could be more than one.

CC was still in love with him, in fact, deeper and madder—as if in a breathing painting, he was the muse and Ryan the artist. He even let Ryan use his naked body as a canvass. CC looked at the final product in the mirror. His entire body transformed. The lines stretched his skin, as if a hole gaped within. And the black paint all over him was a soul clinging to its remaining whole.

But Ryan became like his work: bleak. He was always painting, always in his studio. It was just him and the easel.

On their anniversary, CC's gift was a collection of pictures. He ordered prints of Ryan's sketches and had them framed in mahogany. There was one with a pair of eyes, one of the twins from his school, one was of the *Dama de Noche*, the flower Ryan had been obsessed with. But the biggest one was the drawing Ryan made of their first date. The whole thing cost a lot. CC scraped; he even worked through his breaks. Seeing Ryan smile would be worth it.

Ryan got him a pair of socks.

It wasn't long when they broke up for good. There was no tipping point. It never escalated. No inciting incident.

CC was packing his suitcase. While watching him, Ryan asked, "Why?"

"Because you never say, 'I love you'," CC said. "You only say, 'I love you, too.' Sometimes, 'I love you too' isn't good enough. Not when I've given you everything."

"You did," Ryan said, "but do you know how hard it is to hold someone's happiness in your hand? You gave me your world. And I have to be so careful not to crush it."

"Ryan, I was afraid I loved you more than you loved me. I should've been afraid that I loved you more than you loved yourself."

He slammed his suitcase shut. Anything left, Ryan could keep. Fearing a breakdown, he sat at the bed, taking deep breaths.

Ryan left and came back holding a painting. For the past weeks, he'd been obsessed with this. Every waking moment, he was tirelessly mixing paint and twisting brushes. He never showed works in progress, but this was a special occasion.

Part of his latest collection, the *Dama de Noche,* the painting was a self-portrait: Ryan's face contorted in all directions across the canvass. There were violent slashes of red and black. His eyes were dotted with holes. CC recognized every single stroke. It was beautiful and broken. Just like Ryan.

"What's it called?" CC asked.

"The Self-Hating Faggot Doesn't Kill Himself At The End."

CC hadn't spoken to Ryan since he left though he enjoyed seeing his name on the paper. He was proud of Ryan's accomplishments. And it was hard to let go.

"Tell me one thing," CC said. "Why did you invite me? Accident?"

Ryan looked at him. "There are no accidents."

"I missed you." This was painfully true. Taking his chance, CC leaned his head on Ryan.

"I don't know why I invited you," said Ryan. "That's the truth. I just wanted to. And sometimes wanting to do something is reason enough."

CC kissed Ryan. He held Ryan's face and grazed his lips. "I'm sorry," CC said. "I just wanted to."

They kissed for a few minutes. The cold didn't bother CC anymore. He clung on to Ryan's shirt and pushed him against the tree. He rubbed Ryan's hair. Cars passed. CC didn't care.

After they kissed, they sat looking at the road. Ryan fixed his hair. "I think that's enough."

"You think too much." CC's fingers clasped on to Ryan's. "Wanna go somewhere else?"

Ryan nodded. But as CC stood up, Ryan clarified, "I want to go with you. But I can't."

"Why not?"

Ryan stood up. "I have to go back."

"Fuck the party!" CC held Ryan, his tone pleading.

Ryan wiped his eyes. "Yeah. But I have to."

CC wanted to put Ryan across his shoulders and run through the night, run far away, run to where demons can no longer hunt them, run to where they'd spend days laughing in bed. But he understood.

Instead, he walked Ryan back. The trip home was quieter. There was no need to talk when two boys were holding hands.

CC had planned to head home after dropping Ryan off, but, needing to piss, he followed Ryan inside. "I think this is it for us."

"What happened to thinking too much?" Ryan asked. "But you're right. This was a shit day. I want my ignorance back."

"Oh, baby, you were never ignorant."

Ryan laughed, as he punched CC's shoulder. "I thought I wanted closure. But, hey, closure is overrated sometimes."

Walking toward the bathroom, CC winked. "No closure. Only frustrations."

"Hey, Clarence Cordero," Ryan called out. "Blow me!"

CC turned around laughing. He put his palm to his lips and blew Ryan one last kiss.

Raise Your Glass

VYN WAS GLAD the voice was gone. It'd come back later. That he was sure of. But for now, Ueliton's pitchy questions and Long's monotone were enough. Around him, the conversations were dying out. He saw Angelo and Joule with their coats on near the door when Ryan came back in.

At the bar, King was wiping the counter. It wasn't his job, but it was the least he could do for Percy. As Ryan sat in front of him, King asked where he'd been. Ryan shook his head and asked for a drink.

Ryan took the Bloody Caesar from King. *Delicious, even by smell.* Perfect for a wrap-up. The clamato taste chilled Ryan's throat. But as the drink settled, his eyes jolted. *Shit!* So much had happened tonight, he almost forgot.

Percy was enjoying a massage from Naveen. *Ah, nothing tops a doctor's trained hand.* Ryan had to interrupt. "Percy, camera! We don't have a picture. The seven of us, then everyone, okay?"

Near Percy, Sugar was chatting with Badger when he heard Ryan's suggestion. He was sad to leave Badger again, (all night, their conversations were cut) but Ryan's idea was genius. He went around to gather the gang. Long and Vyn were too happy for a chance to get away from Ueliton. King almost tripped on his feet rushing over. *But where was El?*

Close to the door, Drew spotted El coming out from the bathroom. "Your friends are calling you," he said. "Afterward, I'm booking one-on-one time with you."

There they were. Long stood at the back, to the right of King, while Vyn was on King's left. King's arms draped across both their shoulders. "Come on!" Long stifled a yawn. El scrambled to sit in the middle of the sofa. Sugar reclined on the left armrest, his feet on El's lap. Percy sat, crossing his legs, to the right of El. With the sofa full, Ryan squatted on the floor.

"Let's go!" El said. *Tonight was a good night.* "It's our first group photo since, well, y'know."

Ryan knew better. Eyes sat beside him, his mouth stretched to dramatic proportions. Ryan nodded his way before turning to the camera. Naveen counted to three and *snap!* Perfect.

"Everyone!" Sugar called out. He didn't want people to be left out. Awkward enough for someone like Mickey whose hand was already on the door. Tonight deserved to be preserved.

Getting everyone to fit in one shot was challenging. Si helped Ryan choreograph the scene. Their combined artistic brains were no match for the chaos. Percy scooted, letting Naveen take his spot before sitting on his boyfriend's lap. Drew squeezed in between Sugar and El. Badger sat on the armrest, an arm around Sugar. Si stood beside him.

Mickey leaned on the back of the sofa. *He's so beautiful.* Zeke wrapped his arms around him. He kissed Mickey's neck. He missed this. This felt right.

Joule and Angelo found a place at the back. They were embracing while Reyes hid behind them. Joule had none of it. He and Angelo grabbed Reyes's legs and lifted him.

Timmy and Wallace sat cross-legged on the floor beside Ryan. Timmy rubbed his eyes. People liked to put him and Joule side-by-side. It was tedious. Joining them, Ambrosius crawled toward the center. Timmy pulled him back so he wouldn't block the camera.

Ueliton didn't want to be in the photo. He wasn't dressed up, he'd broken up, and he'd just received information about his brother's death. He offered to be the cameraman, but El said, "Don't be absurd, there's a self-timer." Resigned, he went to the only available spot—by the right of the sofa beside Lee. *Yaaaay.*

Inconspicuously, CC sat down beside Ryan. Their hands found each other. The moment of serenity was broken by Chase diving on the sofa. He looked comfortable lying on top of everyone's lap. Percy shrieked, but that only made the stripper more handsy.

Look at all these boys. Eyes had been sitting beside Ryan, but as the timer went down, he left. *Take your own bloody advice. Besides, it's more fun to watch.* He observed the group from behind the camera.

Three. Two. One. "Happy birthday," Ryan mouthed toward Eyes. Flash.

Percy rushed to the camera. *Lovely! Absolutely lovely!* He'd never say it, but he was happy Ryan got him to host this. People were telling him to tag them later. Time check, *is it 5 a.m. already? Why aren't they leaving? Oh, but this was fun. But they had to leave.*

Ryan had other ideas. "Hey, everyone, everyone." Ryan's voice was drowned out.

"What is it, sweetie?" asked Sugar.

"I'd like to say a few words."

This was Long's specialty. Using his teacher's voice, he ordered everyone to be quiet.

Lee scurried over. Chase had been giving him his number when Long's command shushed them right up.

All eyes were now on Ryan.

"So, yeah, everyone, thanks for coming."

"That's not how you open a speech, my dear," Eyes said, lingering beside him. "You should end this whole damn party with a bang, and it all hinges on what you say right now."

"No backseat driving. Bitch," Ryan muttered.

But Eyes had a point. Public speaking wasn't Ryan's forte. "I'm sorry, everyone. It's 5 a.m., and you wanna go home. Please indulge me one last time. Can we all please grab a glass?"

Reyes groaned. *Ryan's gotta be kidding.* Reyes couldn't take another shot. Neither could Angelo. Joule could, and maybe Timmy or King. Reyes's fears were alleviated when Ryan backtracked, "For those who can't drink alcohol, get a glass of water or tea."

Ryan's sentence wasn't finished when King started flipping glasses at the bar. Though not a bartender, Chase's experience at the club proved an invaluable help. Together, they fulfilled all drink requests within minutes.

"Hurry up!" Percy snapped. His irritation was a put-on, but it scurried people back from the bar.

Wallace blew on his tea. Around him, everyone settled. King handed Ryan another Caesar.

"Some of you know why we're here, but I know most are confused. No. It's not my birthday, we're not celebrating me. It is someone's birthday though, and I'm here to talk about him.

"Eyes was a lot of things to most of you. His friend, his brother, his boyfriend, his lover, his rival, his classmate. When Eyes died, there weren't a lot of people at his wake. I'm embarrassed to say I wasn't there. Few of his friends were. I mean,

Sugar went, but that's because he's Sugar, right? It's impossible to dislike Sugar."

The crowd chuckled while Sugar blushed. Ryan's forehead sweat. He turned to Eyes. "Help me."

"Always, my dear. Always."

Okay. Breathe.

You're not alone.

Take your time.

Three.

Two.

Smile.

"Raise your glass if your body's sticky with paint, when your whole life escapes into a painting, and you move through the colors and lines to untangle from the past. Raise your glass if you're in pain, when pills are your savior, when pills are your jailer, when healing is hurting and the pain is within. Raise your glass if you are the new normal, when boys are but bodies that hold you in the cold but whose souls are lost in the hiss.

"Raise your glass if you absolve your guilt in the streets, equating the shame with inaction, and justice for mercy. Raise your glass if you play the world but the world has played you, and the one thing unfixed is the one thing desperate for fixing. Raise your glass if you're gone, gone, gone, but not forgotten. Raise your glass if you've moved heaven into hell, you've gnashed your hair, you've jumped off the cliff, but the world needs more than a try. Raise your glass if you stare at the mirror, throwing invectives and spilling blood, in the search of perfection.

"Raise your glass if you've hurt the one person you shouldn't have, and the chaos took charge of your fist. Raise your glass if you've had ten thousand strange hands frolic on your body, unyielding to resistance, unstoppable, and you are left a husk, the broken-down reflection. Raise your glass if all your life, everything touched is broken, with every step blocked, every road leading back to hell. Raise your glass if you don't care what people say: bitch, slut, whore, prude, freak, but the words stick and words hurt because sticks and stones may break my bones but words are fucking words.

"Raise your glass if you have a perm, or you dye your hair, or you wear a skirt, because you are twice the man your haters are. Raise your glass if you dance in sequins and boas, if your kisses are teases, and the night is your home. Raise your glass if a 'happy ever after' is a dream that you'll fight for knowing you'll lose.

"Raise your glass if questions haunt your dreams, dazed in a stream of pictures down memory lane. Raise your glass if you hear voices, when the voices are fun, when the voices are evil, when the voices sing you to sleep, when the voices play with your lips, when you are a prisoner of your mind, and your only cellmate is him.

"Raise your glass if you burn through games, in pillars of flame unstoppable. Raise your glass if you walk through the halls uncertain, and their glares are flying daggers. Raise your glass if you annoy yourself, and all they see are the ruins of the past. Raise your glass if, at death's door, you fling middle fingers under the grace of a divine.

"Raise your glass if you live in a world too advanced for this, when fantasy and reality collide in a straitjacket. Raise your glass if you find solace for the unforgiven at the bottom of your twentieth vodka. Raise your glass if you wear pink and eat your trauma. Raise your glass if closure is at arm's length, floating and reappearing at its whim in a final kiss.

"All my underdogs, raise your glass!"

The room roared. Everyone stood up, chanting, "Raise your glass! Raise your glass! Raise your glass!" Silence. Glasses were raised. Forgiveness. Friendship. Gratitude. Bliss. Above all, love.

Ryan put his glass to his lips. Across the room, Eyes leaned against the wall, his arms crossed, and an understanding smile on his face. Ryan tipped his glass to Eyes. After he drank, Eyes was gone.

A funny thing came over Chase after Ryan's speech. He was one with the crowd: he stood up, raised his glass, and drank. As soon as his glass was down, he walked toward Ryan.

Tomorrow he's back at the club. Tomorrow he'll be dancing again. Tomorrow nothing will matter but the biggest tipper. He grabbed Ryan and sucked on his neck.

CC was supposed to leave. That speech was the last thing he needed. Tomorrow he will serve coffee, its aroma a mocking testament to tonight. But here he was, hovering one inch behind Ryan, wrapping his arms around his waist, while Ryan's breath floated to his mouth.

Ryan had let go. Tomorrow he can search for closure. *Let go.* His shirt was being unbuttoned. *Let go, let go.* It was peeled off him.

Drew was dead man walking. Tomorrow he will start chemo. He sat on top of El, brushed the boy's hair all the way to the back, and kissed him.

Tomorrow El will complete his signature campaign. His arms were pinned down as Drew licked his body from side to side.

Mickey and Zeke were hesitant. Tomorrow they will fix their relationship. Zeke pushed Mickey to the floor and, though sleepy, he jumped on top of him. Their arms locked, they rolled while kissing.

Another body entered their embrace. Tomorrow Long will nurse his hangover while preparing a lesson plan. His facial hair stroked Mickey's chest while Zeke untucked his shirt. His naked torso lay with the two of them.

Percy was sitting on Naveen's lap during the speech. He turned to give him a peck, but Naveen pulled him closer. For lust, safety, and comfort, Percy clung on to his shirt. But it was in Si's hands, which were unbuckling his belt, that he found truth. Tomorrow the three of them will be confronted with a choice. Percy kissed Si. He kissed Naveen. Si kissed Naveen. Then the three of them kissed.

Joule's hand was on Angelo's crotch as he bit his ear. Tomorrow they will see if they can make it. Angelo grabbed Joule and slammed him against the wall as he dove into Joule's face.

Another bite on Angelo's ear. Timmy was joining in on the fun. Tomorrow he and Joule will plan out a future. He made sure Angelo was watching as he swooped in and kissed Joule. Their tongues fenced with each other. Even in kissing, they were competitive.

By chance, Reyes was sat beside King. King was whistling when Reyes pounced. And he wasn't gentle. He bit King's lip while his hands grabbed on to King's elbows. Tomorrow he will not sleep to catch up on his studies.

There was no way King would lose a wrestling match. He flipped Reyes over and grazed his chin. Reyes giggled. *So, he's ticklish. Good to know.* Tomorrow he will show a group of fifty-year-olds the historic downtown churches. He underestimated Reyes's strength; now, he was at the bottom, and Reyes was tickling his ribs.

Sugar was asexual, yes. But sensual was not sexual. Badger was behind him, smelling his hair, fingers down his legs. Tomorrow he will be yelled at by irate customers. He turned around and held Badger intimately, the rise and fall of Badger's chest mimicking his.

Badger was drowning. When Sugar hummed into his ears, his instincts kicked in. He traced the front of Sugar's shirt to find the nipple. *There.* Pinch. Sugar's eyes clenched. Tomorrow he will focus on the alumni basketball team. His hand entered Sugar's shirt and pinched the naked nipple.

None were as passionate as Vyn, Wallace, and Ambrosius. Vyn was already naked, the two others were almost there. Tomorrow these three have serious meditation to do. Vyn bent

Ambrosius over, lowering his boxers. He kissed the boy from the ankle to the ass. When Wallace took off his boxers, Vyn's eyebrows went up. *If we had known about that in high school, maybe he wouldn't have been an outcast.* He lowered himself and submerged in Wallace's Apollo's belt.

Earlier, Lee had refused to sleep with Chase. But here he was, straddling the young boy's legs, while allowing him to rip open his shirt. Behind them, a familiar breath tickled his back, as Ueliton's fingers moved down his spine. Tomorrow they will say goodbye. He turned to Ueliton. There was so much he needed to say. They laid their foreheads together.

Shirts were taken off, and pants were dropped. Even those who had already put their jackets on were left with fewer clothes. One will lose track of who kissed whom, whose lips were on whose nipples, or whose hand was groping whose cock. All they were was a collection of bodies, contorted, flexed, and beautiful.

My dear, it is hard, nay impossible to understand these boys unless you were one of them. To know pain that never left, to lose serenity, only to find yourself in the midst of an orgy. Fully naked, Ryan was moaning on the pool table, every body part moving independently, each teased by a different tongue, finger, or crotch. He couldn't count how many hands were on him at any given time; perhaps it was all of them.

And soon, he was just another naked body among naked bodies piled on top of each other: twenty-three boys in various states of euphoria, madness, and eroticism. No one knew whose body they were touching. The boy they were kissing earlier was now lost in the body pile. Who cares? Go make out with another one. Who was it? Does it matter? It was hot.

It was the night Eyes and Ryan first had sex. Already naked on the bed, Eyes chuckled at Ryan's nervous expression while he slid off his shoes.

But he won him over. Eyes gently unbuttoned Ryan's shirt and kissed his nipples. Ryan's back arched in pleasure as Eyes's warm tongue explored every crevice on his body, from his armpits, feet, and then dick.

As they fucked, Eyes continued to kiss Ryan. This moment had to be documented. There was no way Eyes would let him down.

"Is it always this bad?" Ryan asked afterward, as they passed cigarettes. "Or was it just me?"

Eyes pinched his shoulder. "My dear, it is never that bad, and it is always just you."

"I think I got you figured." Ryan searched for an ashtray. "You think you're saying something smart when all you do is reverse what the other person said. *My dear.*"

Eyes passed the ashtray from his side of the bed. "Well, Jesus, lord, sodomites, and bedwetters, you got me."

They looked at each other, then they laughed. Ryan was so cute Eyes had to kiss him on the forehead.

"What was that for?"

"There's this flower called the *Dama de Noche*." Eyes looked steadily at Ryan's face. Creased lines and crow's feet. How he loved this face. "It's beautifully fragrant but only in the dark."

Ryan flicked ashes over Eyes's body. "Are you calling me ugly?"

"It's also highly poisonous."

"Lovely."

Eyes smiled and gave Ryan another kiss.

Ryan gripped on to someone's shoulders, (he thought it was Naveen's) as all the warmth and all the love transferred from end to end. He groaned as his nipple was bitten and his balls were teased. He opened his eyes. It was beautiful, watching all these boys, of different skin colors, hair, sizes, features, and temperaments collide into one.

One by one, all twenty-three boys came. They lay, drenched in sweat, in tears, and cum, holding and hugging for relief, warmth, and just because.

Ryan will remember this moment. The contour. The musk. The pain. This will be the centerpiece of the *Dama de Noche.*

The sun's first rays shone.

We are the underdogs. Sleep was creeping on Ryan. Around him were snores. We are freaks. We are fools who party alone.

He closed his eyes as the dawn pierced through the patio. We are the people you never get the best of. We are the family portrait. We are the Lady Marmalade. We are trouble. We are sluts like you. We are the beautiful trauma. We are the fistful of glitter in the air. We are just like fire. We are stupid boys. We are fucking perfect.

As sleep overcame him, Eyes's words rang: We are the boys who wear pink.

O

ACKNOWLEDGMENTS

This novel is a work of love.

We want to thank everyone who has worked on this project. From our awesome readers, Marizpan, Jov, Chris, Evered, Cain, Carla, Kyra, Virginia, Kiria, Olivia, Zoey, Raven, Anteria, Asher, Kasper, and Rosie, to our editors, Ally for the line edits, Ash for the copyedits, and Maddy for the proofreading, to Hetvi for the cover design, Leandro for the social media marketing, Michelle for the typesetting, George for the trailer music, Twine for the trailer narration, and Gabiche for acting.

We also acknowledge the invaluable support of Alistair, Corin, Victor, Jesse, Martin, Uel, and people whose names may be escaping me right now.

Finally, to P!nk, whose songs have served not just as inspiration for this work, but who artistry has continued to guide several outcasts like me.

REVAN BADINGHAM III

Revan Badingham III is a queer Filipinx multidisciplinary artist.

As a theatre creator, they are the founding artistic director of Voices of Asia International, a Filipinx theatre company based in Montreal. Their last major production was Beats Around the Bush: The Word Opera, which ran in Newfoundland to critical acclaim. They have done work for Tuesday Night Theatre Café, Theatre NDG, and Sigaw ng Bayan CKUT.

Revan has also been involved in the spoken word scene. They were part of Spoken Word St. John's and Throw Poetry Collective. As a poet-performer, they have performed in stages across Canada, including McSway, The Words & Music Festival, and the 100 Thousand Poets for Change. They have also facilitated workshops, including the Axana Poetry Spa.

Their work has been anthologized in BKL: Bikol/Bakla and The Queer Monologues.

In addition, Revan is a trained actor, musician, and designer. They can also speak ten languages.

To The Boys Who Wear Pink is their debut novel.

RevanBadingham.com